Readers are falling in love with *I See London*!

"A sassy, steamy read that had me racing to the next page to see if Samir would be on it. Mmm, Samir."
—*New York Times* bestselling author Chelsea M. Cameron

"*I See London* is fun, sexy, and kept me completely absorbed."
—Katie McGarry, award-winning author of *Pushing the Limits*

"Lots of drama. Lots of partying. And just a little bit of studying. Guess what? It's New Adult at its finest."
—*T's Bookish Moments of Escape*

"Holy smokes, this book was very addicting. I loved everything about this book, from the beautiful cities of London, Paris and Italy that Maggie gets to see, to the swoon worthy guys that have captured her attention, jealousy, secrets, and of course the sizzling romantic chemistry."
—*Jess Time to Read*

"I read a lot of books, and I've read a lot of New Adult books that blend together, but weeks after reading it, I can still remember *I See London* vividly."
—*Book Labyrinth*

"I absolutely loved this book! It was different enough from others in its genre that it set itself apart from the beginning and it kept getting better as it went along."
—*Examiner.com*

"I was in awe, I was hooked, I was mesmerized—I couldn't get Samir out of my mind!!!"
—*Book Freak*

"*I See London* is by far my favorite New Adult novel I have read so far!"
—*Lost in Believing*

Also by Chanel Cleeton

The International School Series

I SEE LONDON
LONDON FALLING
FRENCH KISSED

For a complete list of books by Chanel Cleeton,
please visit her website at chanelcleeton.com.

I SEE LONDON

CHANEL CLEETON

CANARY STREET PRESS

CANARY
STREET
PRESS™

Recycling programs
for this product may
not exist in your area.

ISBN-13: 978-1-335-00486-4

I See London

First published in 2014. This edition published in 2023 with revised text.

Canary Street Press
22 Adelaide St. West, 41st Floor
Toronto, Ontario M5H 4E3, Canada
CanaryStPress.com

Printed in U.S.A.

I SEE
LONDON

1

I couldn't find my underwear.

Knickers, as the British called them.

It should have been easy; there wasn't much to them. They were black, lacy…and shit, I was going to miss my flight home if I kept looking.

"Start by thinking of the last place you had them," my grandmother would always tell me when I lost something. The bed seemed like the best place to start. Or had it been on top of the dresser? Or against the wall by the window?

I'd been a busy girl.

"You leaving?"

I stared down at the boy lying in bed. His voice was heavy with sleep, the sheets tangled around his naked body. The sight of all that skin sent a flash of heat through me.

I wasn't ready to handle the morning after. Screw my underwear.

"Don't worry about it." I leaned down, pressing a swift kiss to his lips, barely resisting the urge to climb back into bed with him. "See you next year," I whispered, grabbing my shoes and heading for the door.

I paused in the doorway, wondering how the hell I'd gone from spending my Friday nights studying to doing the walk of shame sans underwear.

I blamed the Harvard admissions committee.

Ten months earlier

I was going to die, and I wasn't even wearing my best underwear.

My Southern grandmother loved to tell me a girl should always look like a lady—even down to her "unmentionables," as she liked to call them.

"But no one's going to see them."

It doesn't matter. You could be in a car accident and then what? Would you want people to see you in those?

I wasn't sure if the underwear rule applied to plane crashes. But if it did? I was about to die in the world's ugliest pair of black cotton underwear.

"Are you okay, dear?"

I loosened my grip on the armrest, turning slightly to face the woman in the seat next to me.

"It's just a little bit of turbulence. Perfectly normal." She looked to be about my grandmother's age; unlike my grandmother's smooth Southern drawl, though, her voice had a clipped British accent. "Is this your first flight?"

I cleared the massive, boulder-sized knot of tension from my throat. "It's been a long time."

"It can be scary at times. But we're only about an hour away."

The plane hit another bump. I gripped the armrests again, my knuckles turning nearly white.

"What takes you to London?"

"I'm starting college."

"How exciting! Where?"

I struggled to focus on her questions rather than the possibility of the plane plummeting from the sky. The irony of my fear of flying wasn't lost on me.

"The International School."

According to the glossy brochure I'd conveniently received the day my dreaded thin-envelope rejection letter from Harvard arrived in our mailbox, the International School boasted a total of one thousand undergraduate students from all over the world.

"Do you know anyone in London?"

I shook my head.

"I'm surprised your parents let you move by yourself. You can't be more than what, eighteen?"

"Nineteen."

My dad hadn't been a big fan of the whole London idea. *He* could travel the world and live overseas. I just couldn't go with him. I'd heard all the reasons before. He couldn't be a fighter pilot and a single parent. It was too difficult for him to predict when he would be sent away on another assignment. If my mom were still around—

It hung between us, the rest of the words unspoken.

I could fill in the blanks. If my mom were still around, we would be a family. But she wasn't. When she left my dad, she took our family with her, my dad's parents assuming the role of my legal guardians. I loved my grandparents, and they loved me.

But it still wasn't the same.

"You must be pretty brave to come to London by yourself. Especially at such a young age."

Brave? I wasn't sure if it had been bravery or desperation spurring my sole act of teenage rebellion. But ever since I'd received that rejection letter in the mail, my thoughts had been less than rational.

It was all I'd ever wanted—Harvard. It was the best. I'd imagined my dad beaming with pride at my high school graduation, the one he'd ended up missing anyway. Harvard had been my chance to change everything. It was the reason I didn't date and skipped parties in favor of doing SAT prep on Friday nights, the motivation behind me joining every student organization. In the end, none of it was enough.

I wasn't enough.

She nudged me. "We're nearly there."

I turned toward the window, peering through the glass. Fog filled the sky, the air thick and heavy with it.

"It's hard to see anything."

"Just wait for it. Keep looking."

Lights. Scattered throughout the fog were lights. Hundreds, thousands of lights. Like a Christmas tree. Beneath us was a carpet of lights.

"Welcome to London."

I peered out the taxi window, watching as the city passed me by.

The ride from the airport took a little under an hour. As we drove, we crossed into more urban areas where the landscape of little houses disappeared, replaced by large blocks of mul-tistory apartment buildings and small shops on street corners. Little by little the traffic increased, the driver laying on the horn several times and shouting out the window. BBC Radio blared through the car speakers.

The sidewalks were filled with people, their strides long and confident. Everyone looked as if they were in a hurry, as though wherever they were going was the most important place in the world. And it was noisy. Even over the radio, I heard the city, so different from anything I'd ever experienced.

When the cab passed by the infamous Hyde Park and then Kensington Palace, only to turn onto what the cab driver re-ferred to as Embassy Row, the reality of my new life began to sink in. We passed rows of expensive buildings—mansions, really. Some had guards stationed out front and flew flags of various countries, no doubt how Embassy Row got its name. Others were private residences, each one large and imposing. The taxi pulled through a set of enormous gates, traveling down a long gravel driveway. The driver let out a low whistle.

I stared out the window, barely resisting the urge to panic.

The school was huge. The grounds were perfectly mani-
cured; large trees dotted the landscape. Security buzzed around
as students gathered in small groups, greeting each other and
joking around. Ridiculously expensive cars, the like of which
I had only seen in movies, passed by.

Thank God for my scholarship.

I stepped out of the cab on shaky legs, offering a quick smile
for the driver before sliding three crisp twenty-pound notes into
his hands. I rolled my two black bags up the drive, ignoring the
group of boys lounging in front of the school's wooden doors.

"Samir, check out the new girl."

"Not my type," an accented voice, smooth and rich, called
out behind me.

I stiffened, turning to face the speaker.

A boy stared back at me, lounging against the railing leading
up to the school steps like he owned the place. He was average
height and lean, dressed casually in jeans and a black T-shirt.
His hair was an inky black, curling at the ends, his eyes dark
brown, his lashes full and thick.

The boy—Samir, I guessed—did a once-over, starting at
my long brown hair, drifting down my body, lingering on my
boobs—my eyes narrowed—before coming back to rest on my
face. There was something appraising in his gaze—a flicker of
interest—followed by a smile that had my heartbeat ratchet-
ing up a notch.

He flashed me another cocky smile. That smile was lethal.
"Sorry."

He looked anything but.

I wanted to say something clever, wanted to say *something*. But
as always, words failed me. I'd never been good with guys—in
high school I was prone to what I not so lovingly referred to as
deer-in-the-headlights syndrome. If a guy I liked showed any
interest in me, I would freeze, standing there awkwardly, all

clever thought evaporated. It was a spectacularly effective way to ensure I never had a boyfriend.

Get me out of here, now.

His laughter, warm and smooth, filled the space behind me.

I walked into the school on shaky legs, cursing my rocky start. But as soon as I stepped into the entryway, nerves gave way to awe. The building was incredible, like a work of art.

A woman at the front desk greeted me with a smile. "Welcome to the International School. We're so glad to have you joining our family. Name, please."

"Maggie Carpenter."

"Nice to meet you, Maggie. I'm Mrs. Fox. I'm in charge of Residence Life. My staff and I will be responsible for your dorm room and for getting you settled into your new home here." She thumbed through a stack of blue folders before pulling one out of the pile. "Here you go. You'll find the code to get into your room in this folder along with your schedule. If you need anything at all, don't hesitate to come to my office. It's on the map."

I took the folder from Mrs. Fox's hands, struggling to keep the instructions straight through the haze of jet lag. I headed toward the stairs, moving through the crowd of students. At the end of the hallway, I stared up at the narrow staircase in front of me.

"Need some help?"

A tall blond boy with a British accent smiled at me. He wore a blue polo shirt with the words *Residence Life* stitched on the front.

I hesitated. "No thanks. I can manage on my own."

"Are you sure? Trust me, these steps are intense." He peered over at the sheet of paper in my hand. "And you're on the third floor? That's four floors up."

"Huh?"

"Four floors. Not three. In London the main floor is considered the ground floor and the next floor up is the first floor. It's different from how you do things in America." He grinned. "Your accent sort of gave it away," he offered by way of explanation. He reached out, grabbing the handles of my bags. "Come on. I'll help you get to your room. I'm George."

I followed him up the stairs. "Thanks. I'm Maggie."

"Nice to meet you, Maggie. Where are you from?"

"South Carolina."

His brow wrinkled for a moment. "Is that near New York City? I've been there."

I grinned. "Unfortunately, it's light-years away from New York City. I'm from a small town. There's not exactly a lot to do there."

I followed George up another flight of stairs, struggling to keep up with him. I couldn't stop gawking at my surroundings. I'd seen some pictures of the school online, but I'd figured those were the best shots. I hadn't expected it to live up to the advertising. The place looked like a museum.

"So, who are your roommates?"

I stared down at the piece of paper clutched in my hand. "Noora Bader and Fleur Marceaux."

George turned around, a strange expression on his face. His voice sounded like a strangled laugh. "Did you say Fleur Marceaux?"

I nodded.

This time he did laugh, the sound filling the narrow stairway. "Good luck with that one."

2

George dropped my bags off at the front of a long hallway.

"This is as far as I go."

"Do you turn into a pumpkin past this point or something?"

He laughed. "No. But your roommate is number one on Residence Life's hit list."

"Please tell me she's not that bad."

"Oh, she's worse."

"Worse, how?"

"We call her the Ice Queen."

I groaned. It was hardly an original nickname, but also not particularly encouraging.

"She thinks she's better than everyone else and isn't afraid to let them know it."

"Awesome. What about Noora?"

"I don't know her. She must be a freshman."

"Why don't they put all the sophomores together?"

"Because none of the sophomores would have Fleur as a roommate. She was supposed to have a single room, but something fell through. She'll probably be even more difficult now."

Fabulous.

"Look, if you want to apply for a roommate change, come by our office. We're on the ground floor."

I smiled weakly. "Thanks."

I walked down the hall, dread filling me as I searched for room 301. I looked down at the room code on the piece of paper, struggling to punch in the numbers on the little metal keypad, my mind muddled by the time difference.

I swung open the door, dragging my first bag over the threshold, stopping short at the sight of the room that was to be my home for the next year. It was small...three small beds, three small wardrobes, three small desks...and two big windows. I walked over, peering out at the view of Hyde Park. The lush green trees, the expanse of grass, the heavy iron gates—the magic of it all—made up for everything else.

I spent the next hour unpacking my suitcases. Thankfully, I was the first one to arrive. I set a few things out—my favorite books, a few mementos from home, pictures with friends.

The sound of the door opening startled me.

"Hi."

A girl stood in the doorway, bags on her shoulders. Her hair was covered by a gorgeous purple silk scarf.

"Please tell me this is the right place," she announced.

"I'm Maggie. Are you Noora?"

She waved with her free hand. "Nice to meet you."

I grinned. "Nice to meet you, too."

She dropped her bags down on the empty bed. "Is this it?"

"Yeah. Hard to believe they mean for three of us to live here, isn't it?"

"Have you met the other girl?"

"I haven't. I heard she's a sophomore, though." I didn't mention the rest. No sense in worrying Noora, too.

"Are you a freshman?" Noora asked.

"Yep."

"Me, too."

"Nice. Where are you from?"

"Oman."

We chatted for a few more minutes, talking about our backgrounds. I liked her immediately. If Fleur was the Ice Queen, Noora was her polar opposite.

As soon as Noora left to go visit with a friend from home, I called my grandmother. It was early morning in the US, but she'd always been an early riser.

"How are you settling in? Have you made any friends?"

A wave of homesickness rushed over me at the sound of her voice.

"The people seem nice so far." I didn't mention Fleur. My grandmother worried enough as it was.

"Have you been getting enough to eat?"

I grinned. "I promise I'm going to eat lunch soon. Although I bet the food won't be anywhere near as good as yours."

I took a deep breath. "Have you heard from Dad?"

"Sorry, honey. I haven't."

I pushed down the familiar hurt that rose in my throat, forcing the words out. "Do you know where he is now?"

"You know how these things are, honey. He can't say where."

"When will he be back?"

"Hopefully, by Christmas. He said he might be able to come home this year. We could spend Christmas together."

I hadn't spent a Christmas with my dad in at least three years, possibly more.

"That sounds great, Grandma."

We talked for a few more minutes before I hung up the call, tears welling up in my eyes.

For a moment I just sat there, homesick.

I'd been traveling for fifteen hours. I needed a shower. I grabbed a towel and my bath stuff, heading for the door.

The bathroom, like my dorm room, was a bit of a disappointment.

I settled into the shower just as the first tears began to fall.

It felt weird walking back to my room in just a towel, but the only places to change in the bathroom were public.

Luckily, the hallway was still empty. This was the first day students could move into the dorms, but school didn't start for a few days. I stopped in front of my door, shifting my bath caddy to the other hand so I could punch in the code. This time I got in on the first try.

Shutting the door behind me, I set down my bath stuff and unwrapped the towel from my body.

It dropped to the floor.

"I was wrong. You're my type."

I whirled around in shock at the sound of that voice, smooth and teasing, the boy from the steps standing before me.

3

I stood there, gaping at him, convinced this was some sort of nightmare I would eventually wake from.

I blinked.

Still there.

Samir lay sprawled on the empty bed—Fleur's bed—his hands behind his head, ankles crossed.

I shrieked.

Lunging to grab the towel from the floor, I wrapped it hastily around my body, as if its mere presence was enough to erase my nakedness from his memory.

"What the hell are you doing here? What is wrong with you? Why the hell are you spying on me?"

"I wasn't spying. I was waiting for someone. The show was just a bonus."

I crossed my arms over my chest.

I wanted to die. More accurately, I wanted him to die.

Samir laughed, the sound sending a flutter through my body. "I'm pretty sure I'm going to be enjoying this little memory for a while." He rose from the bed, his body uncoiling, the move graceful and unhurried.

"What are you doing?"

He stopped inches away from me, close enough that the scent of his cologne teased me. He was taller than I'd originally thought, forcing me to tilt my head up to meet his gaze—

"Samir!"

The voice broke me out of my stupor. I whirled around, staring at the door.

A girl stared back at me through narrowed eyes and a pissed-off expression. She was tall. Dressed in an outfit that looked like it belonged in a magazine. Shiny brown hair and boxy bangs framed a slender face with high cheekbones. One perfectly shaped eyebrow arched at the sight of me. There was only one person it could be—

I'd never seen a French music video, but I could imagine *her* in one.

She brushed past me, her eyes only for Samir. *He* didn't even have the decency to look embarrassed. They hugged in a tangle of limbs, my presence forgotten.

This time I did bolt. I grabbed my clothes, heading for the door. Hell, at this point changing in the middle of the hall was preferable to spending another minute in their presence.

My roommate's boyfriend was the hottest guy I had ever seen.

And he'd just seen me naked.

Fifteen minutes later I was fully dressed but no less flustered. I hovered outside the room, hoping I'd given them enough time to go somewhere else. Anywhere else. I would have stayed out longer, but I was hungry, and my wallet was sitting on top of my desk. I punched in the code, my hand getting ready to turn the knob when the door swung open.

I stared up into Fleur's perfect face.

"Let me guess, you're one of my roommates." Her voice had a heavy French accent; her hand fisted on her hip. The words escaped in a bored drawl, hinting at some irony in us being roommates.

"I'm Maggie. Maggie Carpenter."

She turned her back to me. "American. Of course.

"The rooms suck," Fleur called out, a note of satisfaction in her voice. "The American kids always have a hard time adjusting. Especially if they haven't been to Europe before. They say everything in the US is *bigger*."

A burst of French came from the other side of the room.

"Don't poke the new girl, Fleur." Samir's voice filled the room, speaking English now. He winked at me.

Of course, they were a couple.

It was official.

I had the worst living situation ever.

For a school as expensive as the International School, the dining hall was a bit disappointing. Like the dorm rooms, it was small, but I suppose given the cost of real estate in a city like London that was to be expected.

"Go with the curry. Trust me, it's the only thing remotely edible."

I turned to the girl next to me—a tall Black girl with long black hair. Gorgeous blue beaded earrings hung from her ears, a matching silver-and-blue scarf wrapped around her neck.

"Thanks for the advice."

"No problem. I'm Mya. Are you new?"

"I'm Maggie. I'm a freshman."

"Welcome. American?"

It had to be the accent giving me away.

"Yeah."

Or my outfit. I stared down at my jeans and flip-flops, wishing I'd put something more glamorous on.

"Don't worry. There are lots of Americans here." She gave

me a friendly smile, one of the first genuine ones I'd received since I arrived. "This is probably a bit of a culture shock."

"It's different," I hedged. "Where are you from?"

"Nigeria." She shrugged. "We spend most of the year here now. My dad works at the Nigerian embassy." She gestured toward one of the empty tables. "Do you want to sit together?"

"That would be great, thanks."

I followed Mya to one of the tables, sliding into the chair across from hers. "Have most students arrived yet? It seems kind of empty."

"Most probably have, but there are always the ones who push it right up to the last minute. Not everyone lives on campus or eats in the dining hall, either. A lot of students have their own flats and do their own things."

From the other side of the partition, I heard people speaking French. I turned in my seat, a groan escaping my lips. Fleur walked in, Samir trailing behind her.

"Fabulous."

Mya followed my gaze until she settled on Fleur. Her lips quirked. "Ahh, I see you've met the reigning queen."

"She's my roommate."

Mya's eyes widened. "You're going to have your hands full."

I ducked my head, hoping I wasn't turning bright red. "What's the deal with that guy? Samir, right? He was in our room earlier."

"You *have* had a busy morning. That's Samir Khouri. He's Lebanese. His dad is a politician in Lebanon. His mom's French."

"He seems like an asshole."

She laughed. "Yeah, you're not far off the mark with that one."

"Hi, Mya."

My head jerked up at the sound of Fleur's voice.

"Are you going to the party tomorrow night?" Fleur asked, completely ignoring me.

Mya grinned. "I never miss a boat party."

Fleur tossed her light brown hair back over her shoulder. "A bunch of us are going out after if you want to come."

"I might. Thanks."

Fleur nodded, not even bothering to glance my way, her red-soled heels clipping on the wood floor as she walked away.

"Are you friends?"

Mya shrugged, tearing off a piece of bread from her plate. "Not really. I would call us acquaintances that occasionally hang out. We went to boarding school together in Switzerland for a few years."

"So, about that party Fleur mentioned. You're going, right?" Mya asked.

"I don't know. I hadn't thought about it, really."

"You must go. Everyone will be there."

"I don't know. I don't have anything to wear."

"You're coming. I can't allow you to miss your first boat party. Besides, if you need an outfit, you came to the right city. We're going shopping."

She hadn't been kidding about the shopping. Thanks to Mya, I was now the proud owner of a hot-pink dress made of some sort of stretchy fabric. It barely covered my now highly enhanced boobs, courtesy of Mya's padded bra suggestion. The hemline fell just below my butt. High heels completed the look.

A knock sounded at the door.

Mya greeted me on the other side in a gorgeous red dress.

She whistled. "Girl, you look hot. My friend Michael's going to give us a ride."

"Sounds good to me."

We walked out to the front of the building, where a guy leaning casually against a black SUV waved to Mya. He walked up to her, pressing a swift kiss on each cheek before turning to me.

"I'm Michael."

"Maggie."

He grinned. "Where are you from, Maggie?"

"South Carolina."

"A Southern girl. Nice. I'm from Connecticut."

He was cute—sandy blond hair and green eyes. He was dressed in a cool-looking T-shirt that looked distressed in a way that wasn't accidental and equally worn jeans that probably cost more than my car payment back home.

"You girls look great tonight."

I fought off the blush. "Thanks."

Mya grabbed my arm before we slid into the back seat of his SUV. "He's gay," she whispered. "I didn't want you to get a crush on him. He's a great guy and I thought you guys would get along. There are a lot of fake people here. Michael's as real as they come. He's an amazing friend."

As we sped off into the city, I couldn't help but feel like Cinderella on my way to the ball.

4

The boat was packed, students crowding around the bar area and filling the dance floor. The DJ played some song I'd never heard before. In one corner a guy climbed on top of a table, spraying the dancing crowd with champagne.

"Ladies, anyone care to join me for a drink?" Michael stood behind us, a gold-colored bottle of champagne in hand.

Mya grinned. "You got the good stuff. Nice." She turned to me. "Do you like champagne?"

I had no idea. "Sure."

Michael handed the bottle off to one of the girls serving drinks at the tables and guided us over to a table in a reserved section cordoned off by velvet ropes.

The waitress opened the bottle of champagne, filling up three glasses.

"A toast!" Michael announced, grabbing the first glass and raising it high in the air. Mya and I followed suit. "To the start of another fabulous year!"

Our glasses clinked together. I took a sip of my drink, the bubbles exploding in my mouth.

"I love this song!" Mya grabbed my hand. "Come on, we have to go dance."

I followed Mya out to the dance floor.

"Your roommate's here," she yelled over the pumping beat. I turned.

Fleur strolled into the party, a group of guys in tow. Samir walked next to her.

Tonight, he wore dark jeans, an expensive-looking black jacket and a gray collared shirt. I hadn't thought it possible for him to look even *better* than the day on the steps.

I was wrong.

He exchanged handshakes with a few guys before heading over to the table next to Michael's. He moved confidently, as if he owned the room. Suddenly Samir's head turned, his gaze meeting mine.

Samir's eyes widened. The look he gave me was long and languid, surprise flickering in his deep brown eyes. I felt the full weight of his stare, each glance leaving a trail of heat in its wake.

No one had ever looked at me like that before.

Fleur tugged on Samir's arm. He ignored her. She tugged again—saying something to him now—and he turned his attention away from me.

"They'll probably go out later if you want to come."

I forced my gaze back to Mya. She shot me a curious look.

"That whole group is pretty big on the club scene," she explained. "They're going to this club called Babel tonight. It's in Mayfair and it's amazing."

I struggled to calm the nerves exploding inside me. "Mayfair?"

"It's one of the nicest neighborhoods in London." She grinned. "In that dress you'll fit right in."

If not for the massive throng of people standing on the sidewalk waiting to be let in, I would never have pegged this as one of London's hottest nightclubs.

You couldn't even get into the club from the street. The

street level led down a flight of concrete stairs that looked haz-
ardous to my health, especially given my ridiculous high heels.
A gray door remained firmly shut at the bottom of the stairs,
while a burly guy in a black dress shirt and trousers stood guard
in front. Thirty or so people stood in line behind a red velvet
rope blocking the entry to the steps. A girl with a clipboard
held court next to the rope.

"How long is it going to take to get in?"

Mya grinned. "Watch this."

Samir brushed past us, walking to the front of our group.

There were ten of us. Best case, some people would get in before others. I didn't have to guess where I would be in the line.

But rather than heading toward the back of the line, Samir
walked up to the girl with the clipboard. He gave her the
same air kiss on both cheeks everyone seemed to use in this
city. She smiled back at him before reaching down and un-
clipping the velvet rope. Samir turned back, waving everyone
through. One by one, we started filing behind him, descend-
ing the stairs without a second glance for the people standing
on the pavement.

"What just happened?"

"Samir's a member at all the best clubs in London. He can
always get people in." Mya nudged me forward. "That's why
everyone puts up with the fact that he's also a bit of an ass."

"But what about all those people? How long have they been
waiting in line?"

Mya shrugged. "Probably an hour or so."

"That doesn't seem fair." I shuffled forward, grabbing the
metal railing as I made my way down the steps.

"Welcome to London."

I felt as though I was entering a secret world—one open only
to the wealthy and glamorous.

The club wasn't big; the compact space was littered with tables, most already full. There wasn't really a designated dance floor. Rather, people grouped together, dancing in all empty spaces. A DJ stood in the corner mixing while a giant video screen played strange patterns of swirling bright colors. I figured it was the kind of thing you enjoyed if you were on something. Otherwise, it just looked strange. The main focal point, though, was the bar. It covered nearly the entire back wall, its surface lit up in eclectic light patterns, matching the colors on the video screen. Girls danced on top of it.

I had felt out of place at the boat party. Here I felt as if I had walked into Oz.

Samir led the group over to a small table, everyone cramming in together. I slid in between Michael and Mya. Immediately, a waitress came over with the biggest bottle of champagne I'd ever seen. Things that looked like sparklers exploded from the top of the bottle. No one else seemed to think there was anything unusual about the pyrotechnics or the giant-sized bottle of champagne.

Right. No big deal.

"I think I'm going to head to the bar for a second," I whispered to Mya.

I got up from the table, wondering for the millionth time what I was doing with them. Everyone acted like Samir was footing the bill, but I couldn't help but feel guilty that he barely knew me and yet he was buying me champagne. I figured the mini fireworks display, which no one else at the club had gotten, meant something special. And by *special* I meant *expensive*.

I pushed through the crowd of people, making my way up to the bar. I paused for a moment, trying to find the biggest gap of space between the dancing girls.

I leaned across the bar top, struggling to catch the bartender's attention. There were at least twelve other girls trying to do the same. My gaze caught with a guy standing next to me at the bar. His arm grazed mine, his hips bumping against me as the crowd pushed us together. He grinned.

"Hi."

Hello.

He was tall, really tall, with a gorgeous head of dark, chocolate-brown hair. He was dressed in what was clearly the standard uniform of a pair of dark jeans and a suit jacket with a collared shirt underneath.

He wore it well. Really well.

He grinned at me. "Can I buy you a drink?"

There was no way I was ordering a soda now. Even though I was underage in the US, here I could legally drink.

For a moment I felt the familiar rush of nerves and fear filling me. But whether it was the dress or the champagne, this time I didn't freeze. I managed a nervous smile and prayed the club's darkness masked any flush that might cover my cheeks. "Sure. Thanks."

He signaled to the bartender. "What do you want?"

I hesitated for a beat and then gave him my order.

He relayed it to the bartender for me.

The guy turned his attention back to me. "I'm Hugh."

"Maggie."

"You're American. Welcome to London. How long have you been here?"

"Just a few days."

"What brings you to London? Work?" He leaned against the bar, propping his arm against the frosted glass, his body dominating the space around him. Colors lit up beneath the bar top, alternately flashing pink and red.

This could not possibly be my life.

"I'm doing a master's." The lie flew out of my mouth before I could stop it. For some reason I didn't want to tell this guy I was only nineteen.

The bartender handed me the drink.

"What do you do?" I asked, leaning my elbows against the bar top.

"I own a bar in Chelsea. Cobalt." He reached into his jeans pocket and pulled out a business card. He handed it to me, our fingers grazing as he slipped the card into my hand. His fingers lingered on mine for a beat. "You should come by sometime, bring some of your friends. I'd love to take care of you."

He leaned in closer. His lips grazed my cheek, hovering near my ear. A shiver ran down my spine. He smelled good. Really good. Like citrus and pine and something smoky I couldn't quite identify. He leaned back, that same smile still on his face. "I have to head out. I was just settling up my tab." The bartender walked over, handing Hugh a platinum credit card. "It was nice to meet you, Maggie from America."

I grinned, unable to keep the silly expression from my face. "It was nice to meet you, too."

"Come and see me sometime."

When he was just a dot in the sea of dancers, I stared down at the card in my hand. *Hugh Mitchell. Cobalt. Owner.*

I turned back to the bartender, draining the last of my drink. "Can I have another?"

5

I was drunk. Really, really drunk. I'd never been drunk before, but I still recognized it when I saw it.

And I was a hot mess.

"Are you sure you're okay? You're swaying."

I struggled to focus on Mya. Her dress sparkled back at me. "I'm great." At least that's what I meant to say. The words came out a bit jumbled as I tripped over my tongue.

"I can't find a waitress. Sit down and I'll get you water from the bar."

I sank down on one of the small leather stools, grateful for the break on my feet, tugging on the hem of my dress in a desperate attempt to pull it down.

Not so much.

We'd been here for a couple hours now, and the group had scattered, leaving me alone.

"Nice dress."

Speak of the devil…

Samir appeared seemingly out of thin air, sinking down next to me at the table. I looked straight ahead, ignoring him. At least I tried to. He shifted and our legs brushed against each other.

I had just enough liquid courage to voice my thoughts aloud.
"Go away."

"It's my table," he countered smoothly.

"Fine. Then I'll go away."

"Come dance with me."

"I don't feel like dancing."

"You're already swaying, you're halfway there," he teased.

"Not funny."

"You smiled a bit."

God, he had a beautiful mouth.

"I did not."

"Yeah, you did. See, right there, that's a smile." His finger
reached out, brushing against my lips as if to prove his point.
He pressed down gently, tracing the shape of my bottom lip.
His eyes darkened.

Warmth flooded me.

What the hell was wrong with me?

"It's not a smile."

"If you say so." He winked.

My thoughts were a muddled, jumbled mess, confusion war-
ring with desire. How could he hit on his girlfriend's roommate?

"Has anyone ever told you that you're a giant pain in the
ass?" I blurted out.

"All the time. Come on." Samir held out his hand.

I swayed forward, teetering on the tiny heels. "Crap." I
grabbed Samir's hand, more for balance than anything else.

"Dance with me."

I lifted my chin a notch, meeting his gaze. I felt as though
we were playing chess and he was five steps ahead of me. I
could blame the alcohol, but he was a little drunk, too. I still
couldn't keep up with him.

"Dance with me," he repeated. His dark eyes sparked with
amusement—and something else, something infinitely more

dangerous. For a moment, everything seemed to stand still. We stared at each other, our hands still joined. His palm moved, his fingers curving, linking with mine.

My heart pounded furiously in my chest.

Samir made a gap in the crowd, pulling me along with him. A techno song blared from the speakers. He began moving to the music, surprisingly graceful. I struggled to follow his lead. The boy had moves. It wasn't hard to imagine other places he could put those moves to good use.

"You can dance."

Samir laughed. "Don't look so surprised." He leaned in closer to me, his lips brushing against my ear, his arm wrapping around my waist to pull me closer to his body. "My mother used to make me take dance lessons."

I giggled despite myself. "I can't see that at all."

"I was pretty good." He glanced down at me. "You're not so bad yourself."

His hand traveled downward, hovering just at the small of my back. Through the dress's thin material, the heat of his skin pressed against me. His hand stayed there for a moment, its presence both reassuring and discomfiting. He began stroking my lower back, his movements slow and lazy, his fingers tracing patterns on my body. Each touch lit a fire within me.

The beat changed, couples moving closer together. I let Samir pull me toward him, enjoying myself too much to stop. His body was lean, but judging by the hard muscles pressing against me, he knew what to do with it. He moved against me, and suddenly everything stilled again.

My body rocked against his, relishing the feel of him pressed against me. His hand slipped an inch lower, hovering below the small of my back.

His lips moved toward my ear, rubbing against the curve and down to my earlobe. His teeth grazed the lobe with a nip. I shivered. His lips roamed down, tracing the curve of my jaw.

He pressed soft kisses there, setting off a new wave of emotions. I was hot and achy all over, his face buried in the curve of my neck, his lips doing all sorts of naughty things to me.

I'd never lost control like this. I was logical, cautious when it counted. This was something else entirely.

Samir's lips drifted to my cheek. I froze, no longer dancing, hovering on the brink of what would happen next. We stood there, our bodies against each other, unmoving.

Somehow, I knew he was going to kiss me. I don't know how I knew it was coming, but some instinct in me just *knew*. I blamed the champagne for the fact that I didn't move away. Or maybe it was just my own curiosity. Or perhaps it was the desire reflected in his eyes.

Samir's lips brushed against mine, soft at first. Teasing. Then more insistent, his tongue brushing against mine, licking into my mouth, bolder now, his mouth opening wider, the kiss deepening. It wasn't anything like I expected for my first kiss. It was hot, and reckless, and completely unexpected. It only took me a beat to catch up before my mouth moved against his. I had no idea what to do, if I was even doing it right, but none of that seemed to matter anymore. I just felt, giving myself over to his lips, his hands, his body. My needs.

His body still pressing against me, he maneuvered me through the crowd, his hands in my hair, his lips devouring mine. We bumped into people, neither one of us bothering to break apart. He sucked on my bottom lip, drawing it into his mouth, giving me soft little bites, following the motion with the soothing sweep of his tongue.

I moaned against his mouth. I wanted more. More kissing, more touching. *More.*

This was unfuckingbelievable.

The wall pressed against my back. My eyes fluttered open. Samir had guided me into a dark corner, just off the dance floor. His body blocked out most of the crowd, his lips made the rest of the club disappear. His hands were *everywhere*, leaving a trail of heat in their wake. Parts of my body I never knew could be sensitive tingled—the curve of my neck, my collarbone, the little spot behind my earlobe. I had no idea what I was doing, but somewhere along the way—between the dancing and this—I'd learned the moves. He was good. Very, very good. And I never wanted him to stop.

His hands played with the neckline of my dress, his fingers trailing along my skin, dipping underneath the fabric. They hovered dangerously close to my breast.

And then suddenly he wasn't touching me at all.

Samir broke apart from the kiss first. My eyes widened, staring at him in breathless anticipation, frustration flooding my body.

Samir stared back at me, something that might have been shock flashing across his face. It was there for only an instant before his cocky smile slipped back into place.

"Sorry. Got carried away."

A girl bumped into me. I stumbled forward. Samir reached out, catching me. "Want to sit down?"

I nodded, my brain still running in circles, my body a mass of confusion. As soon as he pulled away from me it was like a bucket of cold water had been thrown over me. What had I just done—what had I nearly let him do—*in public?* The worst part? As horrified as I was that we'd even started making out, part of me was just as upset we'd stopped.

What the fuck?

Samir walked me back to the table, his arm around me keeping me from stumbling. Just that touch was enough to send another wave of desire running through me. I tried not to lean into the curve of his body.

"That never should have happened. I don't know what I was thinking. I *wasn't* thinking. Please don't tell anyone," I blurted out, struggling to not freak out.

I was the new girl. The last thing I needed was for Fleur to hate me more than she already did, and there was absolutely no excuse for the horrific mistake I had just made.

"Promise," I repeated, my tone desperate.

For a second something flickered in Samir's eyes. But as quickly as it appeared, it was gone. "Sure. Have it your way." He hesitated for a beat, his gaze running over me. "I'm going to go say hi to some friends at another table." He placed a swift kiss on my cheek. "Thanks for the dance." He winked. "And everything else."

I watched him walk away, my jaw hanging open in shock. I somehow still couldn't wrap my mind around what had just happened. My first kiss wasn't supposed to be like this. I'd had it all planned out. I was supposed to go to Harvard, meet *the* guy at Harvard. He would be my first kiss, the guy I would have sex with for the first time, the guy I would eventually marry. Maybe it sounded naive, but I didn't care. I had it all planned out. This had not been in my plans.

I ran my fingers over my lips. They felt soft, swollen. My breasts felt sensitive, my nipples tight. My body felt as if it belonged to someone else. No one had ever touched me like that before. I'd never wanted anyone to.

"Where'd you go?"

I jerked my hand away. Mya stood in front of me, a bottle of water in hand.

"Bathroom," I lied. "I just needed to get away from the loud music and everything."

"I think we're about ready to go soon. Michael's gathering the group."

I took the water from her, taking a long swig from the bottle. Mya plopped down next to me on one of the stools.

"Do you know where everyone else is?" she asked.

I wasn't going to fess up to knowing anything about Samir's whereabouts. "No idea."

Mya groaned. "Well, I'm leaving in fifteen minutes regardless of who is ready to go. I'm exhausted and my feet are killing me."

"Same."

"You ladies had enough for the night?" Michael appeared in front of us.

I nodded, beyond relieved to see him. "Yeah, I'm pretty tired."

"Come on, then. We can make our exit. The rest of the group can find their own way home."

My hand clutched in his, I followed Michael out of the club. Mya trailed behind us, her hand pressed against my back. I turned my head to the right, my gaze drifting across the room to the tables pushed up against the far wall.

I couldn't help it.

Samir sat at one of the tables. His head jerked up and he met my gaze across the crowded room.

My cheeks warmed.

I tore my gaze away.

So much for my first kiss.

6

Firsts. There was something about the first day of school. Today felt like the start of everything, not just the start of classes. Today was the day I would finally get to focus on subjects I cared about rather than sitting through boring biology classes and the like.

My inner nerd hummed with excitement.

I stood in front of my wardrobe, deciding what to wear. When I packed for London, my clothes had seemed fine. But after Saturday's party I began to realize fashion was a serious business at the International School, and I had no idea how to play the game.

"That really doesn't go together."

I kept my gaze trained on the wardrobe, too embarrassed by what had happened between me and Samir that night at the club to risk facing her. I had been avoiding her since the kiss, and thankfully, she neither seemed to care nor notice, and Samir seemed to have kept his word and not mentioned it to anyone. We were just lucky no one saw us.

Fleur thrust something orange and pink in my line of sight. "Try this. It'll help the outfit out." She paused. "Without it you look a little sad."

I grabbed the scarf out of her hand. I had ten minutes to get to my classroom building. I couldn't imagine anything worse than being late on the first day.

"Thanks," I mumbled, wrapping the scarf around my neck. I stood back, studying my appearance in the mirror. She was right—it was better.

When I turned around, Fleur was gone.

"You look great," Noora called out from her side of the room. "I like the dress."

"Thanks. Do you have class this morning?"

"Not until the afternoon. What class are you headed to?"

I had my schedule memorized, printed out and tucked in my planner in case I forgot.

"Intro to International Relations with Graves."

Noora wrinkled her nose. "Have fun with that. It sounds like the kind of class that makes me glad I'm an art major."

It was the class I was most looking forward to.

I rushed out of the room, hurrying through the hall and down the stairs, weaving my way through the groups of students standing in the lobby. I left the building, trying to settle the nerves in my stomach.

King's House was the main residence hall at the International School. The building housed most of the dorms along with the cafeteria, several staff offices and a common room. Our classes were held one street away in a separate building.

I made the trip in seven minutes, barely walking through the classroom door in time for class to start. The room was small, but filled with students. There was only one empty seat.

"You have got to be kidding me."

Samir lounged in his chair, his legs crossed at the ankles, right next to the only open chair. He grinned. "Miss me?"

"Hardly." I rolled my eyes, sliding into the seat next to him. "Are you even supposed to be in this class? Aren't you a soph-omore?"

"Junior."

My eyes narrowed. "Why are you in an intro class? What's your major?"

He beamed at me. "IR."

"Bullshit."

He laughed. "I speak the truth."

"You're a junior and you're just now taking Intro to IR? How is that even possible?"

"It used to be at eight. I don't do morning classes."

"You don't do morning classes?"

"I like to keep my mornings open…for other activities." He winked at me.

"I can't deal with this right now."

"You love it."

"Does this whole persona you've got going normally work for you?"

"All day…and night long."

"Okay, it looks like it's time to start." My head jerked up at the sound of our teacher's voice. He stood at the front of the room—somehow, I had completely missed his presence. "If you're in here, then you're supposed to be enrolled in Introduction to International Relations."

I spent the next hour furiously scribbling down everything he said. International Relations—as the professor explained it—studied the relationships between countries. He walked us through introductory concepts, handing out the syllabus and going over his expectations for the class. Even Samir's presence couldn't distract me.

I was hooked.

Few people spoke in the first class; the professor just lectured while we all took notes. Well, some of us took notes. It was easy to tell the students who were really into the subject and the ones who wished they were anywhere else.

Samir didn't bother picking up his pen.

"Good class," Samir commented when class came to an end.

I tossed him a skeptical look. "Were you even paying attention?"

He grinned. "Can I help it if I was distracted by the great pen shortage? The suspense of whether you would run out of ink was way more compelling than anything Graves had to say."

I stared down at my desk. Four pens stared back at me.

Was that unusual? It seemed prudent to have backups. For my backups to have backups.

"There's nothing wrong with being prepared."

He grinned at me, an almost goofy grin that seemed totally at odds with his cocky persona. I waited for him to say something, waited for a joke that never came. He just stared at me. Not the stare that made me feel like he'd seen me naked, but another stare. One that made me feel like he saw through me, one that felt impossibly more intimate.

We hovered in the doorway for a moment. Out of the corner of my eye I caught sight of Fleur leaving one of the other rooms. Guilt and nerves filled me. Time to move on.

I took a deep breath. "See you around."

For a moment, he looked like he was going to say something in response, but instead he nodded and walked away toward Fleur.

By Friday I had somewhat settled into academic life at the International School.

After classes got out on Friday afternoon, I took the Tube down to Westminster. I was still learning the way the complicated system worked, trying to feel like a real Londoner. Luckily the color-coded lines helped a bit. I took the green line down a few stops from High Street Ken. When I left the station, I turned my head, struggling to get my bearings. Then I saw it.

The Houses of Parliament were one of the most awe-inspiring

things I'd ever seen. I crossed the street, standing in a grassy square opposite the buildings.

I hadn't totally chosen the International School on a whim. When I received that horrid letter from Harvard, I panicked. I didn't have a backup plan—not a good one, anyway. I had no desire to stay in the same town where I'd lived my whole life, feeling like I never quite fit in. I wanted a chance to do something different. If I couldn't make one of my dreams happen, I wanted a chance at another one.

London had been a dream, one I promised I would indulge when I graduated university and made something of myself. Now, standing in front of Parliament, I felt the sense of accomplishment that had eluded me since my Harvard rejection. I was living my dream now.

7

"So how is it? Are you homesick?"

I leaned back against my pillow, shifting the phone in my hand. My roommates were out for the day, and it was the first time I had really had any privacy to call home. I talked to my grandparents before calling my best friend, Jo.

"It's amazing. Even better than I thought it would be."

"I'm so jealous."

I grinned. "Whatever. You're probably hanging out with all the frat guys at Carolina."

"Okay, yeah, maybe I've been to a few parties. How are the guys there?"

I grinned. "I did meet one."

"Spill."

I filled Jo in on the Hugh story.

"Are you going to go to his bar?"

"I don't know."

I wanted to, but what if he didn't remember me? Or he was just being polite by offering his card?

"Have you met anyone else? Have you kissed anyone yet?"

I blushed, grateful she couldn't see my face. "Ughh. Sort of."

Jo shrieked into the phone. "Oh, my God, Maggie. I can't believe I missed your first kiss. I need details on these things."

I laughed. "I'm sorry. You're right. I've been a bad friend. I should have called you instantly and filled you in."

"Well, you can make it up to me now. Spill. Now."

"It's not the greatest situation. I don't even like him. And he's my roommate's boyfriend. And she already hates me even without knowing what we did. It was a huge mistake."

"Why did you kiss him, then? That doesn't sound like something you'd do."

"It just happened. I don't know. We were both drinking a lot, and then we were dancing, and we kissed. It was just a random, one-time thing. It was a mistake. One I feel terrible about."

"Was it good?"

I hesitated. *So good I couldn't stop thinking about it.* "Yeah, I guess it was. Objectively, I mean. If you stripped everything else away. But you can't change the fact that he has a girlfriend. Or that he's kind of an asshole."

"Are you going to do it again?"

Only in the strangely erotic dreams I couldn't seem to shake. "No chance."

There was a pause on the end of the line.

I sighed. "Fine. What?"

"I'm not saying anything."

"I know you aren't. I've also known you long enough to know that means something. So spill."

"Don't take this the wrong way—"

I laughed. "Well, that's an encouraging start."

"I just want you to be happy."

"I am happy."

"You do realize that making out with a random guy is the first spontaneous thing I've probably ever seen you do."

"That's not fair," I protested. "I came to London. What was that if not spontaneous?"

"Okay, fine. You're right. You going to London was a little spontaneous. But you have to admit, you weren't *really* going outside of your comfort zone. You've been talking about London since we were kids."

"And drunkenly making out with a random guy is now your definition of spontaneity?"

"For you? Yes."

Silence filled the line. I thought back to the dreams I'd been having since the night Samir and I kissed at Babel. This shit was way more complicated than I expected it to be. "I don't know how to handle him. He's way out of my league."

"Try."

"He's dating my roommate, remember."

Jo sighed. "Oh, Mags. When you go in, you go all in."

"Tell me about it."

"So, what's on the agenda for tonight?" Mya leaned back in her chair, pushing a half-eaten plate of food away.

I shrugged. "I don't know. Want to watch a movie or something? I should probably get started on homework."

Mya frowned at me. "It's Friday night. We just got through our first week of school. We're not staying in and watching a movie. And homework is out of the question. My brain needs a break." Her eyes lit up. "Let's go to Cobalt."

Apparently filling her in on meeting Hugh had been a mistake. "Absolutely not."

"Why not? You said you liked the guy. The least you could do is check out his bar."

The idea of seeing Hugh again sent a little thrill down my spine. And a wave of nausea in my stomach.

"I don't have anything to wear."

"You can wear one of my dresses."

"I don't know what to say to him. I feel silly just showing up."

"He wouldn't have invited you if he wasn't interested."

"I can't just go to some bar. What if we don't get in?"

"Get in where?"

I turned around, surprised by the sound of Fleur's voice. She stood over the table, her long hair pulled back in a high pony-tail. She was dressed in workout clothes—a hot-pink stretchy top and fitted black pants. Trust Fleur to make going to the gym a fashion show.

"To this bar in Chelsea," Mya answered, ignoring my dirty looks. "Cobalt. Have you heard of it?"

I kept my gaze averted, unable to meet Fleur's eyes.

"Yeah, it's a decent place. Who's going?"

"Me and Maggie."

"We haven't decided yet," I corrected. As much as I didn't want to go to Cobalt, I really didn't want to go to Cobalt with Fleur.

Fleur sat down in the chair opposite mine, not bothering to wait for an invitation to join us. "Why Cobalt?"

She posed the question to Mya, ignoring me.

I shot Mya a look.

"Maggie met a guy at Babel. He owns Cobalt and invited her to stop in to say hi."

Fleur's gaze shifted to me, lingering on my face. Her eyes narrowed for a moment—I had no idea what she saw there but I couldn't help but feel I'd been judged and found wanting.

"What are you going to wear?" There was just a hint of scorn in her voice.

"She's going to borrow one of my dresses," Mya volunteered. Her eyes lit up. "Why don't you do her hair and makeup?"

Fleur shrugged. "Why not? I don't have any plans tonight anyway." Her voice trailed off and a frown crossed her face.

A boy, the likes of which I had only seen in movies, strolled in with a stunning brunette tucked against his side. He had similar coloring to Fleur's, his dark hair and eyes suggesting some Greek or Italian heritage. For a moment his gaze traveled over the table, before it stopped, lingering on Fleur.

She stiffened, ducking her gaze. She pushed back from the table.

What was that about?

"Fine, we'll meet at nine."

I blinked. Did Fleur just make a plan to hang out with me? Part of me wanted to go. Part of me was still scared. Hugh had been cute—and he'd seemed a little interested in me. I didn't want to spend my college years single. Besides, Jo had a point. I needed to be more spontaneous, needed to put myself out there more. I did *not* need to focus on a certain kiss I couldn't get out of my mind.

"Fine. But no guys, okay?"

Fleur nodded, her voice sounding relieved. "It'll be a girls' night."

She left, leaving me and Mya sitting alone at the table.

"What was that about? Who's the guy?"

Mya frowned. "Fleur's ex, Costa."

"Was that the guy she dated before Samir?"

"Samir?" Mya laughed. "They're not a couple."

"Wait—What do you mean they're not a couple?"

"Fleur and Samir? Not even kind of."

"But they're always together."

Now that I thought about it, I'd never seen them kiss or any-thing. And Samir didn't really look at Fleur like that. But they were so close, I'd just assumed...

"They're friends. Best friends. Besides, Samir's kind of a player. I don't think he does girlfriends. He kind of has *bad idea* written all over him."

I waited for Fleur and Mya on the front steps. I was beyond nervous. I didn't do things like this—chase after a guy. At least the old version of me didn't. I wasn't quite sure what to make of the new me. She seemed a little reckless.

"Hot date?"

My head jerked up as my stomach did a somersault. I knew that voice.

Samir stood in front of me, dressed in a collared dress shirt and jeans. A flush spread across my cheeks.

"Maggie?"

"Hi." It came out as a squeak.

Was it my imagination or did his gaze sweep over my body, lingering on my boobs? I crossed my arms over my chest.

He grinned. "You look good."

So do you.

"Thanks."

"On your way out?"

"Girls' night with Fleur and Mya."

His smile widened. "So, you and Fleur made peace?"

I laughed. "I wouldn't say we made peace. That might be overly optimistic."

"You'd be surprised. She's not so bad. It just takes her a while to warm up to people."

That seemed like the understatement of the year, but I let it slide. I still couldn't get past the fact that they weren't dating.

Samir shoved his hands in his front pockets, a flash of tan skin showing at the motion. My gaze was riveted to the spot. My fingers itched to reach out and touch him there. I fisted my hands on my hips.

"So, are we going to talk about it?"

I jerked my head up. A knowing smile spread across Samir's lips.

"I don't know what you're talking about."

He quirked a brow at me, his head tilted to the side, his expression considering. "So that's how you're going to play it?"

"Pretty much."

Samir grinned. "Fine. I have my memories to keep me company." He winked at me. "And believe me, I have plenty of good memories."

I reached out and shoved him, the move reflexive, my hand fisting the expensive fabric of his shirt. I froze mid-motion, my hand half pulling him toward me, half pushing him away.

"Why won't you admit you want me?" Samir asked. "It was obvious when your body was wrapped around mine."

I flushed. "My body was never wrapped around yours," I snapped, releasing my hold on his shirt. "It was a one-time, stupid, drunken thing. It'll never happen again."

"Sure, it won't."

"You haven't told anyone, have you?"

"Told anyone about what?"

He was utterly impossible.

"You know what I'm talking about."

He tossed me a knowing smile. "I thought you didn't know what I was talking about."

"The kiss," I hissed.

"I remember a lot more than just a kiss. I remember exploring you with my hands, tasting you, your body pressed up against the wall—"

"Did you tell anyone?"

"No."

He took a few steps forward, closing the distance between us. Something tumbled in my chest. His lips brushed against my cheek, pressing a swift kiss there. Just as he'd done at Babel before we'd parted ways.

I stood frozen, too surprised to move.

"See you around, Maggie."

I stood on the steps, watching him walk away, hating the part of me that wished I were going with him.

8

Walking into Cobalt I was struck by three things. First, as tacky as it sounded (and I only said it in my head), if Hugh really did own this place, he was loaded. Loaded in a very adult sort of way, in which I didn't fit. Two, I had no idea what I would even say to Hugh when I saw him. And, finally, whatever else happened tonight, this "girls' night" was something I never could have predicted.

I wouldn't have gone as far to say Fleur was *nice*. She seemed to be grudgingly accepting my presence because Mya wanted me there.

Fleur led us to a small table in the corner. She sat down first, crossing her legs. "Do you see him?"

I scanned the room. The decor was sleek and modern, the bar filled with well-dressed people, the majority of whom looked several years older than us. I had felt glamorous on the way here, but being in a bar like this, so far from how I had grown up, surrounded by so many beautiful people who looked way more secure in their skin than I ever was, I felt that confidence slipping away.

I shook my head.

"What's his name?"

I hesitated, not sure I trusted her with anything. "Hugh."

The backflips in my stomach started up again. "This was a bad idea. He probably won't remember me. Let's just go somewhere else."

Fleur frowned. "I'm not leaving. We just got here."

"What's up?" Mya asked. "You seemed excited on the way here."

"I didn't know what all the girls would look like on the way here."

"It's London," Fleur interjected.

"I was talking to Mya."

Fleur shrugged, completely nonplussed by my angry face. "It's London," she repeated, her French accent creeping in. "There will always be girls. There will always be beautiful girls. You can either stay in and lament that fact, or you can go out and be one of the beautiful girls. It's not about what your hair looks like or the dress you're wearing. It's about how you feel inside. How you see yourself is how others see you."

"That's easy for you to say. I'm not sure it's like that for the rest of us."

Fleur ignored me, signaling to a waiter. "London is all about perception. With the right attitude you can have any guy you want. You just have to play your cards right." The waiter hovered near her side. "Now, what was the guy's name?"

I gaped at her. It was strange to think she'd just given me something akin to advice.

"Hugh. His name is Hugh."

Fleur turned to the waiter, a beaming smile on her face. "Is Hugh here?"

The waiter nodded, clearly speechless.

"Excellent. Will you tell him Maggie from Babel is here to see him?"

My heart pounded madly in my chest. "We didn't order drinks," I protested, desperately needing liquid courage.

Mya grinned. "I don't think we're going to need to."

★ ★ ★

The waiter came back with a bottle of champagne and three glasses. Fleur nodded her approval before turning her attention to a group of guys at the table opposite ours. My gaze darted back and forth around the room. I didn't see any sign of Hugh.

"Maybe we shouldn't have bothered him on a busy night."

Fleur rolled her eyes. "If you're going to keep complaining, I'm going to leave you and go sit with those guys. Stop freaking out. He sent over a very nice bottle of champagne. He's interested. This is just all part of the game."

"That's the problem. I don't know how the game is played."

"Let me guess. You've never had a boyfriend?"

"I've been busy," I shot back defensively. "Focusing on school. Getting into a good college." *Trying to get into Harvard.* "I didn't exactly have time for boys and parties."

"What a little saint you are." Fleur's tone was mocking. "And yet you're here. So, a part of you doesn't just want to stay at home doing homework on the weekends."

"Okay, fine. What do you suggest?"

"Flirt. Make eye contact. If you get nervous, ask him questions about himself. Guys love talking about themselves. You can make a whole date go by, saying practically nothing at all."

Mya nodded, taking a sip of her champagne. "She has a point." She nudged me. "I think you're about to get your chance."

My hand tightened on the stem of the champagne glass.

Hugh walked toward us, looking even better than I remembered.

"Nicely done," Fleur whispered under her breath.

I couldn't help but agree. Tonight, Hugh was dressed in a perfectly tailored black suit, no tie, and a cream dress shirt underneath.

"By the way, he thinks I'm doing a master's," I mumbled.

Fleur's eyes widened. "Maybe I misjudged you. You're learning already."

I rose from my seat, my normal five-feet-four-inch height helped by the pair of red heels Mya had lent me. He still towered over me.

Hugh smiled widely, his gaze roaming down my body. "Hi." He reached out, gathering me close. Through the soft fabric of his shirt his muscular chest pressed against me, his strong arms embracing me. His lips brushed each of my cheeks in greeting before he pulled back. I stood there, my brown hair tumbling around my shoulders, my curvy body wrapped in Mya's tight dress, a faint blush spreading across my cheeks as his gaze took me in.

"You look gorgeous."

The gymnasts that had been working out in my stomach moved farther north. Something tumbled in the vicinity of my heart. When he said it, I believed him.

"Thanks."

His gaze shifted from me to Mya and Fleur. I quickly made the introductions, bolstered by their presence. Hugh asked how everyone was enjoying themselves before he led me off to a table tucked in the back.

My hand in Hugh's, our fingers linked together, I followed him through the bar. Occasionally, he paused to shake hands with someone.

I followed his lead, sitting down next to him on a comfy couch. Hugh moved closer, his suit-clad leg brushing up against my bare one. The movement sent a flash of heat through my body.

He waved over a waiter. "Do you want a drink?"

I nodded, leaning back as he ordered drinks for both of us. I had no idea what to talk about. Ask him about himself, Fleur had suggested. It couldn't hurt to give it a shot.

"How long have you owned the club?" I leaned forward,

closing the space between us. I wasn't completely unaware of the fact that the move gave him an excellent shot of my cleavage.

Hugh's gaze dipped for an instant before returning to my face. He grinned, taking hold of my hand once again, lacing my fingers with his. A thrill ran down my spine. His fingers stroked back and forth.

"About a year."

I would never get tired of hearing that accent. I struggled to concentrate on the conversation. "What did you do before that?"

"Traveled, mostly."

I grinned. "I'm jealous."

When I was a kid, I'd been obsessed with the idea of traveling. I'd had a globe in my room, and I used to place pins in all the places my dad had been—the ones he could talk about, at least.

Hugh's fingers moved up my arm, tracing small circles on the inside of my wrist. "I spent some time in Asia and Europe. Backpacked around, mostly. I got bored with that after a while and I ended up coming back." His fingers traveled farther up my arm. "Besides, my girlfriend wanted to settle down back home."

I froze. Girlfriend?

Hugh smiled ruefully. "We broke up a year later. She wanted to get married. I didn't. And then I opened the bar."

I didn't even know what to say to that. He'd almost been engaged? I hadn't ever even had a boyfriend. "How old are you?" The words tumbled out of my mouth before I could stop them.

"Twenty-seven."

Shit. Eight years.

"How about you?" His voice was low, a strand of my hair wrapped around his finger.

I couldn't tell him I was nineteen. "I'm twenty-three," I lied, the number appearing out of thin air.

"You're a baby."

He had no idea.

"I'm not that innocent," I teased, the words slipping out, adding to the weight of my lies.

Hugh's eyes widened, a grin spreading across his face. His fingers traveled higher, stroking the sensitive hollow of my neck. "Oh, really?" His lips whispered over my ear, moving up to press a swift kiss against my temple. "I'm beginning to wish I didn't have to work tonight. I'm tempted to test that statement."

His lips brushed against mine.

Holy shit.

"That is a shame." The words tumbled out of my mouth with the same seductive tone I'd slipped into since we sat down at the table. It was like someone had taken over my brain. "I'm tempted to let you."

I was flirting. I was actually flirting.

All these years Jo told me it would be easy if I could just let go a bit. She was right. Now that I'd let go, I didn't want to go back to the old Maggie. I liked this version—liked the flutter in my chest when Hugh looked at me like he wanted me.

He grinned at me. "I'm really glad I met you, Maggie."

My own smile echoed his. "Me, too."

Hugh glanced down at his watch. "I have to get back to work. You around later?"

I thought about saying "yes." Part of me wanted to. I liked the way I felt around him—shinier, more glamorous, simply more. But somehow Fleur's voice appeared in my head. *Play hard to get. Make him work for it.* "Sorry, I have plans."

Hugh nodded, the gorgeous grin still on his face. "I'm glad you stopped by." His lips wandered downward, grazing the corner of my mouth. "See you around, Maggie. I can't wait for next time."

9

"What the hell happened? He didn't even ask for my number."

Mya leaned back in her chair, an oversize pair of sunglasses covering her eyes, a coffee cup clutched in one hand. Last night after we left Cobalt, we'd made plans to meet at our neighborhood Starbucks for coffee.

"Dating in London is challenging," Mya replied.

"It's not like it was even a date. I sat with him for like a nanosecond."

"He looked interested."

I pulled off an end of my croissant, stuffing it in my mouth. "I guess. The whole thing was just confusing."

"That's London."

"He's twenty-seven."

"That's a little old."

"It's eight years." I sighed. "Well, as far as he thinks, I'm twenty-three. So, it's only four." I groaned. "You're the expert. Help me. What do I do next?"

Mya drew off her sunglasses, setting them carefully on the small Starbucks table. "He's playing the game."

"Yeah, that's kind of a problem, then, considering I don't know the rules."

Mya leaned back, studying me. "I'm surprised you didn't have a boyfriend in the US. You're cute. What was wrong with those American boys?"

I laughed. "I'm not great with guys."

"Why?"

"I don't know. I just get uncomfortable. Like in high school, there was this guy I liked. He was really popular, captain of the soccer team, really hot. We had, like, five classes together and I still couldn't manage to talk to him. Finally senior year came around and our chem teacher assigned us as lab partners. I spent the whole time planning out exactly what I was going to say to him. There may have been note cards involved." Mya snorted. "One day I got so nervous I knocked over one of our experiments."

Her eyes widened.

"Oh, yeah. I started a fire. So, for the rest of senior year, he knew me as the girl who started the fire in our chem class."

Mya cracked up.

"It was bad."

"You seem to at least be doing better here. No chemical fires."

I threw my napkin at her. "Laugh all you want. It sucks being this inept with guys. I do want a boyfriend. I just have no idea how to actually get one."

"I can only help you so much. I haven't dated a ton, either. You need Fleur."

I grimaced. "Trust me, that's the last thing I need." I hesitated. "What's the deal with you and Fleur? Why'd she come out last night?"

"I think she's lonely. It's a bad situation. A lot of their friends jumped ship with the breakup. I don't think she has anyone besides Samir and his crowd."

"Maybe she would have more friends if she was a bit nicer. She still barely speaks to me as it is, and I live with her."

She was marginally kinder to Noora. I figured she just hated

Americans. Or it was something I'd done. When I'd thought she and Samir were a couple, I considered the possibility that she might have noticed my attraction to him. But now that I knew they weren't, I couldn't understand it.

"She's hard to get close to," Mya replied. "But once you get to know her, she's not bad. And despite all the shit with Costa, she's really good with guys."

"I don't think there's anything to help me with. If he was interested in seeing me, he would do something about it."

Mya waved her hand dismissively. "There are a ton of other guys in this city. If this guy isn't the guy, you'll find someone else."

Mya and I separated at Starbucks. She had some shopping to do, and I had been dying to go to Hyde Park. From my dorm room window, I could just see the tops of the trees. I'd started going on these little walking adventures, exploring the city I'd come to love.

I crossed the street, walking through the oversize iron gates. It was still early for London and the park was fairly empty. I loved the city when it was like this. It felt like it was my own secret place to explore. I wrapped my coat tighter around my body, trying to ward off some of the morning chill. It might have been late September, but London was starting to get cold. I sat in the quiet for an hour, lost in my thoughts.

Brunch on the weekends was served until one; luckily, I had just caught the tail end of the meal. The cafeteria was mostly empty. I made my way through the line, frowning at the meager food offerings. Somehow, unbelievably, the weekend food selection was even worse than normal. I grabbed some cucumbers and white rice, the only appetizing options. I scanned the room for a seat.

Fleur sat by herself at one of the tables. I hesitated, shifting the tray in my hands.

"Can I join you?" I asked.

Fleur's head jerked up from the fashion magazine she had been reading. She paused for a moment before gesturing toward the empty chair. "Go ahead."

I sat down across from her. Fleur continued reading her magazine, her fingers flipping the pages at a rapid pace.

Costa walked by with a group of his friends. He didn't spare a look for Fleur, but her head jerked up at the sound of his voice. The stricken expression on her face said it all.

"I'm sorry."

Fleur's eyes narrowed, her gaze jerking away from Costa and focusing on me. "I don't need you feeling sorry for me. I'm fine. How about you? What are you going to do about that guy? The one from last night?"

"Hugh? I have no idea." I hesitated for a moment. "Mya thought I should talk to you. She seems to think you're some sort of guy whisperer."

"I'm not sure I'm the example you should hope to emulate."

I shrugged. "I'm massively out of my league here."

"Aren't we all?"

"Fair enough."

We ate the rest of the meal in silence before we went our separate ways. But I couldn't help but wonder if I'd seen the beginning chinks in the Ice Queen's armor.

Or maybe it was just wishful thinking.

10

Little by little, I began settling into life at the International School. I enjoyed my classes, loved getting into debates with my classmates. Here students from all over the world mingled together, forming friendships transcending their backgrounds or identities. The school wasn't Harvard, but it was special.

Most of all, I fell in love with London. I spent my free time walking around the city, exploring new places daily. Since my visit to Westminster, I'd added trips to Buckingham Palace, Harrods, the National Gallery, and the Tower of London. Sometimes I went with friends, but I often went on my own. It was the kind of place where you could never get bored.

"Are you staying in tonight?" Noora asked from across our dorm room. As usual Fleur had gone off somewhere.

"Yeah. Probably just doing some work. You?"

"I'm meeting some friends for a movie. Want to come?"

"I think I might pass this time. Thanks for the invite, though."

Noora nodded, grabbing her purse. "See you later."

My phone rang. Mya. "What's up?" I asked.

"We're going out."

I stared down at the textbooks spread out all over my bed. I had a ton of reading this weekend. And I was behind.

I pushed away the guilt.

I could study another time.

London was calling.

I followed Mya down the steps, stopping dead in my tracks.

Samir stood on the street in front of the building, leaning against a sleek black sedan. Fleur stood next to him.

Mya tugged on my hand. "You're coming."

"You could have mentioned that two of my least favorite people were included in our little group." I didn't even bother lowering my voice. Samir was a flirty thorn in my side and Fleur's thawing seemed to have been a temporary moment, never to be repeated.

Samir grinned at my words. Fleur just looked upset.

"You wouldn't have come if I told you the truth," Mya answered, nonplussed. "Besides, you need a night out. You've been way too good lately."

Samir turned to Fleur, a torrent of French escaping him. He didn't seem angry, but there was intensity behind his words—and a definite chill in her reaction.

Whatever he said to her, Fleur didn't look happy.

I already felt ridiculous enough, playing dress-up in one of Mya's dresses, too tight on my curvy frame. Now I felt like an unwanted interloper. "You know, maybe this was a bad idea," I called out, ready to turn around and go back in the building.

"You're coming," Mya snapped, shooting both Fleur and Samir a dark look.

Samir said something else in French. Fleur glared at me.

I really needed to learn another language.

Fleur turned her back to me, sliding into the back seat without another word.

"Come on." Samir jerked his head toward the car.

I hesitated.

"Come on." His lips curved into a grin. "Are you really going to let Fleur push you around like that?" He leaned in closer to me. "Trust me, your best play is to show no fear."

He had a point.

I slid into the back seat next to Mya, glad to have her as a buffer between me and Fleur.

Samir's friend Omar got into the front seat. I instantly recognized him as Samir's partner in crime from the first day on the stairs.

I leaned back into the leather seat, desperately wishing I were anywhere else. Fleur didn't talk most of the car ride, staring out the car window instead. Samir and Omar spent most of the drive speaking in Arabic. We ended up at Babel again.

As we walked toward Babel, I felt a nervous flutter in my stomach. Was Samir thinking of the last time we were here together? Because as soon as I set foot in the club, I couldn't get the memory out of my mind. At the same time, I couldn't help but wonder if I would run into Hugh again. It felt a bit like returning to the scene of the crime.

"Sorry it's a little tense tonight," Mya whispered.

I laughed. *That* was a massive understatement. "Why are we even here?"

"Samir called me and practically begged me to come out."

I gaped at her. "Are you joking?" Somehow, I couldn't see Samir begging anyone for anything.

"Fleur's not having the greatest day. It's her birthday."

"What's so bad about that?"

"Her mom was supposed to come to London so they could spend it together. But she bailed at the last minute to go to some spa in Switzerland."

There was nothing worse than being disappointed by your parents.

"Fleur was set to spend her birthday by herself, but Samir found out. I think this was his attempt to throw her a party."

My gaze flew to Samir. A few girls stood next to him and Omar, one of them pressing a swift kiss to Samir's cheek.

"And he told you it was okay to invite me?"

Mya shook her head. "It was his idea. He thought you would have fun." She grinned. "He said something about you seeming tightly wound lately? An excess of pens in class? I couldn't understand what he was talking about."

I laughed. He still gave me shit about the first day. At least now I was down to two.

"There's more to Fleur than what you see. A lot more. I wasn't popular in Switzerland. I was one of the only Black girls and some of the girls were really mean. Fleur wasn't like that. I'm not saying she's sweet, but she's not as bad as everyone makes her out to be. She has her good side. You just have to work to find it. It'll be fun. Promise."

There was a weird energy at the table tonight. Fleur was knocking back drinks, her expression hard. Samir hadn't broken apart from a girl he'd hooked up with when we first arrived. Omar didn't speak to anyone, leaving Mya and I to our own devices. I doubted I was good company. The last thing I wanted to do was sit at a table watching Samir make out with someone else.

I opened my mouth to plead my excuses so I could get out of here when Fleur leaned over to me and Mya. "Let's go dance."

Mya groaned. "I'm not in the mood. I think I'm just going to go home."

Relief filled me.

"I'm going to go with you," I shouted over the loud beat of the music.

Samir broke apart from the girl. His gaze met mine across the table. Something lurched in my chest as I hurried to look away, afraid he would see the confusion and inexperience reflected in my eyes. If I didn't get up from the table soon, I was going to have to leave. This was beyond awkward.

"I'll dance with you," I blurted out, turning away from Samir to face Fleur.

Mya stared at me.

Fleur looked surprised for a moment before she nodded. "Fine. Come on." She grabbed my hand, pushing her way around the table. She stopped in front of a raised platform, on display for the whole club to see.

"Up there?"

She rolled her eyes. "I don't dance on the floor like everybody else."

Of course she didn't. I stared back at our table—Samir was still ensconced with the group of girls. *What the hell*. I climbed up to the platform.

"This is such a bad idea," I muttered under my breath.

Ignoring me, Fleur began dancing to the music, moving her hips in a way I could only hope to emulate. My gaze roamed over the crowd.

I moved closer to Fleur, moving my body to mimic her moves. Our hips swayed to the beat of the music, our bodies nearly flush with each other. We were putting on a show and judging by the whistles we were getting from the crowd, they liked it. A photographer came over and snapped our picture. Fleur threw her arm around me, pressing a kiss on my cheek.

The flash went off.

So, this is what it was like. This is what it felt like to be wanted. To be one of the cool kids.

I loved it.

I grinned at Fleur. She had a point—on top of the platform it was impossible not to feel as though you were on top of the world. She flipped her hair back, tossing me a smug little smile.

I locked eyes with Samir across the room. He sat nursing a drink, the girl finally dislodged from his lap.

This time I didn't look away. I met his gaze head-on, shaking my ass to the music. Fleur grabbed my hand, pulling me into a twirl—and then I was facing Samir again. He hadn't stopped staring.

I didn't care.

I wanted this feeling, this rush, to last forever. I jerked my gaze away from Samir, passing over the crowd until it rested on—

A very tall, hot guy in a black jacket.

Hugh.

11

Hugh's lips spread into a wide grin as he nodded his head toward me.

Fleur nudged me. "Aren't you glad you came up here and danced? Now he sees he has competition."

"What are you talking about?"

"Look."

I followed her gaze. Sure enough, guys were standing near the platform, watching us dancing. Hugh made his way through the crowd, walking toward the platform.

"Hi, gorgeous."

I grinned. "Hi."

"Can I give you a hand?"

I took his outstretched palm, putting my hand in his. Our fingers locked as he pulled me down from the platform, one hand firmly on my waist. As I slid down, our bodies brushed against each other.

"Fancy seeing you here."

I grinned. "I wondered if you would be here tonight."

"I'm glad I am. Can I get you a drink?"

I nodded.

We walked to the bar together. He ordered our drinks and

guided me to a bench near the DJ booth. He draped his arm around my shoulders, his lips just skimming my ear. His hand played with the ends of my hair, the backs of his fingers barely touching the exposed skin above my collarbone. His touch was soothing...and not. It felt like the start of something. I just wasn't entirely sure what.

Hugh pulled back slightly, his gaze meeting mine. "I've been wanting to touch you since the first day we met."

Holy shit.

"Here." He pressed a swift kiss to my neck. "And here." His lips grazed my skin. "And definitely here." Hugh's head leaned in closer, his minty breath filling my nostrils. His lips brushed against mine. I opened my mouth slightly, a sigh escaping.

It was all the invitation he needed.

Hugh deepened the kiss, his hands reaching out to pull me forward onto his lap. His arms wrapped around my waist, pulling our bodies closer together. His body felt hard beneath mine and I couldn't resist the urge to press against him, to wrap my body around his strength.

Instinctively I looped my arms around his neck, bringing our bodies in closer contact, pulling him toward me. Someone—possibly me—moaned. His hand moved from my waist, sneaking up my leg, beginning at my ankle, gradually, leisurely, traveling north.

My body burned everywhere.

Anywhere else our behavior would have earned some strange looks and—given the way his hands roamed over my body—possibly an arrest. But this was London. We were just another couple in a long line of couples making out in the nightclub. The anonymity of the dark and the music made it feel like we were in our own private world. It was so easy to get lost in his kiss.

"Come back to my place," Hugh whispered, his hand high on my thigh.

I stilled, my heart pounding.

"Maggie?"

I jerked away from Hugh. Mya stood behind me, a knowing grin on her face.

"We're about to go. Do you need a ride?"

I was a virgin. He was twenty-seven. And so obviously not a virgin. If we went back to Hugh's place, he was going to want to pick up where we left off. And I doubted he would stop with a kiss. He was hot—and he was an *amazing* kisser—and I totally wasn't ready for him.

I turned toward Hugh. "I should go. I had a great time, though."

He pulled out a cell phone from his jacket pocket. "Why don't you give me your number and we can go out to dinner sometime?"

"Sure." I struggled to keep my voice nonchalant as I pressed the number into his phone.

Hugh leaned back on the bench, his face flushed, his lips swollen. He looked every inch the satisfied male. "I'll see you around, babe."

I walked out of Babel feeling as if I was walking on air.

As we gathered our stuff to leave, my gaze met Samir's. He looked through me, turning to Fleur, not even bothering to speak English so I could understand what he was saying. He acted like I didn't exist.

Was he judging me for making out with Hugh in the same spot I'd kissed him? A pang of guilt hit me.

Inexperienced or not, Samir had *unavailable* written all over him. If I gave an inch, he would take my heart and put it through a blender. I'd already suffered enough disappointment at the hands of a man, thanks to my father; I didn't need to add to my losses.

Hugh seemed different. He was a chance. One I wanted to

take. With Hugh I could be someone else. I wanted that opportunity…

Samir didn't speak to me the whole way home.

I couldn't sleep.

Nervous energy poured through me. There was something
about tonight. I felt as though I had become a different person,
changed the path my life was on with the risk I'd taken dancing
in front of all those people, with the kiss I'd shared with Hugh.

It felt good.

I grabbed a book, shutting the door behind me gently so I
wouldn't wake Noora. It was still late—or early, really—we'd
gotten back from the club at 4 a.m. I had no idea where Fleur
was.

I headed down to the common room, hoping it would be
empty. It was usually the site of large groups watching football
(soccer) matches but hopefully there wasn't one going on right
now in any part of the world.

I pushed open the door.

Fleur sat curled up on one of the couches, on the phone,
yelling in French. I'd seen her upset before, but I'd never seen
her this angry. Suddenly, she threw the phone at the wall. It
bounced before hitting the floor. I watched, mesmerized, as
the first tears began to fall. She sobbed, her body rocking back
and forth, her body curled up in a little ball.

I hovered in the doorway.

I remembered what Mya had told me about it being Fleur's
birthday, and also, what she had told me about her mom. Fleur
cried as though her heart had been broken in a way I understood all too well.

I closed the door behind me, walking toward her. "Are you
okay?"

Fleur's chin jerked. A flush spread across her cheeks. For a
moment I didn't think she was going to answer me.

"I'm fine."

I sat next to her on the couch, silent for a moment. "You don't look fine."

Her face was splotchy, tears still running down her cheeks. She laughed bitterly. "Go away." Her lip trembled.

She may have been telling me to leave, but her eyes said otherwise. She looked lonely. Maybe Mya was right, maybe she really did just need a friend.

I sat down next to her on the couch. "Do you want to talk about it?"

Fleur laughed again. "What, we danced together—I let you hang out with us once—and now you think we're friends?"

The words stung. But I could tell by the look in her eyes that she meant them to and I knew a thing or two about pushing people away.

"Mya told me about your birthday. And your mom." I shrugged. "I've been there. I've seen my dad a handful of times in the past five years. My mom left us when I was a kid. I barely remember her."

I threw out the words like they meant nothing, like they weren't a part of me, like I wasn't pretending that maybe the reason I played things safe was because I'd had my heart so irrevocably broken so long ago.

It was a few moments before she answered. "She's getting a facial in Switzerland." Fleur wiped her eyes. "I wanted her to come so badly. And she blew me off to go get a facial."

"I'm sorry."

Fleur shook her head. "I don't know why I bother anymore. She does shit like this all the time."

"What about your dad?"

"He's even worse. He's so busy that he doesn't even bother with me. He didn't call. Didn't even send a card."

I felt bad for her. At least I had my grandparents.

"That sucks."

I knew it was wholly inadequate considering the pain that she must be feeling, but there were some things that there simply weren't words for.

Fleur sighed. "It definitely does suck." What might have been embarrassment flashed across her face. "There's no need to babysit me. You can go now."

"What's your deal with me?" I asked her.

"What do you mean?"

"Why do you hate me? I didn't do anything to you. I've heard your rep, but still you're nowhere near as mean to Noora or anyone else. What gives?"

"What rep?" Her eyes narrowed. "The whole Ice Queen thing?" I nodded. "What else have you heard about me?"

Fleur was pretty much a legend around here. The rumors ranged from the bizarre to the truly unbelievable.

"You know."

She rolled her eyes. "I do. People have entirely too much time on their hands and impressively vivid imaginations."

"Fair enough."

She hesitated for a beat. "And I don't hate you."

"Right."

She shook her head. "I don't." She made a face, her tone reluctant. "You were kind of fun tonight. You're not so bad."

I laughed. "You really have a way with compliments. I'm going to head back to the room. Happy birthday."

I reached the door when Fleur called out to me—

"He's my best friend."

I froze, my hand on the doorknob.

"He's my best friend. He doesn't have girlfriends, doesn't hang out with other girls. But he wants you around."

My heart pounded in my chest. I didn't have to ask who *he* was.

I turned. "Samir and I aren't friends," I protested.

"He likes you."

That made me laugh. "I'm pretty sure you're wrong about that one. I don't even want to be friends with Samir."

Fleur shrugged. "Suit yourself."

"Is that seriously why you've been so tough on me?"

"I don't share."

"So, what you're saying is that Samir is yours?" I asked incredulously.

"Not like that."

"Well, whatever you think, you're wrong. I can't stand him most of the time. He's a pain in the ass and he seriously needs to be taken down a peg or two. I'm not trying to screw up your little best-friends-forever vibe you have going on. Seriously. I'd just like to not be saddled with a roommate who loathes me for the rest of the year. I thought we had fun tonight. And at Cobalt. You have your moments where you're almost nice."

"Gee, thanks."

"Can we have a truce? Please? It's going to be a long year if we keep this up. Not to mention the fact that I'm getting sick of taking your shit."

Fleur was silent for a moment and then her lips curved into a smile. "Fine. You can be part of the group."

"That's it?"

Maybe Samir had been right about the show-no-fear thing.

"Like I said, you're not that bad." Coming from Fleur that sounded like the highest of compliments.

I laughed. "Really? You sure about that?"

She grinned. "Yeah. I am."

12

Fall came to London, the leaves in Hyde Park changed, the weather turned cooler, and I adjusted fully to the rhythm of life at the International School.

Noora and I became closer. Rather than going out, I stayed in with her, watching movies in the common room and eating my way through British candy. Sometimes Fleur joined us. After our common-room truce, things improved with her. Slowly at first and then somehow, as unlikely as it was, we sort of became friends. As roommates the three of us got along well. Our interests were different enough that we each had our own space.

For the first time since I had gotten to the International School, I finally felt like I belonged. I had a solid group of friends now, and little by little I was starting to get to know everyone. In high school I never quite felt like I fit in. Here I hit my stride. My love life, on the other hand?

Sucked.

Hugh didn't call. Two weeks passed with no word from Hugh, not even a text. And I checked my phone. Constantly. But every time my phone rang it wasn't him. I finally gave Hugh his own ringer to cut down on the agony that came up every time my phone went off.

It didn't help.

I knew on some level I could have called him. Mya was solidly in the camp that I should, whereas Fleur said something about me losing all the power if I did and advised against it. I listened to Fleur. It wasn't that I believed she was some sort of guy whisperer so much as it was that I just couldn't call him.

I tried.

But every time I pulled his number up on my phone, and my finger hovered over the send button, I chickened out. Just like I'd chickened out on the offer to go back to his place that night at Babel. My lack of experience with guys was catching up with me. And I felt totally out of my league.

I didn't bother with the club scene. I figured I'd done something wrong that night at Babel—I hadn't kissed well enough, I should have gone back to Hugh's place with him. I had cocked it all up and now here I was sitting in the common room on a Friday night.

"This is pathetic." Mya tossed the television remote to me.

"What's pathetic?"

My head jerked up at the sound of Samir's voice. He walked into the common room, a bottle of Jack Daniel's in hand.

Fleur eyed the bottle greedily. "You better share," she warned.

Samir handed the bottle over.

Fleur took a long swig of the liquid before passing it over to Mya. She took a few sips from the bottle, wiping stray drops of whiskey from her mouth.

"So, what's pathetic?" Samir repeated, flopping down on the couch next to me.

I stiffened. Why did he always have to sit next to me? The Samir sex dreams had tapered off a bit, but I still didn't feel totally comfortable in his presence. And I knew he knew it. He was always taking little opportunities to brush his arm against mine in class or for his foot to touch mine under the desk. His little not-so-accidental innocuous touches drove me insane.

Mya groaned. "Us. We're pathetic. Here it is Friday night. In London, no less, and we're hanging out in the common room watching movies."

Samir's eyebrows rose. "No hot dates?"

"Fuck off." Fleur shot him a dirty look. "Trust me. You don't want to go there."

I winced.

Guys were not the topic to bring up around Fleur right now. I still couldn't figure out the deal with her and Costa. Despite our budding friendship, Fleur wasn't big on sharing her feelings. And Mya didn't seem to know a lot about the breakup. But whatever had happened between them, Fleur was clearly devastated. For the life of me I couldn't figure out how someone like her ended up in knots over a guy. Sure, Costa was hot, but was it worth it?

I wanted no part of her brand of heartache.

"What about that guy you were making out with at Babel?"

It took me a second to realize Samir was talking to me. I glared at him. "Shhhuut up." The words slipped out in an awkward tumble.

He blinked in surprise, a slow smile unfolding on his lips.

I flipped him off.

"Go away, Samir," Fleur called out, handing the bottle over to me. I flashed her a grateful smile. I took a swig, wincing at the overpowering alcohol.

"No way. This is much too entertaining." He turned toward Fleur. "I don't have to ask why you're upset. I've seen the way Costa has been with his girlfriend." Fleur's expression darkened. "But I'm curious to hear what has Maggie upset."

"Maggie's fine." My words were slurred. And I had just referred to myself in the third person.

Samir's eyes widened. "Maggie doesn't seem fine."

He sounded positively gleeful.

"Well, I am."

"Boy troubles?"

"Boys are assholes."

Samir leaned forward, propping his elbows on his knees. "Do tell."

Fleur sighed. "He might be helpful," she mused, whispering conspiratorially at me. "And he's obviously not going away." The last bit was delivered with a pointed look at Samir.

Which he ignored. *Of course.*

Samir shrugged, leaning back on the sofa. His arm draped behind my head. "It's up to you. You need guy advice. I'm a guy."

I didn't trust him at all. I didn't need my pathetic love life to become fodder for the International School gossips. It had been two weeks, though. Desperation set in. Besides, being quasi friends with Samir seemed safer than anything else we could be.

Samir rolled his eyes. "Are you going to share or what?"

"Fine. Yes. I'm upset about the guy from Babel. He hasn't called."

"Hmm."

"She should call him, right?" Mya suggested from across the room.

"No. Terrible idea," Samir scoffed.

"See, I told you." Fleur smiled triumphantly.

"Why shouldn't I call him?" I hadn't wanted to originally, but now that two weeks had gone by I was seriously wondering if I would ever see Hugh again. My pride seemed to be a little thing to hang in the balance.

"Because you'll look pathetic."

My gaze was skeptical. "Is that your interpretation or guy code?"

"Mine and guy code. Trust me. No guy wants a girl who throws herself at him. We like the chase."

"Right. That's why you let girls sit on your lap and make out with them. I didn't see much of a chase going on then."

"Jealous?"

He shrugged.

My eyes narrowed. The words just popped out of my mouth. "Your shrug is bullshit."

Samir stared at me, blinking twice. "What did you say?"

I had a tenuous grasp on my dignity, but I could have cared less. "Your. Shrug. Is. Bullshit." I carefully enunciated each syllable, my stare defiant. Samir's shoulders began to shake, his body erupting into full-on laughter.

I crossed my arms over my chest and frowned. "It's not funny."

He grinned. "It really is. You're so *American* it's adorable."

"News flash, I am American," I snapped.

"Well, my shrug is a French thing," he countered smoothly.

"Fleur doesn't shrug like you do."

"Haven't you figured it out by now, Maggie, no one does things like I do."

The way my name rolled off his tongue did things to me, a warmth settling low in my belly.

"Besides, you're only half-French," I sputtered.

He *shrugged* at me.

Fleur and Mya dissolved into giggles.

"My cousin can be a pain in the ass," Fleur called out, in between bouts of laughter.

I froze. *Cousin?*

My gaze darted to Fleur and back to Samir. "The two of you are cousins?"

"Our mothers are cousins. They're both French," Fleur volunteered. "So technically we're second cousins. But still. Family."

Mya shook her head. "How did I never know that?"

Samir winked at me. "I'm the black sheep of the family."

"That I can believe," I muttered.

Samir let out another shout of laughter.

"I'm glad I amuse you," I shot back tartly. I couldn't believe I'd kissed this asshole. Then it hit me. The Jack Daniel's spoke to me again. *Samir kissed me.* He wasn't just an opportunity to ask for guy advice. It was even better. He was the only person who could give me feedback on what I'd done to turn Hugh off. If I had the guts to ask.

An hour later Mya and Fleur decided they were tired and headed to bed. Samir hung back, flipping between TV channels before settling on a soccer—excuse me, football—match. I studied him carefully, trying to pretend I wasn't. My heart pounded wildly in my chest.

Was I really going to do this?

At this point it seemed like I had little to lose. I was pretty sure I'd given up my sanity a long time ago.

"Can I ask you something?"

Samir set down the remote, facing me. "Sure. What's up?"

I sucked in a deep breath. "That night we kissed—" My voice was barely above a whisper. "Do you think my kissing maybe has something to do with why I haven't heard from Hugh?"

I blamed the alcohol.

Samir leaned in closer to me, his face inches away from mine, our lips nearly touching.

A shiver slid down my spine.

"Yes."

13

"I think you need kissing practice."

He did not just say that. "You're joking."

"I'm not." Samir grinned. "I'm just saying. If you want to be good at it…"

"I don't want it that badly." This was *horrible*.

"Suit yourself. It's your loss." He winked at me, moving closer and wrapping an arm around my shoulders. I was too upset to shake it off.

"I find that hard to believe."

"How about this—why don't you explain the problem to me?"

"Fuck off."

Samir chuckled. "There's that attitude."

"Why are you such an ass?"

"Why are you so uptight?" he countered.

I got up from the couch.

Samir sighed. "Fine. Come back. I'll help you." He paused meaningfully. "After all, I have some firsthand knowledge of your kissing style."

My hand froze on the doorknob. I whirled around. "If you tease me—if you tell anyone about this—I swear I'll make your life a living hell."

I wasn't sure how I could make good on my threat, but he didn't need to know that. The smile tugging at the corner of his mouth suggested he wasn't as afraid of me as I would have liked.

I walked back to the couch, sitting on the end, putting some distance between us.

"From what I remember, your kissing skills are fine."

My eyes narrowed. "Fine?" That hardly sounded promising.

"Yeah. You weren't a bad kisser or anything. For the most part you seemed to know what you were doing."

"What do you mean 'for the most part'?"

"I mean, sure, I could tell you weren't super experienced kissing guys. But it wasn't bad or anything."

He didn't even have the good grace to look embarrassed by his words.

"It was my first kiss," I mumbled miserably, staring down at the worn sofa fabric. I regretted every time I'd turned down Jo's offers to go to a party in high school. Maybe then I wouldn't be in this mess.

Samir's eyes narrowed. "I was your first kiss?"

"Yes."

Why had I thought this was a good idea? Why couldn't the floor just swallow me up?

"I kind of like that," he announced after a long pause.

I rolled my eyes. "That's just great. Amazingly enough, feeding your ego wasn't exactly on the top of my to-do list this evening. Can we please move on to more important things?"

"So, you're not experienced. I think we've hit on the problem." He paused. "Who else have you kissed? Besides me?"

The blush deepened. "Just Hugh."

"And he's older?"

"A lot older."

"Then you have a problem."

"No shit. That's why I'm talking to you."

Samir sighed. "Okay, fine. Look. Just don't freak out. Kissing is about attraction. Just go with it and you'll be fine."

I blushed. It felt weird talking about this with Samir. But this was what friends did. And being friends seemed safer than the other thing...

Mya's words came back to me...

Samir has bad idea *written all over him.*

"Attraction isn't exactly the problem. It's more of a technique issue. I just don't know what to do. Or where to put my hands. I thought I did, but what if I've been doing it wrong the whole time?"

Samir's grin widened. "I can help you with that. Come here."

"No."

Samir rolled his eyes. "Stop being a drama queen. You want to learn how to kiss? Come here."

I felt like Eve being tempted by the serpent. I hesitated for a second, his offer lingering. "You can't tell anyone about this." I hesitated. "Or what happened before. And it's just this once—"

I closed the gap between us.

"The kissing lessons?"

"Yes, fine. Whatever you want to call them. Just this once. This is not a thing."

He grinned wickedly. "Fine."

Against my better judgment, I moved closer, like a moth to a flame. Our faces were inches apart. Having him this close made it hard to think.

"Kiss me."

I blinked. *Was he joking?*

"Kiss me," Samir repeated, his tone lazy.

I shoved against his chest. "You're not helping. Be serious."

"I am being serious. You want to learn how to kiss? Kiss me. Knowing how to initiate a kiss is just as important as knowing how to receive one. It's not enough to be seduced, you need to know how to seduce."

My hands remained on his chest, my fingers curled into the fabric of his black sweater. Curled into his warmth. Up close, I couldn't resist the opportunity to study Samir. His eyes were a dark coffee color, framed by ridiculously thick, long lashes. Dark curls of hair brushed against his collar. His skin was tan, certainly far tanner than my own pale skin. He was beautiful. Absolutely beautiful.

"Scared?" he teased.

Yes.

I was tired of being ruled by my fear and nerves. I closed the gap between our lips, lingering just a breath away from kissing him. My hand traveled north, releasing my grip on his sweater, moving up his neck. My fingertips brushed against his bare skin, the feeling silky smooth. My hand continued its upward path, growing bolder now, threading through Samir's hair, loving the feel of his silky curls beneath my fingers.

He stiffened.

Our gazes met. I held the force of his stare, shocked to see desire flaring in his eyes. It was all the encouragement I needed. My lips brushed against his—hesitant, exploring, hungry. Once, twice. Samir sighed, his mouth opening slightly. His breath tingled with mine, his tongue grazing my lips. He wasn't quite kissing me back, but he wasn't moving away, either. Clearly, he was going to make me work for it.

"Kiss me." He whispered the words against my mouth, taunting me with them, goading me further, pushing me over the edge.

"Shut up. This would be so much better if you didn't talk."

He chuckled, his lips vibrating against mine.

I opened my mouth, deepening the kiss, my tongue reaching out and grazing his. Suddenly everything exploded. The taste of him swirled in my mouth, the feel of his body against mine sent sparks through my body. He kissed me back. He kissed me like he was drowning, and I was his lifeline—mad, desperate kisses that had my body tightening in anticipation and my mind blown. *This* was nothing like I'd ever experienced before. And it was way better than our kiss at Babel.

"Better," Samir mumbled, the word nearly lost between our mouths. His words might have been noncommittal, but by the way his hands were moving over my body—cupping, stroking, squeezing—the way his mouth plundered mine—he was just as affected as I was.

I might have been naive, but the desire I felt pressing against me was enough to erase any doubts. He wanted me just as much as I wanted him.

I moved against him, emboldened now, deepening the kiss, throwing whatever inhibitions I had out the window. His body moved over mine, covering me, pushing me back until I was lying down on the sofa. I felt the worn cushions hit my back, shifting slightly until he was directly settled between my legs. I hooked my right leg over his back, putting our bodies in closer contact.

Samir reached down between us, lifting my shirt, baring my skin to his eyes. The cool air hit me with a blast, my skin pebbling with goose bumps. It was too much, too fast, too intense, too out of control. I broke away, my face flushed, lips puffy. We were wading deeper and deeper into uncharted territory.

"Stop." I tugged down on my shirt, running a nervous hand through my hair. It was a tangled mess. "Just stop." I scooted up to a seated position, hugging my knees to my chest. "I need a moment."

Samir moved off me, pushing back to sit on the couch opposite mine. When my breathing stilled, I lifted my head and met his gaze. The heat in his eyes was enough to send a shock through me.

What had we done?

"That was better," Samir acknowledged with a tilt of his head. A self-satisfied smirk crossed his face. I would have thought he was totally unaffected...if I hadn't noticed how quickly his chest rose and fell.

"Thanks for the compliment."

"Your kissing is fine. As much as the idea of kissing practice sounds good, you don't need it. Your lips—and tongue—are perfect just as they are. Your body is even better."

I didn't even know how to answer that. I was a mess—

I wanted to run. I wanted to stay. I wanted him between my legs, easing the ache inside me.

"I should go to bed."

Samir leaned forward, closing the space between us. I was riveted by the sight of his lips. I wanted them again. Badly. There was something about him, some temptation I was finding difficult to resist. I just wasn't sure why. My body's response confused me, tied me up in knots, had me searching for answers when I feared there were none. Only want, and need, and lust.

I wasn't thinking as I reached out, my fingers tracing his lips, much the same as he had done to me. His eyes darkened, his gaze smoky as my fingers stroked him, his lips swollen from my kisses. I was mesmerized by him, mesmerized by the feelings he evoked within me.

I burned for him.

As my fingers pressed down on his lips, feeling the weight of them, his tongue darted out, licking my skin before taking my finger into his mouth, sucking on it.

Desire flooded me.

My finger slid from his mouth. His expression was hooded, his chest heaving as though he had just run a race. It seemed to be the same pattern as my own pounding heart. We hovered there, indecision flaring between us. Inches separated us. If I moved forward, we would kiss again. And if I stayed where I was...

His breath mingled with mine before his lips swooped down on me again.

Later I would blame the alcohol and the late hour and the fact that Hugh was twisting me into knots. In the moment, though, it came down to one thing. Samir was there, kissing me. So, I kissed him back.

From the start this kiss was different. We knew each other now—I knew the weight of his body on top of mine, the touch of his lips, the feel of his tongue. I knew that he liked to nibble on my skin, his teeth just barely grazing my flesh. I recognized the groan that escaped from his lips.

Our bodies remembered each other. I would never forget this kiss.

He took me somewhere I'd never been before—a kind of pleasure I'd only read about, only ever imagined. It was just a kiss and at the same time, it was anything but.

I kissed him back, met him stroke for stroke, until his hands skimmed under my shirt, until I felt his hand brush my bra, his fingers whispering along the skin there, inches from my nipples.

It scared me that it was always like this with him, always a spectacular loss of control. It scared me that he pushed me out of my comfort zone and made me crave more than I should.

"I should go," I blurted out, pulling away from him. This time I leaped up off the couch, making my way toward the common room door. I wasn't going to make the same mistake again. But despite myself, I hesitated, my hand hovering over the handle. I tossed out the question behind me, not sure if I asked it more to hear his answer or to try and know my own.

"What was that?"

For a moment I didn't think he would answer me. And then I heard his voice, low and husky—

"Extra credit."

14

"Have you ever been out of control around a guy?"

Jo laughed. "Um, yeah. Why?"

Because I can't seem to keep my hands or my lips off Samir and I don't know what to do about it.

"Just curious." I shifted my phone to the other ear. "Things are weird here right now."

"I can tell."

I sighed. "I think I did something stupid this weekend. I made out with that guy again. The one I kissed."

"Not the British guy?"

"No. The other one."

"Was it good?"

"It was amazing." My voice sounded bleak.

"Don't sound so excited about it," Jo teased.

"It's complicated."

"Why? Because you like him?"

My fingers clutched the phone. "I don't like him."

I couldn't like him.

"Why?" Jo challenged.

Samir has bad idea written all over him.

"Because…" I struggled to find the right words. "I don't like the way he makes me feel."

"What do you mean?"

I sighed. "I don't know. I just don't feel like myself around him. I feel out of control, tied up in knots. I do things with him that I wouldn't normally do."

"Is that such a bad thing?"

It was scary as hell.

"Yeah. It is."

"It sounds like he likes you, though."

I hated the little thrust of hope I felt at her words. "I don't think so. He's always with other girls. And yeah, we hook up and stuff, but that's it. He's never said anything to me that would make me think he likes me."

"So why don't you tell him that you like him? Feel him out?"

I laughed. "Are you joking? I can barely talk to a guy without losing my shit. And besides, I told you—I don't like him. We just have this weird chemistry thing between us."

"Then take my advice—the only way to get over someone—"

"I don't like him," I protested.

"I know, I know. But seriously the best way to get over someone is to get under someone else."

I choked back a laugh. "Thanks. I'll take that one under advisement."

Suddenly my cell beeped. I pulled the phone away from my ear, staring at the caller ID.

Blocked.

My heart thudded. That could only mean one thing. "Jo, I gotta go."

"Okay, Mags. But take my advice."

"We'll see," I evaded, hanging up the phone.

My fingers shook as I hit Accept on the other call. My father's voice filled the line, coming through gravelly.

"How's school?"

I stilled, clutching the cell phone tightly in my hand. I hadn't talked to my father in months. The sound of his voice was enough to put dread in the pit of my stomach. No matter how hard I tried or how much I hoped things would be different, these phone calls never went well.

"Things are good. School is busy." I didn't think he really cared. I was a box he checked off once a month if I was lucky. *Make sure daughter isn't screwing up. Check.* Maybe these little phone calls assuaged his guilt. Maybe my grandparents put him up to it. I had no clue. Sometimes the feigned connection between us hurt more than the absent one.

"Where are you?"

"I'm on TDY for a few months. The phone connection's not great."

Silence filled the line. I struggled to think of something to say. "I heard you might come home for Christmas?"

Static sounded on the other side of the line. "That's the plan."

I felt a tightening in my chest, a familiar lump forming in my throat. And even worse, despite years and years of disappointment, I felt hope. Hope that things would be different. That this would be the Christmas that we would be a family.

Sometimes I hated the hope more than anything.

"How are your classes?"

I shook the feeling off. "They're fine."

"Well, hopefully you're at least getting a decent education out there. It sure costs enough."

I gritted my teeth, struggling to not point out the fact that he wasn't really contributing to my college expenses. I was here because I worked my ass off in high school and was lucky enough to get a scholarship. He had nothing to do with that.

"Maggie…"

The static became even stronger. A click sounded on the other end of the line.

He was gone.

I stared at my phone, struggling not to cry. I was used to this—phone calls that came at odd hours of the day. Bad connections. Months gone by without talking to each other. It shouldn't still hurt this much. But it did.

No one could hurt me like my dad did.

I shoved my cell into my bag, checking my watch. I had ten minutes to get to my next class. I hurried through the building, making my way up to the classroom and sliding into the seat next to Samir.

As much as I hated to admit it, the call with my dad affected me. It always did.

"You okay?"

The concern I heard in Samir's voice surprised me.

"Yeah. Why?"

"You look a little funny."

I fought off the blush.

"You ready to get your paper back?"

"We're getting them back today?"

Samir nodded. "Yeah, Graves announced it last class. Didn't you hear?"

I shook my head.

He shot me another concerned look.

Professor Graves walked into class, a thick stack of papers in his hands. "I have your papers," he announced from the front of the room, setting the heavy stack down on his desk. "Most of the grades were very impressive. You should all be very proud of yourselves."

He began calling out names. When he got to me, I stood on shaky legs, walking to the front of the classroom to pick mine up.

"Try harder, next time, Ms. Carpenter," he murmured to me.

I stared down at the paper in shock. An unforgiving letter stared back at me, the inky red mark blurring as my eyes teared up. I had gotten a C+. I had never gotten a C+ in my life. "How did you do?" Samir asked when I got back to my seat.

"Not great." My face heated, a red flush settling over my cheeks. Could this day get any worse?

He shrugged. "I wouldn't worry about it. It's just a paper, not the end of the world."

Easy to say when you weren't on an academic scholarship.

I glanced over at him. My gaze settled on the bright red mark on his paper. My jaw dropped.

"You did not get an A."

Samir grinned. "I think I did."

"How is that even possible?"

"My natural genius?"

"You don't even take notes," I sputtered. "Half the time you look like you're almost asleep. I've never even seen you with the textbook. Do you own the textbook?"

Samir laughed. "Nope."

"Life is so not fair."

"Never said it was."

My eyes narrowed. "Is it all an act?"

He grinned, winking at me. "Wouldn't you like to know?"

"Ready to begin?" our professor asked the class, saving me from a response.

For the next hour I sat in class watching Samir. A few times he caught me, tossing me a sidelong grin. He didn't touch his pen once.

He just sat there, lounging in his chair, legs crossed at the ankles. By the end of it the only thing I'd learned was that I couldn't get that stupid kiss out of my mind.

We got up from our chairs, gathering our stuff to leave. Samir walked by my desk. He leaned close, our faces just inches apart.

"Keep looking at me like that and we're going to have to pick up where we left off."

My cheeks turned red yet again.

He walked out of the classroom whistling.

15

If my paper grade in Intro to IR taught me anything, it was that I needed to get serious about school. Somewhere in the array of nights out I'd lost my focus.

I desperately needed to get it back.

"I need a break," Fleur announced.

"You've been studying for twenty minutes." Even at a university where half the school failed to even come to class, Fleur was not going to win student of the year. "You don't need a break after twenty minutes."

I was cracking down on the inhabitants of room 301, myself included.

Noora grinned at me from across the room.

"It's boring," Fleur complained, her algebra book in hand.

"It's math, it's supposed to be boring."

Fleur wasn't the only one who needed a break. Truthfully, I wasn't one to judge her lack of academic motivation. I had decided the only way to get back on track with my classes was to catch up on all the reading that fell by the wayside while I had been discovering London.

There was a lot of it.

"Let's go out."

Noora laughed. "Why do I think you guys aren't going to be getting much work done?" she teased.

I shook my head, not bothering to look up from my book. "No. I have to study. We aren't going out. Considering how little work you do, your grades can't possibly be better than mine. Putting in some extra study time wouldn't be the worst thing."

"Studying is overrated," Fleur challenged.

I hesitated. "Speaking of not studying. What's the deal with Samir? He got an A on our last paper, and I swear I've never seen him with a book."

"Ugh. He's like that. Always has been. He's really smart. My uncle, too." Fleur groaned. "If I have to study for another minute, I'm going to scream."

"You're not helping here."

"Sue me. I hate school."

"I've noticed. What's your major?" I asked.

She shrugged. "Haven't declared one."

Noora shot me an amused look across the room. I pulled a face.

"Need I say more?" I countered. "We're studying. Stop trying to distract me."

Fleur's phone went off across the room. She was silent for a moment, scanning the screen. A smile spread across her face. "I'll make you a deal."

Noora laughed again.

"No deals. Studying." I stared down at the same page I'd been trying to read for the last half hour. It was no use.

"We study for another hour," Fleur cajoled. "Then we go out."

"Fleur, I got a C+ on my paper. I'm on scholarship. If I don't bring my grades up, I'm going to have to leave the International School."

"Fine. Two hours. We can make a late appearance."

I hesitated.

"You aren't going to study past midnight anyway. Please. I

promise we'll spend the rest of the weekend studying. And besides, if we go out you might see Hugh."

"Just give in to her," Noora called out from across the room. "You know she won't give up until she gets her way."

I was so weak. "Fine. Two more hours. Then we'll go out."

We didn't go to Babel. Tonight was a place called Blue, some hot club tucked off a little street in Mayfair. Fleur, true to her word, studied with me for two hours before helping me dress up to go out. Noora stayed behind. As hard as it must have been at times to navigate a social scene that was so often fueled by alcohol and partying, she chose not to go out and I admired the fact that she was never afraid to live authentically as herself. One of the things I loved most about the International School was how we could come from distinct places and share our own beliefs, and yet, respect each other's differences and learn from them.

We met up with Samir and some of his friends. Even though Samir's friends didn't talk to us all that much, they were nice enough and tended to keep an eye out for the girls. If a guy made one of us uncomfortable, they stepped in and broke it up.

From what I gathered, many of them were friends he knew from Lebanon, and the bond between them was evident in the ease of their interactions and the way they were always there to look out for each other. They might not have known me, but because I was—by extension—there as a friend of Samir's, I had no doubt that they had my back.

I imagined that their friendship and connection helped in the moments when they missed home. It was the one thing I had underestimated about being in London—as much as I loved the novelty of my life here, sometimes I missed that shared sense of camaraderie of being around people who understood what my life was like back home.

I leaned back against a pillar, surveying the crowd. I couldn't help that my attention kept straying back to the same place. It really was a cruel twist of fate that Samir seemed to be the hottest guy in any room. Tonight was no exception.

"Who's that?"

Fleur followed my gaze until it settled on a guy in a black jacket talking to Samir.

"Him?" She waved dismissively. "It's Samir's dealer."

"Samir's what?"

"His dealer. It's no big deal. He just gets us stuff sometimes."

"Stuff like drugs?" I didn't bother keeping the shock out of my voice. "Is Samir buying drugs right now?"

Fleur shrugged, seemingly nonplussed. "I don't know. Maybe. Why?"

I gaped at her. "Are you kidding me? I'm not in the mood to get arrested and deported for getting caught with drugs. Maybe you guys have parents who will buy you high-priced lawyers and get you off with just a slap on the wrist, but I promise you, if I get caught my ass is in big trouble." I stood up, smoothing my dress down over my legs. "I know it's not a big deal to you guys, but it is to me. I'm going to head out."

Fleur frowned. "I didn't think you'd care that much. I don't want you to be uncomfortable. I'll go, too. You shouldn't leave by yourself."

"You don't have to."

She shook her head. "I'm not bailing on you. We'll both leave."

We gathered our bags and coats. Samir caught sight of us across the room. His eyes narrowing, he walked over to where we stood.

"What's wrong? Where are you guys going?"

"Maggie's a little uncomfortable. We're heading out," Fleur volunteered.

Samir's gaze shifted to me. "What's wrong?"

I couldn't look at him.

"Did something happen?"

"No. I'm fine. I'm just tired," I lied.

"She's uncomfortable with your dealer being here," Fleur interjected. "Maggie doesn't do drugs."

Samir was silent for a second. "Okay."

He turned away from us and walked back over to the guy. They exchanged a few words before the guy walked away. Samir headed back to us.

"All gone. Stay. Please."

I stared at him, another layer of confusion piling onto my general impression of Samir. "You didn't have to do that. I didn't want to ruin your night or anything."

He shrugged. "Don't worry about it. Want to dance?"

I hesitated, all too aware of Fleur's attention on us now. It seemed dangerous to be close to him. At the same time rude to refuse. And it would probably only draw attention to us.

"Sure."

I was starting to seriously question my willpower—or lack thereof.

I followed Samir out to the dance floor, the night of the boat party rushing back to me. He was just as good a dancer as I remembered. For a minute neither one of us spoke. I wanted to thank him for what he did earlier, but I struggled to strike the balance between showing him that it meant something and not making too big of a deal about it.

"You didn't have to do that."

"Do what?"

"Get rid of that guy."

He smiled. "Yeah, I did."

"Why?" Suddenly I wanted to know. No matter how hard I tried, I couldn't make him out.

"You were uncomfortable."

"I thought you enjoyed making me uncomfortable."

His lips quirked into a little half smile. "There's uncomfortable and then there's *uncomfortable*." The word escaped in a low drawl. "I prefer the latter. Besides, you're my friend. I would have missed you if you left."

"We're friends now?"

"Something like that."

My heart thudded at his smile, the teasing tone. "You really would have missed me?"

"Sure. You're fun to have around. And you're pretty cute, too." I blushed.

"Are you having a good time?" His hand brushed against my back.

He moved closer to me, resting his arms at my waist, our bodies flush against each other.

"Yeah. I really shouldn't be out, though. I'm way behind with school. The paper in Graves's class was kind of the final nail in the coffin."

"You're smart. You'll be fine. Everyone goes through a bit of a transition freshman year. It's normal."

"I don't know anymore. I just feel…overwhelmed. I used to have all these plans. Goals for myself. I just feel like they're slipping away little by little. I'm not even sure what I want anymore."

"You're too hard on yourself. I promise you, you're smarter than most of the people at school. You'll be fine. You don't always have to be perfect. It's okay to fuck up once and a while. I should know, I do it more than most."

I couldn't help but laugh at that.

"It's okay to have a little bit of fun. You don't have to work all the time. You Americans could take a cue from the rest of the world. There's nothing wrong with working hard and playing hard."

"All work and no play?" I joked.

He grinned. "Exactly."

He pulled me closer, and my breasts brushed against his chest. I stiffened as heat flared in his eyes.

All it took was one look, one touch, and I was ready to throw caution to the wind.

"We can't do this again," I mumbled, responding to an unspoken invitation that lingered in his hands and eyes. "Fleur's right back there. We're in public."

"I have very fond memories of doing all sorts of things to you in public. I think you like it in public. I think you like losing control, like feeling reckless. It's so out of character for you, isn't it? You always play it safe. But you're learning now, aren't you, that you weren't meant to play it safe. That you were made for more."

With each word he unraveled something inside me. He saw too much, noticed too much, knew too much about me. He looked at me like he saw through the facade, through the image I put up for the rest of the world.

I wasn't sure I liked it.

"This isn't a good idea."

Unfortunately, my body didn't seem to be getting the memo.

"Why?" Samir challenged. "One reason."

I could give him one hundred.

I was too chicken to tell him the real reason—that I was scared he was going to hurt me, in a way I wouldn't recover from. He wasn't an easy guy to get close to. I was beginning to realize there was more there, a lot more, than was obvious at first glance. The flashiness of him was intimidating enough, but the other stuff? The heat that flared when he looked at me? The fact that I actually liked him?

That was terrifying.

"Maggie…" Samir's voice trailed off as his gaze drifted to a point over my shoulder. His body stiffened, his expression changing.

He released me.

His eyes were different, colder now, as if someone had flipped a switch.

The foolish part of me wanted the heat back. Yearned for it.

"Your guy is here."

I froze in the middle of the dance floor. "What?"

"That guy from Babel is here."

Feeling like everything was going in slow motion, I turned around. There he was, standing near the bar, clad in a gray suit.

Our gazes caught across the room.

A slow smile spread across Hugh's face.

I couldn't make my lips do the same.

I was happy to see Hugh.

Surprised to see him.

I was a lot of things I couldn't quite name.

I turned back and Samir was gone.

16

I stood by myself in the middle of the dance floor. Hugh crossed the distance between us. He leaned down, pressing a kiss to both my cheeks.

"Sorry I haven't called." Hugh's expression was sheepish.

"It's okay." Part of me—the part that spent the past few weeks obsessing and wondering why he didn't text—knew I was letting him off too easily.

"Do you want to get out of here? We can grab a late dinner or something."

I hesitated. Things felt unresolved with Samir. Part of me wanted to go after him and finish the conversation we'd started. But what was the point? After all, Hugh was here, and Samir had walked away.

"That sounds perfect."

We walked over to my friends. I told Fleur bye, struggling not to laugh as she wiggled her eyebrows suggestively behind Hugh's back.

Samir was still nowhere to be found.

We walked outside, the cool London air hitting us with a blast.

"Let me just get the valet to grab my car."

We waited in front of the club. Hugh wrapped his arm

around me, pulling me against his body. He took my hands, cupping them together, blowing warm air against my skin.

"Warmer?"

I nodded.

He pressed soft kisses to my face while we waited for the car. We broke apart, Hugh wrapping his arms around me, gathering me against his tall frame. It felt so good to have his arms around me. I felt comfortable. Safe. Nothing like when I was in Samir's arms.

Hugh nodded toward the valet. "Here we are."

I turned and my jaw dropped.

A bright red Ferrari pulled up to the curb—a convertible.

Hugh walked over to the passenger side, opening the door for me. I slid onto the dark leather, my pulse racing. This was one of those moments I wished I could freeze and take a picture of before anyone would be the wiser.

It more than made up for all those years of sitting on the sidelines.

Hugh strode in front of the car, sliding into the driver's seat. He flashed me a grin. Okay, he knew how hot he looked in the car. He turned away from me, starting the car with a flick of his wrist. The engine revved.

I felt as if I was having an out-of-body experience. My entire high school life I had been the quiet girl, the studious girl. I was never quite a nerd, but I wasn't popular, either. I'd sort of blended or been invisible.

That all felt different now.

We sped through London, the roar of the Ferrari's engine mixing with the sound of the wind rushing around us. Every time we pulled up to a traffic light, cars honked at us, yelling for Hugh to rev the engine, telling him how cool the car was. Even in a city like London this car, and Hugh, stood out.

"Are you in the mood for French?" Hugh yelled over the roar of the engine.

"French sounds perfect."

He maneuvered the car into a parking spot outside of a green-and-white awning. We were in Knightsbridge, the borough that bordered Kensington. I recognized the side street—it was just a few streets over from Harrods.

"This is one of the best French restaurants in London."

I followed him into the restaurant. It was small and quaint, with a sort of understated elegance. A few couples sat at small tables drinking wine and eating desserts. The lighting was low, with soft music playing in the background.

A waiter seated us at a small table in the corner, its surface covered with crisp white linen. A candle flickered on the table between us. Hugh leaned forward, reaching out to grab my hand. He turned my palm up, his finger lazily tracing patterns on my skin.

He ordered for us in French and my heart skipped a beat. His accent was nothing like Fleur's or Samir's, but it was still far more impressive than anything I was used to. And incredibly sexy.

It was strange—he was so much older than me and way smoother than anything I was used to—and yet I didn't feel the same rush of nerves I felt around Samir. My hands weren't clammy, my stomach wasn't in knots.

It was kind of nice.

Each time I saw him, I felt calmer, more confident.

"How many languages do you speak?" I asked, curiosity filling me.

He shrugged. "Enough French to get by. A little Italian, too. Just stuff I picked up during my travels."

The International School was the same way—everyone spoke an enviable number of languages.

"I wish I spoke more languages."

Hugh grinned. "You're too beautiful to need to speak the language. You could get by without it."

A blush formed on my cheeks. I wasn't stupid. It was definitely a line, and a cheesy one at that. But as far as lines went, I was pretty sure all of Hugh's would work.

I took a sip from my wineglass, studying him carefully over the rim. "You're really good at this, aren't you?" My tone was casual, but somehow his answer was important to me. I had been in London long enough by now to recognize that Hugh was what might be called a player. London seemed like the kind of city where you couldn't step without tripping over one.

His dimples flashed in a grin. "A guy has to have game."

"Did you ever consider that you have too much game?" I teased.

"Is there ever such a thing as too much game?"

I made a face.

"Seriously. I'm single, why not?" His gaze met mine. "It's London. London is all about going out and having a good time. London isn't meant to be serious. It's fun. Somewhere you can let loose, let your inhibitions go."

Was there something in the water here?

"I just got over being in a relationship. The last thing I want right now is to feel tied down." He took a sip of his wine, flashing me a wicked grin, his handsome face illuminated by the candlelight. "Unless the tying down involves whipped cream and handcuffs or something."

Holy shit.

"I'm just having fun," he continued, seemingly oblivious to the feelings his words inspired. "Everyone understands it, and no one gets hurt. I'm not looking for a girlfriend or anything."

His tone was nonchalant, the words delivered with deceptive casualness. But we both knew exactly what he was doing. He was warning me off, setting my expectations exactly where he wanted them.

Whipped cream? Fine. Relationship? Not so much.

I had no idea how to respond. His fingers still traced lazy

circles on my hand. With each stroke, my skin felt as if it was on fire. The thought *be careful or you'll get burned* drifted through my mind before Hugh's lips brushed against mine and I forgot my fears.

17

Mya groaned. "This guy is really pissing me off."

"Join the club."

"How did the date end?" Fleur interjected.

We were hanging out at what we termed "family dinner." Basically, we got to dinner right when the dining hall opened and spent three or four hours hanging out and talking. People rotated in and out of the group, dropping in with stories about their days.

Mya, Fleur and I were the heart of family dinner.

"We finished eating—"

Mya interrupted me. "Who paid?"

"He did."

The bill had been astronomical. If I had paid, I would have depleted the majority of my London funds. As it was, my semester expenses left me eating Burger King kids' meals on the days the cafeteria closed.

Fleur nodded. "That's a good sign, at least."

"Well, I'm not sure it did me any good. He drove me back and gave me a quick kiss good-night." I stabbed at the dried-out piece of chicken on my plate. "Oh, and guess what? After four days, still no phone call."

Fleur sighed. "Because the ball is in your court."

"What?"

"He told you. He's looking to have fun. Now he's waiting to see if you're on board with just hooking up."

I grimaced. "What exactly do you think hooking up entails?"

"He's almost thirty, Maggie. I think hooking up in this case means sex."

Mya glared at Fleur. "Don't freak her out."

"She's not freaking me out," I interrupted, defending Fleur. "I had already sort of figured as much."

"So, what are you going to do about it?"

"There's a great lingerie store on the high street," Mya suggested.

I winced. I knew exactly the store she was thinking of. "I think that might be a bit ambitious for me."

Fleur glared at a point over my shoulder.

I turned around.

Fleur ignored us both, her gaze laser focused on where Costa and his girlfriend, Natasha, sat at a table.

Mya shot me a meaningful look, nudging me under the table with her foot. I wasn't sure why I'd been volunteered to have this conversation with Fleur, but I was willing to take one for the team.

"You have to let it go."

Fleur's gaze flew to me.

"I know you're upset," I added. "I know you miss him, but you have to move on. Look, you're gorgeous. And fun. You're adventurous and confident, and you're a pretty good friend. There are a ton of guys who would give anything to date you. Find one of those guys. Date one of those guys. Forget Costa. He isn't worth how upset you're making yourself."

"You don't get it. It isn't just about Costa." She gestured toward the table. "Those were my friends, too. All of those people sitting with him and his new girlfriend were my friends. And when we broke up, they dropped me like I didn't even exist. Sophia and I used to be best friends," she added pointing to a girl with dark hair talking to Natasha. "Now she won't even acknowledge me in the halls."

"You're better off, then," Mya interjected. "What kind of a friend does that? Drops someone because they broke up with their boyfriend?"

"I know. It just pisses me off to see them throwing their new relationship in my face. He acts like we were never anything to each other. Like everything between us meant nothing. It would just be so much easier if I didn't have to see them together every day, but they're always here, in my face."

Mya grinned. "I have the perfect solution to that."

We both turned to her.

"We should go somewhere for fall break."

I hesitated. My budget would probably be exhausted after five minutes of traveling with them. Hell, I could barely afford to be in London as it was. Traveling anywhere else seemed unlikely.

"We could go to Italy," Mya suggested. "Rome or Venice."

"Venice. Definitely Venice," Fleur decided. "I haven't been since I was a kid."

They both turned to me. "What do you say?" Fleur asked. "Venice for fall break?"

It was way too tempting. And definitely way too ambitious for me. "I can't go to Venice."

Fleur frowned. "Why?"

"Honestly? I can't afford it." It was a humiliating thing to admit, but I didn't see a point in lying. There was no way I could keep up with them. Mya's dad was an ambassador and Fleur mentioned something about her dad owning a company in France. I was pretty sure neither one of them was here on scholarship.

Fleur waved her hand. "Don't worry about it."

"Yeah, that's the thing. I can't really avoid worrying about it. There's no way I can afford to go to Italy." I played with my fork. "I'm sorry, guys, I really want to go, but I just don't see how I can make it happen."

"You're going," Fleur announced. "Don't worry about the money—Mya and I are getting a hotel room in Venice, and we want you to stay with us. We can get a cheap flight, and food and everything will sort itself out—"

"I appreciate it, but I would feel so weird about the whole thing."

Fleur rolled her eyes. "You're my friend. Stop being so difficult. If you don't come to Italy with me for moral support, you're a terrible friend."

Mya grinned. "She always gets her way. Why bother arguing?"

18

Our flight arrived in the late afternoon, the sun just setting over Venice. I peered out the window, my face pressed against the glass. The landscape was stunning—a network of waterways and canals and light shimmering off the water like tiny diamonds.

"I needed this."

Fleur grinned from the seat next to me, lifting the monogrammed silk sleep mask covering her eyes. "I told you. This is going to be the most fabulous break ever."

When the plane landed, we grabbed our bags and cleared customs. Fleur had called ahead and reserved a private water taxi to take us to the hotel. We made our way out of the airport, our bags trailing behind us. Fleur walked in front, scanning the rows of boats. A short, dark-haired man stood on the dock, waving a small white sign.

"Marceaux?"

Fleur nodded, gesturing for us to follow her.

The driver—boat captain—took our bags, setting them in the back of the water taxi. Fleur, Mya and I sat on a bench, covered by a crisp white awning. The driver turned around to face us, a rush of Italian flowing from his mouth.

I stared at him blankly. "Er, do you guys speak Italian?"

Fleur waved her hand airily. "Enough to get by."

"Okay, what is he saying?"

She paused. "I'm not exactly sure. Something about a hotel?"

Mya groaned. "Try speaking French. Maybe he knows that."

Somehow between Fleur's French and the driver's Italian we got to our hotel. I spent the ride staring at the scenery as Venice passed us by. Opera played from the boat speakers, adding to the already surreal quality of the setting.

I felt like I was in a movie.

Mya nudged me. "Gorgeous, isn't it?"

I nodded, words failing me. The boat stopped in front of a large building that vaguely resembled a palace. There weren't words for this moment, nothing I could use to do justice to the beauty surrounding me. It was like I'd traveled back in time, to a world I'd only ever read about.

I gaped at the building. It was everything Mya and Fleur had promised and more.

The driver unloaded our bags, handing them off to a hotel porter. Women dressed in fur coats and men in suits walked around outside the hotel. I tugged self-consciously at the belt on my own gray coat. No matter how elegant I felt, I was beginning to realize I would always lack the requisite thousand-dollar designer bag or shoes to really fit in. Still, just being here was enough.

The lobby was all marble and gold and sculpted archways. It was impossible to not feel like a princess. "Are we seriously staying here? I'm afraid to touch anything," I hissed to Mya.

She laughed. "Yeah, Fleur's standards are a bit higher than mine."

"Who doesn't Fleur have higher standards than?" I asked wryly.

Fleur booked us a suite to share. We had a perfect view of the city.

Fleur grinned. "Was this a fabulous idea or was this a fabulous idea?"

"It was a fabulous idea," I conceded. "So, what's on the agenda for the night?"

Fleur shrugged. "Dinner somewhere. I'm sure the concierge can recommend something. Then we hit up this fabulous club Samir told me about."

That sounded expensive.

Mya shook her head, already sensing my argument. "Just go with it. This is Fleur's show. We're all just living it."

The next day we set out exploring Venice. We were only there for two nights and not even three full days, so I wanted to make the most of it. Mya and Fleur had already been to Venice and done most of the touristy stuff, but they were nice enough to show me around. We went to St. Mark's Square, took a gondola ride on the Grand Canal, and ate the best pizza I'd ever had in my life.

We walked everywhere.

That evening we went back to change, throwing on our best clothes to go out again. We went to dinner at a little restaurant the concierge recommended, dining on a feast of pasta, chicken and amazing wine, before we went out to a nightclub Fleur wanted to try.

"Exactly how far away is this place?" I huffed. At least Mya didn't appear to be enjoying the walk any more than I was. Although she did have a height advantage.

"Probably just a mile or two away." Fleur waved her hand vaguely. "It can't be too much farther."

"A mile or two? You said it was close! There's no way I can walk another mile or two in these heels." I glanced down at my watch. "We've already been walking for fifteen minutes."

"We should have just called a cab," Mya complained. "We're lost."

Fleur rolled her eyes. "We're not lost."

"We're definitely lost." I spotted a woman walking across the street. "Look, why don't you go ask her for directions?"

"Or look at the map on your phone?" Mya suggested, obviously annoyed.

"I don't need a map. I've been to Venice before. I know my way around. Besides, my reception is terrible. I keep losing the signal."

"Obviously you don't know your way around," Mya snapped.

Surprise filled me. Mya never lost her temper like this. "Fleur, just go talk to that lady before she gets away. I'm sure she can help us out."

"Fine." Fleur walked away with a huff, crossing the street.

Mya and I watched as she spoke to the woman.

Fleur sauntered back over to us.

"Well, what did she say?" I asked.

"She didn't speak English or French."

"Why didn't you speak to her in Italian?" Mya pointed out, annoyance creeping into her tone.

"I tried, but it wasn't really enough to work things out."

"I thought you said you could speak Italian."

Fleur shrugged. "No, I said I studied in Italy for a semester in high school. That doesn't mean I learned any."

I rolled my eyes.

Fleur fisted her hands on her hips. "Besides, we wouldn't be lost if you had actually followed your phone's directions properly."

She was not blaming me for this one. "The signal keeps cutting out. And I told you I have a terrible sense of direction."

"Obviously," Fleur snapped.

"Okay. Stop it," Mya interjected. "This isn't helping. You both suck at directions. Give me your phone."

I handed it over without any hesitation. Our surroundings looked residential. How far had we wandered off the main road?

"We've been going in circles." Fleur pulled out her cell phone again, stamping her Manolos. "It's one in the morning. We're missing out on the party. We're lost in the middle of Venice. I have one bar. I'm calling for help."

"Who are you going to call?"

"The hotel. Someone. Anyone." Fleur waved her hand impatiently. "I'm not staying around here in this hovel, waiting to end up dead on the streets."

I rolled my eyes. "Drama queen."

"Will you both shut up?" Mya waved the phone in the air. "I figured it out. We were on the right path, we just took a wrong turn back there. We should retrace our steps."

"I'm not walking another step," Fleur snapped. "I'm wearing my favorite Manolos. These streets are cobblestone. Not happening."

Mya studied the map on my phone. She turned in the direction opposite the one we had come from.

"I think if we go down that street, we'll be fine. If we just keep walking the street should intersect with the one we need."

"Sounds like a plan to me. Lead the way."

19

By the time we reached the bar, we were each in varying stages of pissed off.

Fleur made a beeline for the bar, leaving the two of us in her wake.

"She's in a mood tonight," Mya whispered. "Trust me, when she gets like this it's best to just give her some space."

"It doesn't seem like she's really interested in hanging out with us, anyway."

"She'll get over it. She gets really flustered when things don't go her way. Like the situation with Costa. And getting lost tonight."

"I wish she would get over Costa. I thought coming here, taking a break from everything at school would help her out. But she's just as distracted and upset as she was before."

Mya shrugged. "Whatever. I'm not going to spend our whole night in Italy dealing with Fleur's mood."

I couldn't help but agree with her.

We headed toward an empty table. Mya flagged down a waiter. I scanned the crowd, looking for any sign of Fleur. She stood at the bar, her back toward us, talking to a tall, dark-haired guy. I couldn't make out his face.

"Figures," Mya muttered. "Trust Fleur to find someone."

I was surprised by the anger in her voice. "Is everything okay? You seem a little on edge lately."

"Sorry."

I shook my head. "Please. You don't have to be sorry. I'm worried about you."

Mya's lips pursed in a bitter line. "I'm afraid the situation is beyond help."

"It might help to talk about it."

The waiter brought our drinks over, silence yawning between us.

"My dad's been having an affair."

My jaw dropped.

"I don't know how long it has been going on or who she is, but I saw them together outside The Ritz a few weeks ago. After that I started following him. Turns out every Tuesday afternoon he leaves work, and they meet at a different hotel in London."

"I'm so sorry. Are you sure—I mean, is there a chance that maybe it's something else entirely?"

Mya laughed bitterly. "Yeah, not so much. I saw them kissing. And not a friendly European-style kiss. He had his arms around her." She took another sip of her drink. "The girl looked like she was only a few years older than me."

"Oh, Mya. I'm so sorry. Do you think your mom knows?"

Mya shook her head.

"Are you going to tell her?"

"I don't know." Mya gulped down the rest of her champagne. "I thought about it. She deserves to know. But I just can't imagine saying the words." Her expression was grim. "I don't know what to do."

"I'm so sorry."

"It's fine. I'm not mad at you. I didn't tell you what was going on—there's no way you would have known." She sighed. "I'm not really mad at Fleur, either. Things have just been tough lately. The situation just sucks. I can't imagine having divorced parents."

"Well, if you have any questions on the single-parent thing, I can definitely answer them."

"How bad is it?"

"It sucks," I admitted.

"You never talk about your family. What's the deal with that?"

I didn't even know where to begin. Even though Mya was going through shit with her family now, she at least *had* a family. She had two parents who loved her. She would never know what it felt like to not be loved by the people who were supposed to love you the most.

"There's not much to tell. My dad's gone a lot with work, so I live with my grandparents."

"And your mom?"

"I have no idea where she is. She left when I was practically a baby. I don't remember her, or anything. And it's not like she keeps in touch."

"That must have been rough."

I'd never told anyone how I felt about my mom. My dad certainly didn't talk about her. I didn't even know how to explain it—

I felt abandoned. Completely abandoned.

"I guess. I mean, it's not like I could miss her when I don't remember what it was like to have her around."

Lies. All lies.

The truth was, not a day had gone by that I hadn't felt the absence of my mother. There were so many times I wished she was there to talk to, to ask for advice. My grandmother tried her best, but it wasn't always easy for us to connect with such a huge age difference between us. And it wasn't so much my mother's absence that hurt as it was what her absence meant.

She hadn't loved me enough to stay. Or to take me with her.

I hadn't been enough for her to want me.

I tried to smile, reaching out and squeezing Mya's hand. "I'm sure everything will be okay. If there's anything I can do to help, just let me know. Even if you just need to talk."

"Thanks."

I turned my attention back to the bar. "Do you see Fleur?"

She scanned the crowd. "No."

"Maybe she's in the bathroom?"

"I'll go check it out." Mya sighed. "I probably owe her an apology anyway."

I sat at the table, sipping my drink, waiting for them to both come out. A few minutes later Mya emerged by herself.

"Did you find her?"

"No, she's not in there and no one has seen her."

I pulled my phone out, dialing Fleur's number. The call went straight to voice mail. *No answer,* I mouthed to Mya. I left Fleur a quick message, telling her we were worried and asking her to call us. "What do we do now?"

"I have no idea. I guess we just wait around to see if she comes back. We can't leave her here."

We sat at the bar waiting for Fleur for an hour. She never showed. Neither did the guy I saw her talking to earlier.

She didn't call us back, either.

"Maybe she went back to the hotel," Mya suggested. "Wherever she is, she definitely isn't here."

We grabbed our coats and headed toward the exit. Mya hailed a cab. We rode in silence.

"I'm worried about her."

Mya's voice was grim. "So am I. She's just been so off the rails lately. She isn't handling any of this well."

"What's the big deal with Costa? I don't get it. I mean, yes, he's hot, but there has to be more to it than that."

Mya sighed. "They'd been together for years. Since before we came to London. When I knew her in Switzerland, she and

Costa were dating. I really think she loved him. And he can be very charming when he needs to be. He was always taking her on romantic trips, buying her expensive jewelry. We were all jealous of her back then. He was the perfect boyfriend—except when he wasn't. I think he probably always cheated, but it wasn't in her face enough for Fleur to realize it until they came to London. That girl he cheated with—Natasha—is now his girlfriend."

I winced. "Ouch."

"She hasn't been the same since. She even was out of school for a while—a month or so. When she came back she seemed different. Broken, somehow."

Surprise filled me. A month of missing school over a guy seemed extreme at best.

"It's way worse this year. Before, she had her moments, but now it's like she's doing everything she can to push herself over the edge."

"What do you mean?"

Mya hesitated. "She's drinking a lot. Partying harder than normal."

When we got to the hotel, we moved through the lobby quickly. Mya led the way down the hall, pulling out her room key to open the door. I followed her through, the lights just as we'd left them, the bed perfectly made.

My heart sank. "Okay, now I'm really worried."

Mya pulled out her cell, dialing Fleur's number. She stood with the phone pressed to her ear. She shook her head. "Straight to voice mail."

"Shit."

Mya left a terse message asking Fleur to call us.

"What do we do now?"

"I have no idea. Wait, I guess. I don't think you can call the police until someone has been missing for twenty-four hours." She glanced at her watch. "It's only been two."

"Do you think she left with that guy?"

"Probably." Mya squeezed my hand. "Don't worry about Fleur. I know you're scared, but I promise you, Fleur always lands on her feet. I'm sure this is just a blip and she'll turn up later with some story about the hot guy she hooked up with."

I wanted to believe Mya. I just wasn't sure I could.

When we woke the next morning, there was still no sign of Fleur.

"Okay, now I'm starting to get worried," Mya announced. "I really thought she would waltz back in during the middle of the night."

I sat up in bed, running my hand through my hair. "Our flight is this evening. What do we do if she doesn't get back in time?"

"I don't know."

"Should we call her parents?"

"No way. Trust me, that would be the last thing Fleur would want."

"Well, we have to do something. We can't just sit around like this, hoping to hear from her."

"I don't know what to do."

There was only one person I could think of who seemed to know how to handle Fleur. "Do you have Samir's number?"

"Yeah." Mya pulled out her phone, handing it to me. "That's not a bad idea. He's probably the closest person to Fleur." She hesitated. "Why don't you call him? I think he likes you better, anyway."

I dialed the number, my heart pounding as the phone rang. I glanced down at my watch. It was only 10 a.m. in Italy, probably still too early for Samir to be awake in London. He answered on the fourth ring.

I sucked in a deep breath. "Hey, it's Maggie."

"Maggie?" His voice sounded sleepy, his accent heavier than

normal. "Why are you calling me?" He didn't sound annoyed, just confused.

"I'm here in Italy with Fleur." I paused. "Well, that's the problem, and why I'm calling you. We can't find Fleur."

"We?"

"Mya's here, too. She's the one who gave me your number," I added as an afterthought. "The three of us came to Italy for the weekend. Venice."

"Yeah, I know. Fleur told me."

"When was the last time you talked to Fleur?"

There was a pause. "I don't know. A couple of days, maybe? I don't exactly keep track." A rustling sounded on the other side of the line. "What happened?"

"We went out to this bar—"

"What bar?"

I looked to Mya for help.

Travinia, she mouthed.

I repeated the name to Samir.

"Yeah, I know it."

"Well, we got lost on the way there and everyone was a little annoyed with each other, so Fleur took off right when we walked in. She went over to the bar and started talking to some guy. The next thing I knew she was gone.

"We waited for her for an hour, looked in the bathroom, asked around, but no one had seen her. We tried calling her cell, but it just goes straight to voice mail. She hasn't returned any of our messages or texts. Her social media is silent. We came back to the hotel, but she wasn't here." With each word, the rising note of panic increased. "It's morning now and she still hasn't come back. Our flight leaves in a few hours and we don't know what to do. Mya thinks we can't call the police this early, but we don't want to leave without her, either. Should we call her parents?"

"You won't be able to reach them. Fleur can barely get in

touch with them as it is. Besides, even if you do talk to them, there isn't much they're going to do. At most her dad will send someone to Italy to find her. It's not unheard of for Fleur to go off on her own like this."

"I'm worried about her."

"Just relax. Don't panic. Stay in the hotel in case she comes back. I'll be there in a few hours."

"What?"

"I'm coming to Venice. It's a short flight. It shouldn't take too long to get there."

"You're going to buy a ticket to come over here?"

"My dad has a plane. I'll be there soon. Just sit tight."

"Are you sure? Mya and I can take care of this on our end."

"It's no big deal."

I hesitated, relief filling me. "Thanks, Samir."

20

Four hours later someone knocked on our hotel room door.

I leaped up from the bed. "Maybe it's Fleur." I padded over to the entrance, pulling open the door. Samir stood on the other side. I'd never been so glad to see him.

"Did you hear anything from her?"

I shook my head, opening the door wider and inviting him in.

"Thanks for coming," Mya said.

"Have you tried calling her?"

Samir nodded, his gaze sweeping around the room. "Yeah, she's not picking up. I called one of my dad's investigators and he's running a check to see if any of her credit cards have been used."

"You can do that?"

"This guy isn't exactly aboveboard, but yeah, you can."

Mya glanced down at her watch. "Our flight is this evening. I don't know what to do."

Our bags were lined up by the door, packed and ready to go.

"If you guys need to leave, I can take it from here."

I grimaced. "I don't feel right leaving her like this. I don't have class until tomorrow afternoon, so it's not a big deal if I get on a later flight. I want to help find her." I didn't add that there was no way I could afford to pay for it. Right now all that mattered was making sure Fleur was safe.

"If you miss your flight, I can give you a ride on my dad's plane," Samir offered.

I hesitated. "Thanks." I turned toward Mya. "You have a test tomorrow, don't you?"

She nodded.

"If you need to go, I can stay back here with Samir."

"I don't want to leave you by yourself."

"I'll look out for her," Samir interjected.

Funnily enough, I believed him.

"Really, it's fine. Samir and I can take care of Fleur. Why don't you head over to the airport now so you don't miss the flight? I'll call if we hear anything from Fleur."

Mya's gaze darted from me to Samir. "Are you sure?"

"Go." I reached out and hugged her. "Don't worry about anything here. Fleur and I will be in London tomorrow for dinner. I'm sure of it."

Samir called down to the front desk and ordered a water taxi for Mya. We said goodbye before he helped her downstairs with her bags. A few minutes later, he walked back in.

"She's off to the airport."

"Thanks."

Samir sank down next to me on the edge of the bed. Our knees brushed against each other. A shiver slid down my spine. He pulled out his phone, running through the messages and emails.

"Anything?"

He shook his head.

"What do you think happened to her? Do you think she's in danger? Or do you think she just went off with some guy she met?"

Samir ran a hand through his hair. For the first time since he arrived, I realized how tired he looked.

"I don't know. I think she's probably fine. She does stuff like this sometimes. More so now after Costa. She could have just been upset and decided to take off for a bit."

"Why wouldn't she tell someone? You would think she would at least text someone and let them know not to worry about her."

Samir shrugged. "I've given up trying to predict what Fleur's going to do."

"You guys are close."

"I care about her, yeah." Samir hesitated for a beat. "She's the person I'm probably the closest to in my family. Unfortunately, that doesn't mean I always understand what she's thinking."

Silence hung between us.

"What are we going to do?"

Samir leaned forward, bracing his elbows on his thighs. "I don't know. We can leave a message with the front desk to let us know if she comes back here or calls. Maybe the best bet is to go back to the bar and see if there's any sign of her or anyone who saw her."

I didn't have a better plan. I followed Samir out, stopping at the front desk while he spoke with the concierge. Money changed hands between them.

"Come on. They're calling a water taxi for us."

For the first time I realized that the whole conversation between Samir and the concierge had been in Italian.

"You speak Italian?"

"Why do you look surprised?"

"I don't know. I just didn't peg you as being interested in foreign languages."

"I like girls from foreign countries." He winked at me, some of the tension leaving his face. "Knowing the language does tend to help things go more smoothly." He grinned. "Although it isn't always a prerequisite. I have other skills."

I rolled my eyes.

"I'm just saying. I have a good ear for languages, but the really impressive thing is what I can do with my hands...and my mouth..."

"Is everything sexual with you?" I asked, exasperation filling my voice.

He flashed me his trademark grin. "Isn't that how you like it?"

I couldn't help but laugh. "You don't know I like it," I bluffed, fighting the urge to blush.

Samir's smile slipped just a notch. His voice lowered. "I think I do know. I remember what you feel like in my arms."

"You really should stop thinking about that."

"Maybe I can't. Maybe I can't stop thinking of you."

I stepped back. Samir moved forward, closing the gap.

"You should probably know—I always get what I want."

"Maybe. But you can't have me."

He grinned. "Oh, I promise you, I *will* have you." Heat flared in his eyes. "In my bed, against the wall, on the floor, everywhere."

I couldn't even respond. Images flashed through my mind. His body. Mine. Pressed together. Naked. Limbs entwined.

"It's not a question of *if*, it's a question of *when*."

I couldn't handle this. Couldn't handle him. I could play at this, but any time he upped the stakes, I folded.

The concierge walked over toward us, speaking with Samir in Italian. It was a welcome interruption that allowed me to get myself under control. Or at least to try. When they'd finished talking, Samir walked back over to me.

"How many languages do you speak?" I squeaked, struggling to break the moment. I needed something to ease the tension in my chest, a distraction to banish the image of Samir's bare skin from my brain. We'd only been alone for half an hour and my lips were already this close to his. I was so screwed.

Samir shot me a knowing grin. "French, Arabic. English, obviously. Some Italian, enough Spanish to get by."

I couldn't help but be impressed.

"I went to a special language school before going to the International School," he added. "To learn English."

"Where? In London?"

"Yeah."

"If you went to school to learn English before starting university...how old are you?"

"Twenty-two."

I wasn't entirely surprised by his answer. He seemed older. "Is it weird being here with the rest of us? I mean—the age difference and everything?"

"Not really." His mouth quirked. "Although sometimes you do make me feel like a debauched old man."

I rolled my eyes again. "Are you ever serious?"

"Not if I can help it."

No one at the bar had any leads on Fleur or the guy she was talking to. We decided to head to the mainland and take a car to the airport to see if maybe she had decided to leave on an early flight back to London. As far as options went, it wasn't great, but now it was all we had to go on.

A sleek black Maybach with dark-tinted windows pulled up at the curb in front of us.

"You ready?"

I nodded, allowing Samir to open the door for me. I slid into the car's back seat. Samir sat next to me, exchanging a few words with the driver in Italian before hitting a button, the privacy window sliding up.

I stared out the window, watching the city pass us by. When we arrived, we did this trip by water taxi, but now driving to the airport from Venice's mainland, I got a fresh perspective.

Where was Fleur?

Samir reached out, squeezing my hand. I had to physically resist the urge to wrap my fingers around his.

At the same time, I couldn't get my worry about Fleur out of my mind.

"It'll be okay. We'll find her."

I moved my hands out of his grasp, shifting to face him. "I just feel like it's my fault. Like I should have done more to watch out for her."

"You've been a good friend to her. You *are* a good friend to her."

A tear slipped down my cheek. "I'm sorry. I should have just handled it on my own."

"Hey. Don't cry. I'm glad you called me." Samir reached out, his finger grazing my cheek, catching the end of my tear. His fingers stroked my cheekbone, fanning out across my face with a gentle caress.

I froze.

There was something about Samir—for as much as he made my stomach do flip-flops, there were so many other times like now when he made me feel safe in a way I never had before.

My heart thudded.

His fingers remained there, just barely touching my skin. Hovering there. My mouth parted slightly—partly in surprise, partly in anticipation.

Just one kiss. Just once.

21

"Maggie."

My name came out in a half groan, the word torn from his lips. The sound of his voice stirred an ache inside me. Samir leaned forward, his other hand slipping around my waist, his face hovering inches from mine.

I didn't move. I knew what was coming and I didn't move. He said my name again, the sound sending a tingle down my spine.

God, that accent was so sexy.

His lips brushed against mine. The touch was soft, light, teasing. He was testing the waters, exploring me, kissing me as though he had all the time in the world.

Impatience filled me.

I didn't want slow and easy. I didn't want toe-curling seduction. I wanted fire—flash and heat. I wanted to drown in him, for his body to cover mine. I wanted to lose myself in him.

I kissed him back. It wasn't a soft kiss or an easy one. I demanded, changing the tone of the kiss from the start. I was a few layers of clothing away from jumping his bones. I made sure he knew it.

My lips devoured his, my tongue stroking, caressing. I took

advantage of him, using his leisurely kiss to provoke, to demand. My hands explored his body, fulfilling the desire to touch I'd desperately been craving.

For once I wasn't shy. Something screaming inside me, desperate to get out, made me bold...

Samir responded to the change in me, meeting me stroke for stroke, kiss for kiss. His hands explored my body, cupping around my curves, pressing me against him.

He was hard everywhere.

My hands fisted in his hair, winding his dark curls around my fingers. His hair felt like silk beneath my skin. I explored his mouth with my tongue, sucked on his bottom lip, tugging on it with my teeth. I nipped, instantly using my tongue to soothe where I'd bitten him. He'd taught me things along the way—delicious, naughty things—and I was definitely a fast learner.

"God, that feels amazing," he whispered, his voice soaked with lust. He responded by kissing the side of my neck, his tongue darting out, painting my skin with soft licks.

I moaned.

"Take off your seat belt."

I broke away long enough to unclasp the seat belt, my fingers trembling with the motion. My body trembled, my legs weak. Everything within me screamed that even this wasn't enough. I wanted more—

Samir pulled me over, positioning me so I straddled him, my legs wrapped around him, our bodies pressed against each other. Through the thin layer of my pants, I could feel his arousal, pressing against me. Desire, liquid and burning, pooled in my body.

I plastered myself against Samir, wrapping my arms around his neck until there was no space between where his body ended and mine began. His heart pounded against me, keeping time with the rapid beating in my own chest.

Holy shit.

Samir covered my mouth with his, kissing me open-mouthed, his hands working on the belt of my coat. He fumbled with the knot, words in French escaping from his lips.

I would have given anything to know what he said.

"Let me." Impatience filled my voice. Need bubbled up, threatening to spill over. I reached down, grabbing at the knotted fabric, pulling and tugging until the belt came undone. I met his gaze.

Desire blazed back at me. This no longer felt like a game we were playing. It felt like everything.

The car hit a bump in the road, the motion jolting us both. My body rocked against his.

He groaned. "My turn."

His hands came up to my chest, grazing my breasts through the thin fabric. His fingers brushed against my nipples. He teased me, working magic with his fingers, my body growing impossibly more aroused.

"That's so good. Please don't stop. Please. Whatever you do, just don't stop," I whispered against his mouth, pulling him closer to me. Words fired through my brain—*please* and *more* and *yes*—desperate words, triumphant words. Words that told me just how close I was to losing control.

Samir began swiftly undoing each of my coat buttons. I looked down, unable to tear my gaze away from the sight of his long, tanned fingers undressing me. It was the most erotic thing I'd ever seen. There was something so intimate in how he unwrapped me, like I was a present he couldn't wait to open. When the last button was undone, he pushed the coat off my shoulders.

"You're so fucking hot." He buried his head in the curve of my neck, the words nearly lost between our bodies.

He made me feel hot. He made me feel like everything I'd ever wanted to be. He made me want.

Samir's hands slid up the outside of my sweater, cupping my

breasts through the heavy fabric. I relished in the feel of him taking me just to the edge of pleasure as he thumbed my nipples.

I leaned forward, pressing my breasts into his palms. His fingers molded my shape, leaving an imprint of heat and desire in their wake. I reveled in his touch, in the way he made me feel. I felt sexy, desirable, completely and utterly out of control. I was desperate now. My want eclipsed all the reasons I knew this was a bad idea and I'd stopped caring somewhere along the way.

I nipped at his bottom lip, the impatience inside me growing. I wanted to devour him. Bite by bite.

A ringing noise sounded in the background. I ignored the noise, pulling Samir closer to me. Nothing else mattered. My mouth slid down his neck, kissing and nipping at the skin. The ringing continued, the sound breaking into my sexual haze. I froze, pulling away from Samir. Our gazes met. We both grabbed for my phone at the same time, our fingers brushing against each other.

My heart pounded at the sight of the name on the caller ID. *Fleur.*

22

"Fleur?"

"Maggie?"

Relief flooded me at the sound of her voice. "Where are you? We've been calling you for hours. We've been so worried about you."

There was a pause on the other end of the line. "I don't know where I am."

I ran a hand through my hair, then straightened up my clothes. I was out of breath, overheated. I felt as though I'd just run a marathon.

"What do you mean, you don't know?"

"I woke up by myself." Fleur paused. "I'm at a hotel."

"Are you okay?"

"Yeah, I'm fine."

"What happened?"

"Where is she?" Samir interrupted.

"In a hotel," I whispered.

"Who are you talking to?"

"I'm talking to Samir. He's here. I called him this morning when we hadn't heard from you. He flew out to help."

"Oh, God. Can I talk to him?"

Wordlessly I passed the phone to Samir. I looked down, realizing I was still straddling him. And he was still clearly aroused—

I moved awkwardly, untangling my body from his, the whole time keeping my gaze trained away from him. My face heated. At least the other times we'd kissed I could blame things on the fact that I had been drunk. But this time—

I was stone-cold sober.

I sat, playing with the edge of my sweater, struggling to calm the emotions raging through my body. A million thoughts ran through my mind. How had we ended up here again?

A few minutes later, Samir hung up the phone.

"She's going to text me her location and we're going to pick her up."

He didn't look at me, either.

I sat back, staring out the window, while Samir gave the driver our new plans.

"Are you okay?"

I jerked my head up at the sound of Samir's voice. I nodded, still not willing to meet his gaze.

"Maggie."

My heart lurched at the sound of my name coming from his lips. I was not ready to talk about this. "What?"

"Look at me." His voice was husky. I could lose myself in that sound, in the desperation I heard there.

"I can't."

"Maggie, please."

It was the "please" that got me. Gone was the boy who always seemed above me—too flashy, too cool, too everything. For the first time I felt like I had some power, like he wasn't as unaffected as he sometimes pretended to be. I lifted my chin, turning to face him. My heart slammed into my chest.

Samir's face was flushed, his mouth swollen from our kisses. His hair was a sexy mess—tousled by my hands. His camel-colored trench coat was rumpled, the collared shirt underneath untucked from his dark jeans. His expression was inscrutable, his characteristic smirk wiped clean from his face.

He hesitated for a moment, his gaze lingering over my face. He shook his head. "Never mind."

I swallowed, moving over on the seat, putting as much distance between us as possible. It felt so wrong to be near him and not be touching him. I curled my fingers into a tight fist.

"Is she okay?" I asked. "She said she was, but you know her better than I do."

"Yeah, Fleur's going to be fine. She didn't tell me everything, but from what I can tell she went home with a guy she met at Travinia. When she woke up this morning, he was gone. She panicked when she realized she missed her flight."

His phone beeped. Samir pulled it out of his jeans pocket, scanning the message. He relayed the address to the driver.

"How far away is it?"

"According to the driver, twenty minutes."

I nodded as if his announcement had no effect on me. There was no fucking way I could spend another twenty minutes by myself in a confined space with Samir.

I spent the drive staring out the window as if the Italian landscape was the most interesting thing I had ever seen. Not that it wasn't pretty, it was. But 98 percent of my interest in the countryside had more to do with the boy sitting next to me than the color of the trees.

I'd never felt like this. I *never* lost control.

When the car finally pulled up in front of an Italian hotel on the mainland, I heaved a sigh of relief. I scanned the scenery until my gaze settled on Fleur.

Samir nudged me. "Why don't you go talk to her first? I'll wait for you guys here."

I opened the car door.

Fleur's head jerked up. "Maggie!" She grabbed me, pulling me in for a tight hug. "Thanks for coming to get me."

"Of course. I'm sorry I got pissed off for being lost," I babbled. "It was totally stupid. I wasn't really mad at you."

"I shouldn't have left you guys."

I leaned away from Fleur, studying her carefully. Her lower lip trembled slightly, and her hair was a tangled mess.

Worry filled me. "Did anything happen?"

She wouldn't meet my gaze. "It was really stupid."

"What happened?"

She hesitated. "Don't judge me."

"Okay."

"I met up with Costa."

I gaped at her. "Why? How?"

"I don't know. He texted me. Told me he was in Venice and wanted to talk. He knew I was here."

"How could you see him again? I thought this trip was about you getting over him? Why are you back here again? It makes absolutely no sense."

I knew I was being harsh with her, but I just didn't understand. She was so pretty, so funny, so fun to be around. She was so many things and yet she let him take so much from her. She couldn't see it, but she lost her sparkle around him. I hated that the most.

"He said he was having second thoughts about our breakup."

"And you believed him?"

"I don't know."

She looked miserable.

I had to ask—

"Why him? Out of all the guys, why him?" Maybe I didn't have much of a leg to stand on given my hooking up with Samir, but I still didn't get it. She'd been moping over the breakup for months. Why'd she want to get back together with him?

"I can't explain it." Something shimmered in her eyes—a sadness deeper than anything I'd ever seen in her. "It's complicated."

"Try me."

She shook her head. "I can't. Look, I know you don't get it, but the thing is, he wasn't always bad. There's a lot of history there. Some things I can't just walk away from."

"Yeah, that's a ringing endorsement."

"It's complicated. And it felt good to have someone. Just to know I wasn't alone. I miss that."

"I get that, but why can't you find another guy to give you that? A guy who isn't going to screw with your emotions?"

Fleur was silent for a moment. "I'm not great with guys."

I laughed. "I'm sorry, but I don't buy that for a second."

Her smile was brittle. "Oh, I can get guys. In bed. I can make guys want me. But no matter how hard I try, I can't get them to stay. Guys do serious with girls like you. They fuck girls like me."

I gaped at her. She should have guys lining up around the block to date her. She deserved that and so much more...

"I think you deserve more than that. You're incredible. I wouldn't sell yourself short."

I linked my arm through hers.

"Are you ready to go home?"

She nodded.

"Next time you run off, though, will you just let us know? We were really worried about you."

"I'm sorry. I was pissed and I wasn't thinking."

"You scared the shit out of me and Mya."

"Where is Mya?"

"She had to fly back. She has a test in her bio class tomorrow and she was afraid to miss it."

"Is she angry with me?"

"Nah. She understands. We were just worried about you. All we wanted was to know you were safe."

I opened the car door, motioning for her to slide in between me and Samir. Putting some space between us seemed like the best possible idea.

Samir hugged her as she slid into the car.

"Thanks for coming to get me."

Samir visibly loosened, flashing Fleur his trademark grin. "Of course. It's not often I get to play the hero. How could I avoid coming to the rescue of two gorgeous girls?"

I flushed.

Fleur elbowed Samir. "Stop making Maggie uncomfortable," she chided.

I doubted she realized just how *uncomfortable* Samir had been making me earlier.

"I wouldn't dream of getting Maggie all hot and bothered," Samir replied, all innocence.

He winked at me.

The rest of the trip went smoothly despite my choice of companions. If I thought traveling with Fleur was luxurious, traveling with Samir was doubly so.

"Is he always like this?" I asked Fleur, not taking my eyes off him.

"Like what?"

I waved my hand. "This. All of it. The car, the plane. Taking care of everything."

"Pretty much, yeah. Samir tends to take charge. That's probably why he's so popular with the girls. He handles everything. They like the glitz of it all—getting to be on his arm while he shows them a good time."

That was definitely a subject I didn't want to touch with a ten-foot pole. I knew all too well just how Samir *handled things*.

"Hmm." I struggled to keep my face neutral.

Fleur hesitated for a second. "Listen. I don't want to make you uncomfortable or anything, but I've noticed the way he looks at you."

I froze. "What are you talking about?"

"Let's just say that Samir has a tendency to look at you like he wants to eat you in one big bite."

I reddened.

"It's no big deal—he's like that. I just don't want to see you falling for his bullshit. I love him—I mean, he's my cousin and all—but I'm not totally oblivious to his faults. And trust me, Samir has a lot of them. He hurts all the girls he's with. Maybe not intentionally, but somehow he always does." She paused as if choosing her words carefully. "Samir is complicated. He can be the best friend in the world. But he can also be careless with people. I care about you, Maggie. I don't want to see him be careless with you."

I struggled to act like her words had no effect, like they didn't make me feel like a bigger idiot than I already thought I was.

"Thanks, but I'm not interested in him or anything. He's totally not my type."

Maybe if I told myself that enough, I'd start to believe it.

"Good. I figured you had better taste. I just wanted to make sure. I don't want to see you get hurt."

"Thanks. But you don't have to worry about me. I'm not going to be falling for Samir anytime soon."

I couldn't.

"The plane's ready."

I whirled around at the sound of Samir's voice. He stood behind me, holding three Starbucks coffees in a tray in his hand. The look in his eyes said it all.

He'd heard every word we said.

23

We all came back from Italy slightly changed. Mya spent less time hanging around with me and Fleur and more time with her parents. Whenever I tried to broach the subject of her dad, she brushed me off and said everything was fine. I gave her space, knowing easily how often "fine" could fall apart at a moment's notice. All I could do was be there for her when it did.

Samir avoided me like the plague. Every time our paths did cross, he was accompanied by a different girl. He didn't spare me a glance. I told myself I couldn't care less. What had happened between us in the car in Italy was a mistake. I spent the rest of the semester focusing more on my classes, going out less and less. I didn't need any distractions.

Somehow I made it through exams, cramming in the library with my friends. Since our final exams made up most of our total class grade, finals were a big deal at the International School. Late-night pizza runs became a staple around the dorms. I had five finals in total. By the end of the two-week exam period, I was so relieved to be done I didn't even bother obsessing over my grades.

I was officially burned out.

I had one day—and night—left in London before I flew home.

"Is everything set with your flight?" my grandmother asked during our weekly phone call.

"Yep. I get in at two in the afternoon."

"We'll be there to pick you up."

I grinned. "I can't wait to see you guys."

"We can't wait to see you, either, honey. We've missed you."

"I've missed you, too." I hesitated. "Have you heard anything from Dad? Do you think he'll be home a few days before Christmas?"

Silence filled the line.

"Grandma?"

"He said he was going to call you…"

My heart lurched. I already knew what she was going to say before the words left her mouth.

"He hasn't."

She sighed. "I'm so sorry, Maggie."

I knew it.

"What is it this time? Another assignment he just couldn't refuse?" I didn't bother to keep the bitterness out of my voice. "Why doesn't he just say what it really is? He doesn't care about any of us, and he doesn't care about spending Christmas with us."

With me.

"Maggie! You know that's not true."

Actually, I didn't. I loved my grandparents, and I knew they loved me. But my father was their only son. And we were never going to agree on this.

"I'm sorry. It's fine. I'll see you tomorrow."

I hung up the phone just as the tears began to fall.

I stared down at my phone screen. My finger hovered over the keys. I needed a distraction, something to get my mind off my conversation with my grandmother. I wanted to forget, just for a little bit. I didn't want to hurt anymore.

I stared at the cream-colored business card on my desk, lying next to my phone. My fingers traced the raised black ink.

Hugh Mitchell. Cobalt. Owner.

It was now or never.

The cafeteria consensus—Mya, Fleur, Samir and Michael—was three to one that I should call him. Samir, unsurprisingly, had been the lone dissenter. He had shaken his head when I asked the rest of the table what I should do about Hugh.

"You'll regret it," he told me, before turning his attention back to his current girl of the week.

Maybe he was right. Maybe I would regret it. But right now, I didn't care. I didn't want to be good Maggie who always toed the line and never took any chances. I wanted to be someone else.

Fuck it all.

I set the business card down on my desk, picking up my cell phone. With shaky fingers I dialed his number, part of me hoping he would answer, another part hoping he wouldn't.

He answered on the third ring.

"This is Hugh."

I paused for a moment.

"Hello?"

Somehow, I had forgotten how good his voice sounded. That crisp British accent made my toes curl. I sucked in a deep breath, my heart pounding madly in my chest. I should have written down a script or something.

"Hi, it's Maggie."

I could hear the smile in his voice. "How are you?"

I struggled to calm my raging nerves. "I'm good. I've been traveling a bit," I babbled, realizing my best intentions were going awry.

"Where did you go?"

"Italy. Venice."

"I love Venice. One of my favorite cities."

I grinned, the knot of tension in my stomach loosening slightly. "Me, too. It was amazing."

"Speaking of Italian, I know this great restaurant in Chelsea. Best pizza you can get in London. You interested?"

"Yes," I squeaked. "I'm definitely interested."

"Good. Why don't I pick you up for dinner in an hour or so?"

"I'll be there."

"Hold still." Fleur held the curling iron over my hair. "I only have another ten minutes to finish your hair."

I dabbed some lipstick on, struggling to contain all the nervous energy running through my body. "You're a lifesaver."

Fleur grinned. "I know. So, I take it you called him?"

"I did."

"What made you decide to do it?"

"I just…needed a distraction. Or something. Does that make sense?"

"Yeah, it does."

"Where is he taking you?" Noora asked.

"A restaurant in Chelsea."

Fleur ran the curling iron through my hair, the motion releasing a silky brown spiral. "I think it was the right decision. If you hadn't called him, you just would have spent the rest of the year thinking about what might have been. Now you've taken the what-ifs out of things. And he's interested in you if he asked you out to dinner." She grinned. "Now go out and get laid."

I laughed. "We'll see."

Noora came over and gave me a swift hug. "My flight leaves in a few hours. Have a good break."

"You, too."

She left the room, leaving me and Fleur getting ready. Fleur stared at my reflection in the mirror, our gazes locking. The desk and an old glass mirror created the perfect makeshift vanity.

"Take it from someone who knows—don't leave anything to chance. You have a shot with this guy. Make your move tonight."

24

There was something magical about London nights, something in the air that whispered possibilities—and adventure on the horizon.

It was in the air tonight.

I wore one of my own outfits—a black wrap dress with a plunging neckline and short hemline that made up for the demure long sleeves. It had been a massive find at H&M, which was rapidly becoming one of my favorite stores. I paired the dress with a killer pair of black leather high-heeled boots and chunky Lucite jewelry. Thanks to Fleur's hair magic, my long brown hair fell in wild curls around my face.

I could hardly recognize myself. Sometime during the last few months, I had changed. For the most part I still looked the same. My hair was still brown, my hips still curvy, my boobs smaller than I would have liked. It was just the packaging that was different. I was confident in ways I had never been before. I was becoming a version of myself I was getting to know with each day that passed.

Still, no matter how much my clothes had changed, I still felt the same rush of nerves at the sight of Hugh's Ferrari roaring up the street, the same feeling of disbelief.

This was exactly what I needed. I needed to suspend reality, just for a moment. I wanted nothing to do with Maggie from South Carolina. Tonight, I could be someone else.

The car came to a stop in front of the building. Hugh killed the engine and opened the car door, sliding gracefully out of the driver's seat. His gaze settled on me. A low whistle of appreciation fell from his lips.

"Babe, you're a knockout."

I flushed with pleasure, thinking I could say the same about him. He wore an inky-purple velvet jacket, perfectly tailored to his broad shoulders. His long legs were encased in dark denim jeans, a snowy-white collared dress shirt peeking out from the jacket.

"You ready?"

I nodded, crossing the distance between us and taking his outstretched hand, loving the feel of our fingers linked together. Just that little bit of bare skin against mine was enough to send a whole other level of anticipation through me.

I wanted him, and yet—

It was different from how I felt with Samir. I didn't feel desperate; I didn't feel out of control.

It was a welcome change—

We rode through Kensington, the car engine the only sound between us, our hands linked. I told him about my trip while he talked about how busy he had been at the bar. London passed by us, a flicker of lights and sounds I had begun to associate with the city. I tilted my head up, staring at the midnight sky, its expanse teeming with possibilities.

Hugh released my hand, maneuvering the Ferrari into a narrow parallel parking space.

I reached for the door handle.

"Wait."

His voice—the sexy timbre of it—sent a wave of desire through me.

Hugh reached over, wrapping his hands in my hair, pulling my face toward his. He kissed me full on the mouth, his tongue licking into mine. His kisses were nothing like Samir's. Whereas Samir's kisses were urgent and frantic, Hugh kissed me softly, lazily. He kissed me as though this was just a prelude, and we had all the time in the world.

"Seeing you like that, in that dress…" His fingers trailed down my neck, hovering over my collarbone, one reaching out to trace the sharp line. He trailed his fingers lower, leaving a path of goose bumps in his wake. His fingers hovered just above my cleavage.

"We should probably go eat," I whispered, my body a haze of emotions. We had just gone from zero to sixty in no time at all and as always, I was playing catchup.

Hugh got out of the car, opening the car door for me. The move was so smooth, so graceful, it took my breath away.

He led me into the restaurant, my body pressed against his side, his hand on the small of my back, guiding me forward through the crowd. I reveled in the feel of him behind me. The knowledge that he was there, that I was on his arm, bolstered my confidence. Tonight, I felt beautiful.

The restaurant was everything Hugh promised and more. It wasn't as fancy as some of the places I'd been. Rather, the decor was clean and modern, everything sleek while still being comfortable. It was perfect.

We ordered a bacon-and-avocado pizza to share. It was an unlikely yet delicious combo that we topped off with a bottle of champagne. When we finished, Hugh guided me out of the restaurant, his arm wrapped around my shoulders.

"What time is your flight tomorrow?" he asked, his lips grazing my ear.

I had no idea. With him this close, the musky smell of his cologne filling my nostrils, I was pretty sure I could barely remember my own name, much less my travel arrangements.

"Early. Morning, I think," I murmured, wrapping my arms around his neck.

"Want to come back to my place for a bit?"

Did I want to go back to his place? Yes…and no. I definitely wasn't ready to have sex with him; I doubted a guy like Hugh was going to be satisfied by just making out. And I had no idea how to explain the emotions raging through me.

It wasn't that I was even saving myself for marriage. I'd never planned on waiting that long. But I was saving myself for love. For something more. And as hot as Hugh was, and as much as I wanted to see what he looked like under that purple velvet jacket, I couldn't throw away that one last hope that my first time would be with someone I loved.

"Why don't we go meet up with some of my friends?" I suggested.

Fleur had mentioned a bunch of people were celebrating the end of semester at a new club that had just opened in Soho. Fleur had offered to put me and Hugh on the list just in case we decided to stop by. Considering the kiss in his car, the club seemed like the safest bet.

Something that might have been disappointment flickered across Hugh's face before it was replaced by his characteristic charm. "You're going to make me chase you, aren't you?"

Somehow that seemed to be the easiest explanation I could offer. And if it kept him interested, I wasn't going to correct him. "Maybe."

He considered this for a moment, his gaze raking me over from head to toe. He winked at me, and my heart turned over in my chest.

"Could be fun."

25

We pulled up in front of Orion, the line in front of the club already around the block. Whatever concerns I might have had about Fleur failing to get us on the VIP list were dissolved by the way the bouncers drooled over Hugh's car.

He grinned at me, his expression unbelievably boyish. "It has its perks."

No kidding.

As Hugh opened my car door, I spotted Fleur, Samir, Michael and some other kids from school heading toward the club on foot. Samir had his arm around a pretty blonde. She whispered something in his ear and Samir threw his head back, laughter spilling out. Suddenly his head turned, his gaze sharpening on the car first before traveling to me. For a moment our gazes locked. He didn't look happy to see me.

I jerked my head away.

Guilt filled me. Weeks ago, I'd been straddling Samir in the back of a car. Now I was with Hugh. I tried to tell myself Samir didn't care, that none of it mattered. It was hard to do when I read the accusation in his eyes.

I ignored the pang that landed somewhere in the vicinity of my heart.

"Maggie!" Fleur walked over, giving me a quick hug. "I'm glad you made it." She exchanged hellos with Hugh, her gaze drifting to the Ferrari behind him.

"I'm going to go park the car, babe. I'll meet you inside."

I turned away from him, walking toward the entrance, linking arms with Fleur. I wasn't exactly dressed for a club tonight with my long sleeves, but I figured it was enough to get me in. And if I couldn't get past the bouncers, then linking arms with Fleur was the trick. She looked amazing tonight.

"Oh, my God, you did not tell me about the car," she hissed as soon as Hugh drove away.

I grinned. "Pretty amazing, right?"

"That car is seriously hot. Have you driven it?"

"His car is probably worth more than my life."

"I'm sure you guys can come up with some kind of reasonable trade." She winked at me, a knowing grin spreading across her face.

"Ha, ha."

"You look good, by the way. Especially your hair."

"Okay, are you guys not going to fill me in on who the fine guy in the Ferrari is?"

We both turned at the sound of Michael's voice.

"Of course we're going to fill you in," I answered, looping my other arm through his. We followed the group into the club while I shared all the details of my date with Hugh.

"Who do you think made that jacket?" Michael asked. "Gucci? It looks like it's Gucci."

"I have no clue. He's pretty much perfect, though, isn't he?"

"Yes, he is." Fleur pulled a face. "If you weren't such a good friend, I could hate you, you know…" Her eyes narrowed as her voice trailed off. "What the fuck is he doing?"

I followed her gaze. Samir had completely taken over the VIP table leaving no room for the rest of us.

"He's been a pain in the ass lately," Fleur muttered. "I don't know what his fucking problem is, but it's getting old fast."

A girl whispered something to Samir and he threw his head back, laughing.

I grabbed one of the shots the waitress was passing around, tossing it back in one motion. The tequila hit my throat with a burn. I coughed.

Fleur's eyes widened. "You okay?"

"Fabulous."

Samir stopped talking to the girl and stared at me. He opened his mouth like he was going to say something but then he closed it. Annoyance flashed through me like a lightning storm.

"Something you wanted to say?"

"Be careful."

I glared at him. "I'm fine. I don't need a babysitter."

To prove my point, I grabbed another shot of tequila. This time I was ready for the burn, the liquid going down in a smooth gulp.

Something flashed in his eyes. Anger, frustration, judgment—who knew, and I didn't care. The girl on his arm whispered something but he ignored her.

"How much have you had to drink tonight?" he asked me.

Half a bottle of champagne at dinner. Two shots of tequila. I wasn't drunk—just squishy.

My eyes narrowed, my gaze lingering on the flavor of the month. The petty part of me hated that she was my polar opposite. If Samir had a type, it definitely wasn't me.

"None of your business. But thanks for your concern, Mom."

Samir shook his head, hiding those beautiful brown eyes, saying something under his breath before turning his attention back to his *date*. In one move he'd completely dismissed me.

To hell with that.

"Hey, gorgeous."

I jumped at the sound of Hugh's voice. He wrapped his arm around my waist, pressing a swift kiss to my neck.

"Do you guys have a table?" he asked.

"We did," Fleur commented darkly. "Excuse me."

Maybe this hadn't been the best idea. There was a weird vibe in the air tonight. I hadn't expected Samir to be here; he'd mentioned something earlier about staying in and watching a football match. The last thing I needed was for Hugh to find out about our occasional hookups. It was bad enough that Samir had seen me with Hugh. Bad enough that I had to watch Samir all over someone else.

Definitely time for another drink.

"Do you want to head to the bar?"

Hugh grinned, his hand reaching out to stroke my arm. "That isn't the first thing that comes to mind. But yeah, a drink could be good."

I blushed, grateful that the club's darkness hid the stain marring my cheeks. "I'm sure there are dark corners we can check out," I whispered playfully.

Hugh groaned, pressing his lips against my hair.

We headed over to the bar. Hugh ordered for both of us, exchanging small talk with the bartender.

"Did you know him?"

"Yeah, he applied for a job at Cobalt a few months ago. We had already filled the position, though. He's a good guy."

"Do you know everyone in London?" I teased.

"It helps to be well-connected. Especially when you own a bar."

I couldn't help but think there was more to it than that. I figured Hugh would be active on the London club scene even if he didn't own the bar. He was too cool not to be. I'd never met anyone like him. He was this hot, amazing guy, but somehow he managed to look at you and make you feel as though you were amazing, too. And it wasn't just with me. He treated everyone like that. He was genuinely a nice guy to be around.

So why was my mind back on what was going on at the table and not on the guy in front of me?

Hugh leaned down, pressing a soft kiss on my lips. "Come on, gorgeous."

I allowed Hugh to maneuver me over to a corner across the room from my friends. He leaned against the wall, sipping from his martini. I stood in front of him, holding my drink, feeling the beat of the music. I couldn't tear my gaze away from his broad shoulders, that interesting patch of skin peeking out from the unbuttoned collar of his dress shirt. I sipped from my drink, the room tilting slightly. I wanted to unbutton the rest of the snowy-white buttons dotting down the front of his shirt. I wanted to see the rest of his body, feel his muscles beneath my hands.

Fuck Samir.

"What?" Hugh asked, tilting his head to the side. A dimple teased the corner of his mouth. I wondered if he knew the direction my thoughts had taken.

I shook my head, jerking my gaze back to his face. "Nothing." I leaned my body closer to his, closing my eyes at the feel of his hard body pressing against mine. "I was just thinking about how lucky I was to meet you," I whispered, my lips inches from his.

He grinned wolfishly. "I'm the lucky one." He reached out, wrapping an arm around my waist, pulling me closer.

I set my drink down on a small table, locking my arms around his neck. The height difference between us made me essentially eye level with his chest. Given how much Hugh clearly worked out, it wasn't exactly a tragedy.

"This is much better," Hugh whispered in my ear, setting his drink down next to mine. His hand moved under my chin, lifting my face up so that our gazes locked. His lips traveled downward, running along the curve of my jaw before moving up toward my mouth. I giggled, the gesture sending a soft tickle through my skin.

I opened to him instantly, allowing him to control the kiss, molding my lips and mouth in whatever shape he wanted. We stood there, groping each other, doing all the things in public I knew he would much rather do in private.

"I want you," Hugh murmured against my mouth.

After making out for nearly an hour, I was all too aware of how much he wanted me. Every sense felt alive—the feel of his hard body beneath my hands, the smell of his cologne filling my nostrils, sent waves of desire through my body.

"We can get out of here, head back to my place," Hugh suggested, his dark eyes boring into mine. "If you want to."

Why was I fighting it? Hugh was hot and nice, and he liked me. Why not go back to his place?

I grinned, allowing Hugh to wrap his arms around me, pressing my body against his. He released me and my gaze surveyed the crowd. I tried to tell myself I wasn't looking for the one person I had no business looking for—

I found him instantly. Samir stood with his arm around the same blonde he'd been with earlier. She was saying something to him, her body pressed up against his, her hand linked with his free one.

He wasn't looking at her. His gaze met mine across the crowded club. It wasn't a casual stare. His dark eyes blazed with intensity. We faced off against each other, my body tucked against Hugh's, Samir's arm casually wrapped around the blonde. It should have felt totally normal—we were two friends, casual ones at that—out with our respective dates. No big deal.

It shouldn't have made me feel like crying.

The girl I used to be would never have gone home with Hugh. But I didn't want to be that girl anymore.

"Let's go."

Hugh grinned. He pulled me away from the wall, leading me through the club.

Nerves filled me. My legs felt a little shaky; I wobbled a bit in my heels. We passed by my friends.

I couldn't look at Samir.

We walked out of the club, the cold London air hitting us with a blast. Hugh pressed a swift kiss to my lips. "I'll go get the car. I'll be right back."

I watched him walk away, my heart pounding. Was I really going to do this? Was I ready? I didn't even know anymore. But it was time for a change. Time for me to reinvent myself. Time to stop fantasizing about a guy who treated me like an afterthought.

"Don't do this."

I froze.

The voice behind me was raw, angry—and all too familiar.

I turned slowly, coming face-to-face with Samir.

26

"What are you doing here?"

"Don't do this," Samir repeated, walking toward me, his hands shoved in his pockets. "You're drunk. Trust me, it's a bad idea. One you'll regret."

"Are you kidding me? You think you have any right to lecture me on good decision-making?"

"You're making a mistake."

"So what?" I challenged. "It's my mistake. It's none of your business. Go away. Go back inside to whatever girl you're screwing around with today."

His mouth tightened in a harsh line. "Come back inside." He reached out and grabbed my hand, my fingers slipping through his as I jerked away.

"Don't touch me."

"That's not what you were saying in Venice."

"Venice was a mistake."

"Was it? I think you're lying." Samir moved toward me. His body grazed mine, his hips pressing against me. His voice lowered. "Tell me you want him like you want me. Tell me he makes you ache like I do. Tell me you yearn for it. Tell me he makes you lose control like you do with me." He leaned closer;

his lips barely grazed my ear, but it was enough to be my un-doing. "Tell me you don't think of me—my kisses, my hands, my body—when you're with him."

I pushed him away. My voice shook. "I don't think of you at all."

"Liar," he whispered, the sound triumphant, his expression fierce.

I hated that he was right.

"Don't go with him. Don't do this."

"Why? Give me one good reason."

"Because I want you. In my bed. Naked in my arms. Because I can't stop wanting you. Because this thing between us hasn't had a chance to play itself out. You can deny it all you want, but there's something here. I know you feel it."

His words sent a shiver down my spine. The image of our bodies locked together entered my mind. But it wasn't enough.

"Then what? I get, what, one, two nights as your girl of the week?" I laughed, the sound bitter, louder than I intended. "Guess what? You're not worth it."

Samir looked stung. "And he is?"

"Yeah. He is."

I met his gaze head-on. I wasn't sure if it was the alcohol stoking the fire within me or my own frustration over the back-and-forth we'd been doing for months now, but whatever it was, I wanted to lash out at him. I wanted to push him away.

"Maggie—"

"Go back inside." My voice shook with anger and emotion. "Just go back inside. You want to help me? Leave me alone. Because I can't take any more of this."

I turned away, walking toward Hugh, leaving Samir behind me. I didn't look back.

"You okay, babe?" Hugh looked over my shoulder.

Somehow, I mustered a grin. "Yep. Let's go."

I slid into the Ferrari, anger flooding me. *How dare he? How dare he judge me?* Samir knew nothing about me. And he was an idiot if he thought I was going to miss out on a guy like Hugh for a couple nights in Samir's bed. Hugh took me to dinner, took me out on dates. Samir wanted to fuck me. And as good as I knew it might be—I'd seen the parade of girls.

I couldn't be one of them.

And yet...those words... *I want you*... I couldn't push them out. Couldn't push him out.

I didn't want my first time to be like this—angry, confused, unable to get Samir out of my mind.

We stopped at a light.

"Maybe this isn't such a great idea."

"What's wrong?"

I hesitated. "I leave tomorrow and I'm not sure I want to start something we aren't going to have a chance to really finish."

The rest—the truth—was left unsaid. Because there, lingering somewhere in between all my confusion, was the memory of my body wrapped around Samir's.

Hugh studied me carefully. A tinge of annoyance crossed his face, along with something else I was afraid to name.

Would he lose interest if we didn't have sex?

"I'm sorry."

His expression softened. "Don't be sorry. You're offering me a rain check, then? Because it does sort of feel like you're shooting me down."

I nodded, my lips curving at the thought of me writing out a sex IOU. "Something like that. I promise I am not shooting you down. I just need more time."

Hugh leaned over, capturing my lips in another devastating kiss. "Why do I think you're going to keep me on my toes, Maggie?"

I blushed. "Is that such a bad thing?"

My heart pounded as silence yawned between us.

Hugh leaned down and whispered in my ear. "I have a feeling you'll be worth waiting for. And I can't wait to collect on that rain check."

27

"Three, two, one...happy New Year!"

I stared at the TV, watching the glittery ball drop in Times Square. It was depressing as hell to ring in the New Year by myself.

My grandparents had lasted until ten before going to bed. Jo and I were supposed to hang out together, but she got sick, leaving me with a New Year's Eve special hosted by a pop star I'd never even heard of.

If I were in London right now, I'd probably be out at some fabulous club with my friends. In South Carolina I sat by myself in a pair of ratty old pajamas.

Four more days.

My phone beeped. I leaned over, grabbing my cell off the table.

Happy New Year xxxx

It was a British cell number, but not one I recognized.

Thanks. Happy New Year. Who is this? I hit Send and waited for a response.

A minute later—

Samir...what are you wearing? xxx

I burst out laughing. Classic Samir. It had only been a few weeks since I'd last seen him, but I missed him. Even despite our fight. I missed joking around with him—no one else gave me shit like he did and no one else made me want to throw it back. I couldn't resist—

Wouldn't you like to know?

A few seconds later—

Yes.

My heart pounded. My phone beeped again.

I'm sorry about that night. I was worried about you.

I blinked, rereading the text, surprise filling me. I'd never heard Samir apologize for anything. And the fact that he was *worried* about me? That was new. I'd only seen him worry about Fleur.

The thing about Samir—which I would never, ever tell him—was that it was tough to stay mad at him. He was too funny, too charming when he wanted to be, too everything.

I'm sorry, too. I was drunk and angry.

I hit Send and set my phone down, flipping off the TV.

A minute later my phone rang. "Hello?"

"Hi." Samir's voice filled the line.

I grinned. "Hi."

Silence descended.

"Is this a bad time?"

"No. Not at all. I was just getting ready for bed."

"So, it's the perfect time."

"Something like that."

"Wish I could be there."

I chuckled, the knot in my chest slowly unraveling. "Sure you do."

"How's your break going?"

Horribly. My dad hadn't even bothered calling on Christmas. And the "gift" he'd gotten me screamed of my grandmother's attempt to buy something and pass it off as being from him.

"Let's just say I'm ready to go back to London."

"God, you and me both."

"Where are you?"

"Gstaad. Switzerland. Skiing. It's cold. I hate being cold."

"I don't know how you bear it. Rough life."

He laughed. "Sometimes."

I looked around the tiny room I grew up in—the worn carpet, the sheets I'd had since middle school. I doubted our lives could have been any different. It was weird to see my life overlap like this—the old and the new.

We made conversation for a few minutes—small talk about the weather, what our friends were up to. I lay back in bed, curling up under the sheets, listening to his voice, his accent lulling me to sleep.

"Maggie?"

"Yeah?"

"Getting sleepy?"

"Sorry. Yeah. It's late here."

Silence filled the line.

"Are you in bed?"

I blushed. His voice was seductive now, teasing. I doubted he knew how to turn it off. Maybe he didn't want to.

"Yeah."

There was another pause on the line. "I'll let you go to sleep." Samir's voice sounded unusual, strained, even. "Maggie?"

"Yeah?"

Seconds ticked by before he spoke again.

"Did you sleep with him?"

Shock filled me. It was a simple question with a complicated answer. It wasn't his business; he had no right. And yet—

I found the word tumbling from my lips.

"No."

I thought I heard a sigh of relief on his end of the line, a released breath, or maybe it was just my imagination.

Samir was quiet for a moment. "Night. Sleep well. I'll see you in a couple days."

I fell asleep and when I dreamed, I dreamed of him.

This time the flight from Charlotte to London was much easier. I slept most of the way, thanks in part to my ability to land a coveted aisle seat. When we landed in London, I made my way through Immigration with ease, grabbed my bags and hopped on the Tube.

I got off the Piccadilly line at Gloucester Road, lucky enough to snag a cab right outside the station. It was only a couple of miles to the school, but not doable with two massive suitcases trailing behind me.

It was still early, the city quiet. There was an odd stillness to London early in the morning. It was as if the city that never slept was taking a break, recharging its batteries, preparing for the day ahead. In a few hours these streets would be filled with people rushing to work, shopkeepers selling candy, pubs serving lunch. In a few hours the streets would become a sea of languages and people from all over the world.

I loved it.

We hit the park, turning onto High Street Kensington. When the cabbie turned down Embassy Row, I felt the first real sense of excitement—an eagerness to thrust open the door and jump out, bounding up the steps into the school. The building was as beautiful as always, the stone shining in the early-morning light.

"We're here, luv."

I handed the cabbie a ten-pound note. He helped me pull my bags up the front steps and I pushed open the entry doors.

I was home.

I sat at a cafeteria table with Fleur, Mya, Michael and Samir.

"I met someone," Michael announced, effectively silencing the conversation at the table.

I grinned, leaning forward in my chair. "Spill."

"Well, there was this hot guy on my flight to New York."

Samir rolled his eyes. "It's always, 'I met this guy. I think he likes me. But he might not. But he called me. What does it mean?'"

I tried to ignore the fact that his voice sounded a lot like mine. He shot me a pointed look. I scowled back at him.

"You can leave," Fleur snapped.

Samir leaned back in his chair, crossing his arms over his chest. His watch gleamed under the cafeteria lights.

Michael turned back to me. "So this guy was tall and skinny."

I grinned, ignoring Samir's groan.

"The whole flight I was trying to figure out if he was single. Sending out discreet signals and stuff—"

"I love you, baby, but you are never discreet," Mya teased.

Michael balled up a napkin, throwing it and missing Mya, hitting Samir in the elbow. He scowled back at us.

"You're so boring, Samir," I teased. He glared at me. "If you can't handle hanging with the fun people, go sit by yourself."

"Bite me."

My eyes narrowed. The fucked-up thing was that part of me wanted to. Tonight was the first time we'd seen each other since his New Year's phone call. It felt strange to be around him again. Whatever had spurred him to call me seemed to be gone, replaced by a casual indifference.

It was so frustrating.

"No one is listening to my story," Michael complained.

Fleur waved her hand. "Ignore them. Tell us your story."

Michael grinned. "Thank you, Fleur. So apparently, he wasn't gay. But I got his phone number anyway."

I grinned, shaking my head. Michael had the uncanny tendency to fall for straight guys. But I wasn't sure I was exactly one to judge. I guessed in our own ways we all tended to fall for someone we couldn't have.

"When are we going to find you a nice boy?"

"I'll find a nice boy when you do," Michael teased.

"What?" I asked with mock seriousness. "*Moi?* I have found a nice guy, thank you very much. Hugh is a nice guy."

I didn't look at Samir.

"Hugh is a nice *man*," Michael corrected. "He's old."

"He's not old," I protested. Age was relative, anyway. Everyone knew girls matured faster than guys did.

"He is a little old," Fleur chimed in, a teasing grin on her face. She shrugged. "Still fuckable, though."

I laughed. Classic Fleur.

The sound of wood against stone interrupted our banter. Samir pushed away from the table. "I'm out."

Was I supposed to feel bad for talking about Hugh when Samir constantly showed up with other girls? Seriously?

I turned my attention back to Michael, refusing to give Samir the satisfaction of watching him walk away. "So how in the world did you manage to get this boy's phone number?"

Michael winked. "I worked my magic. I've got moves."

"I might need you to show me some of those moves," I joked.

"I take it Mr. Tall, Dark and British didn't call over break?"

"Nope. Not once."

"What an ass," Mya interjected across the table.

Her vehemence surprised me. Mya was usually the calm one. But she seemed a little more tense than usual. So far, she hadn't really shared much about her break.

"I just don't get it," I complained, venting now that Samir was gone. "I thought we ended things on a good note my last night in London. I mean, he seemed interested. So why didn't he call or anything while I was gone?"

"Did you think about texting him?" Mya asked.

"I guess I could have. It just sometimes feels like I'm always the one chasing him. Maybe I want to be the one that gets chased." And hadn't Hugh all but said he was going to do just that?

Mya nodded. "Makes sense."

"Have you ever considered the fact that you might be his booty call?" Michael interjected. Fleur shot him a dirty look. "What? I'm not saying anything bad. We've all been some guy's booty call at one point or another. Now is just Maggie's turn."

"She hasn't given up any booty," Fleur interjected, jumping to my defense. "Despite all my offers to take her lingerie shopping."

Michael grinned. "Lingerie shopping is exactly what she needs."

"Maybe *she* would like for you guys to not talk about her like she isn't here."

"Come on, Mags. A little black lace could make all the difference," Michael teased.

I blushed. "Enough talking about my underwear."

"Which Hugh hasn't seen," Fleur added.

"Fine. Yes. Which Hugh hasn't seen."

Michael sighed. "If you want my advice—" I wasn't exactly sure I did "—you gotta just jump him one of these days and get it out of your system."

"So, your advice is basically that she should just have sex with him and, what—hope for the best?" Fleur shook her head. "Bad advice. If she has sex with this guy, she's going to get all clingy and he's just going to break her heart. Trust me."

It was scary when Fleur was beginning to sound like the voice of reason.

"Guys! Enough talking about my sex life. I didn't realize whether or not I sleep with Hugh was up for a committee vote. I'll do what feels right when it feels right. I'm not going to go into this plan scheming and calculating."

Mya nodded. "Exactly. You should do whatever you're comfortable with. There's no need for you to jump into things."

"Or onto things, as the case may be." Michael snickered.

I balled up my napkin and threw it at him.

"Have you called him?" Fleur asked.

I shook my head. "Not yet."

"You should call him," Michael interjected. "You're never going to know what might happen if you don't."

I knew he was right. But that didn't make it any easier. "I guess. I just don't want to seem too overeager. And I did call him last time," I reminded him.

"Did you tell him what day you were getting into London?" Michael asked.

"No. I hadn't booked my flight yet."

"Then call him."

28

I waited a day. I hadn't been entirely honest with my friends at dinner. It wasn't just the sex that held me back from calling Hugh. It was so much more than that. I had no idea where I stood with him. And I was still having those dreams about Samir...

I decided to text him. Texting was safer, fewer chances for rejection, lower odds I would somehow embarrass myself.

Hi, it's Maggie. I'm back in town now. Hope you had a great Christmas.

The response came half an hour later. My phone pinged as I walked back into the room from the shower.

Hi, gorgeous. Glad you're back. Dinner tomorrow?

Relief, mixed in with nerves, filled me.

I knew I should probably wait to respond so I didn't seem too eager, but I couldn't.

Sounds great. See you then.

I dressed quickly, blowing out my hair and applying makeup. Dinner was almost over. I rushed through the line, grabbing some chicken nuggets and white rice. I maneuvered through the dining hall tables.

Fleur sat at one of the tables. She wasn't alone.

So far, I had been pretty lucky to limit my interaction with Samir. I was careful to only hang out with him in group settings or in public. Public seemed good—safe. Public heightened the chances of me keeping my clothes on and my hands—and lips—off him.

Fleur's gaze met mine across the room. *Rescue me*, she mouthed.

I grinned despite myself, walking up and sliding out a chair opposite hers in the dining room.

"What's wrong?"

"Samir's been sharing his romantic escapades with me. After an hour of this, I need a shower."

I couldn't help myself. I turned to Samir, a grin escaping. "You have an hour of romantic escapades?" My tone was liberally sprinkled with doubt.

Sometimes I couldn't resist the urge to screw with him.

Samir winked at Fleur, but his words were for me. "I have way more than an hour. I have remarkable stamina."

I choked on my soda.

Fleur rolled her eyes. "*Cochon.*"

It took me a second to translate the French word for *pig*.

Samir leaned forward over the table. "Don't be jealous just because you failed to get any action over break."

Did that mean *he* got action over break?

"I didn't fail to get any action," Fleur retorted. "I wasn't even trying to get 'action,' as you so quaintly put it. Some of us had better things to do."

I winced. Fleur looked like a volcano waiting to erupt. Clearly Samir had been needling her for a while.

"Like what?" Samir taunted. "Shopping? Getting your nails done? Crying over Costa?"

Shit. Costa was the one topic that had become off-limits with Fleur.

"Fuck you," Fleur snapped. She got up from the table, grabbing her tray. "There's a reason why no one likes you, Samir. Maybe if you weren't such an ass, you would have friends at school who didn't just use you to get into nightclubs. Maybe your girlfriend wouldn't have left you. Maybe people would care about more than your money."

What? He had a girlfriend? She left him?

Samir's expression darkened, his jaw clenched.

It was impossible to tell which one of them was more pissed off. Fleur's anger came out as an explosion of energy; Samir's was more like a slow burn, no less intense, just more restrained.

Fleur turned to me. "I have to meet up with my group for class. But I'll see you around." She stomped off, leaving me alone with a very obviously angry Samir.

I stared down at my plate of food. "You know I might just get this to go—"

"Stay."

My head jerked up.

"I'm not going to eat you." His lips twitched, the angry line softening some.

I reddened, leaning back in my chair, creating more space between us. We ate in silence. I desperately wanted to ask him about what Fleur said but his mood seemed…unpredictable. I turned my head, sneaking a peek at his profile. He still looked angry, although slightly less so. I turned back to my food, my appetite nearly gone from all the tension at the table. I pushed my food around the plate. Silence. I turned my head again.

"Enjoying the view?"

I jerked back, a familiar flush spreading across my cheeks. "Sorry. I didn't mean to stare."

"Why were you?"

"You seemed upset after Fleur left." The words hung between us. The next words out of my mouth shocked me. "She hurt your feelings." It was so obvious I couldn't just refuse to acknowledge it.

What did your girlfriend do to you?

He looked stung. "She did not hurt my feelings."

"Sure she didn't." I played with my fork. Maybe it was time for me to play peacemaker. "You know, she never would have said those things to you if you hadn't made that dig about Costa. She's still upset by the whole situation and you throwing it in her face didn't help things."

"She doesn't want to hear the truth."

"What is the truth?"

I was curious to hear Samir's take on things. On one hand, he seemed to have the same cavalier attitude toward relationships Costa did. On the other hand, despite their current fight, it was obvious he did care about Fleur.

"Fleur was wasting her time with Costa. The guy was never interested in anything serious. He messed around with her because Fleur's hot and he could. He's a dick and Fleur's way better off without him. Her moping is pathetic. And it's gone on for way too long. She needs to get over it."

"And you've never moped over a girl?" I countered.

Samir stared at me incredulously. "Of course not."

"Not even your ex-girlfriend?" The words slipped out before I could control them.

Samir's trademark scowl slipped back into place. "No."

My eyes narrowed. "I don't think I believe you."

"What?"

"I don't believe you. You seem…" I struggled for the right words. "Thrown by it." I hesitated, pushing on. "When did you guys break up?"

Samir's eyes widened. "Are we seriously having this conversation?"

I was a little surprised by my boldness myself. But it didn't seem fair that Samir knew everyone else's secrets and we knew none of his.

"Guess so."

Samir sighed. "I'm over Vanessa."

Somehow knowing her name made her seem real. I didn't like it. "What happened?"

"Nothing."

"I don't buy that. She's an ex for a reason."

Samir glared at me. "What part of me not wanting to talk about it are you not getting?"

I ignored him. "Was it all the girls? Because I do notice you have a lot of girls around you."

"It was not all the girls," he replied, teeth clenched.

My expression was dubious at best. I couldn't imagine any girlfriend being cool with the way Samir was with other girls.

"It was not the other girls," he repeated. "I didn't cheat on her. I don't cheat."

"Really?"

"Yes, really," he snapped. "I'm single now. If I want to sleep with five girls at once, it's my business. I'm always clear from the beginning. I'm not looking for a girlfriend."

I colored. There was something in the vehemence in his voice that told me I'd disturbed a wound not healed.

"Is that why you don't want a girlfriend now?"

There was a moment where I thought he wasn't going to answer me.

I picked up my tray, ready to leave the table—

"She cheated on me."

My jaw dropped, my shocked gaze meeting Samir's. For the first time I saw pain there—and embarrassment.

"I didn't love her. But I cared about her."

I couldn't tear my gaze away.

"And she humiliated me." He averted his eyes. "Fleur doesn't even know that."

"Is that why you are the way you are?"

"What's that supposed to mean?"

Our gazes locked once more. A conversation passed between our eyes.

"You know what I mean."

His stare held mine. "No. I don't."

I felt the same push and pull I always felt with him, the same impossible sense of frustration.

"Is that why you push people away?"

"Don't try to make me into someone I'm not. I'm not some wounded hero you need to save. I'm a guy. It's pretty simple. I like sex. I like women. And if I'm having sex with a woman exclusively, then she damned well better be doing the same with me."

I shook my head, our conversation driving me nuts. *He* drove me nuts. "What is it with you? Sometimes you seem like a total ass. Other times you're actually kind of fun. Are you the guy who doesn't give a shit about anyone but himself? Or are you the guy who is a decent friend? The guy who flew all the way to Venice because Fleur was in trouble?" My voice was quiet. "Which one are you?" Somewhere along the way, his answer had become important to me.

"Which do you think I am?"

"I don't know," I answered honestly, frustration threaded through my voice. "I haven't decided."

"I suppose that's fair." Silence filled the table. "I feel the same way about you."

"What do you mean?"

"You confuse me."

"Me? That's ridiculous. I'm super easy to read. With me, what you see is what you get."

"Is it?" Samir's gaze lingered on my face. "Somehow I don't believe that."

A ringing sound interrupted us. Samir pulled his phone out

of his jeans pocket, looking down at the screen. He stood up abruptly, grabbing his plastic lunch tray. "I gotta run. See you later."

"Samir—"

"Yeah?"

I sucked in a deep breath, the words rushing out in perfect time with the blood rushing to my cheeks—

"Your girlfriend was an idiot."

He smiled softly. "Thanks."

I watched him walk away, wondering why I felt so off-balance. And wishing I had an answer to my own question—

Who was he, really?

And why did I care?

29

After my lunch with Samir, I desperately needed a distraction. I couldn't ask for more than my date with Hugh.

"I missed you."

I grinned at him across the table. "I missed you, too."

Dinner was at a fancy sushi restaurant in Knightsbridge. I'd already spotted a pop star and Hugh pointed out a few footballers.

"Did you think of me while you were gone?"

"I did." I reached out and traced my finger against his forearm, feeling all that strength through the crisp fabric of his dress shirt.

Maybe *missed* him wasn't exactly the right word. I didn't feel like I saw him enough to get to miss him. But I had thought of him. My feelings for him were a puzzle I couldn't quite work out. I liked him. I just wasn't sure if there was anything else.

"Can I ask you something?" He lowered his voice softly.

"Sure."

"What's going on here?"

I blinked. "What do you mean?"

"You seem to blow hot and cold a lot. And I can't figure it out."

For a moment I could only stare at him. I didn't even know where to begin.

"I think I figured it out."

"Really?"

"You seem…" For a moment he seemed uncomfortable. "Maybe a little inexperienced with guys…" His voice trailed off uncertainly.

The word *virgin* lingered between us, unspoken.

If the floor could have opened and swallowed me whole, I would have gladly welcomed it.

"It's okay, you know."

My head jerked up. I still couldn't meet his gaze.

"It's kind of cool, that you haven't been with other guys. I respect that."

"Really?"

"Really. I just wanted to know if we were on the same page with things. I'm a little confused," he admitted ruefully.

I sucked in a deep breath, trying to gather up the courage to be honest. He seemed to deserve at least that much.

"It's not a religious thing or anything," I explained hurriedly. "I'm not waiting until I'm married. I just always thought that my first time would be…" I trailed off, too embarrassed to finish the thought aloud.

Hugh nodded. "I get it." He leaned over, brushing my cheek with a kiss. "Your first time should be special."

I hesitated for a moment, not sure I wanted the answer to the question I was about to ask. But I was curious.

"I'm guessing there have been a lot of girls for you." I paused. Was I about to ask him this? Did I really want to know? I sucked in a deep breath, the words rushing from my mouth with a great big whoosh. "Just out of curiosity, how many are we talking here? Ballpark. Thirty? One hundred?"

Hugh choked back laughter. He paused for a moment, and I

wondered if he was actually counting. "More than thirty, less than one hundred?"

Holy shit.

Hugh ran his hand through his hair, a laugh escaping his lips. His expression was sheepish. "I know it seems high. A lot of those were when I was younger. I've settled down a bit."

I wasn't sure I believed *that.*

"We're a fine pair, aren't we?" Hugh sighed, pressing his forehead against mine. "I like you, Maggie."

Hope sprang up as the words wound their way into my heart. He leaned forward, placing another kiss on my lips.

"I can be patient."

I walked into the common room, feeling as though I was floating on air. It felt good to clear things up with Hugh.

My phone rang.

Was Hugh calling me already? A smile spread across my face. I stared down at my phone. Instead of seeing Hugh's name like I expected, my caller ID just said **Blocked**. My heart sank.

"Hi, Dad."

His voice came through scratchy on the other end of the line. "How are you, Maggie?"

Angry you never came home for Christmas like you promised. Tired of being without both my parents. Take your pick.

"Fine."

"Good."

"What's up?" I struggled to keep my voice light. These conversations never ended well.

He hesitated for a moment before answering me. "I wanted to talk to you about something."

Something, call it a sense of awareness, settled in the pit of my stomach. My dad's calls rarely brought good news. I doubted this would be an exception. What was it this time? A six-month assignment to Germany? A move to Korea? I was prepared for whatever it was. I'd heard it all. It shouldn't even affect me all that much; I wasn't a part of his life, and he wasn't a part of mine.

I pushed through the common room door, heading toward the front hallway. Static filled the end of the line. I could hear my father saying something, but I couldn't hear what.

I needed fresh air.

I sank down on the stone steps in the front of the building, hugging my knees to my chest to ward off the cold. I was still dressed in my outfit from my date with Hugh—at least tonight I had worn jeans.

"…are you there, Maggie?"

"Yeah, I'm here. The connection was just bad for a minute. What did you say?"

A pause filled the line. "I wanted to tell you I met someone."

A chill ran through my body, a chill that had nothing to do with the cold. My parents split up so long ago, I didn't harbor any illusions they would get back together. But my dad was a military man first. Always. If he didn't have time for me, how could he have time for a girlfriend?

Pain pierced through me.

I knew I should be happy for him. I should be the supportive, understanding daughter. It wasn't entirely his fault my mom left. He deserved to be happy, too. But the overwhelming feeling swamping me wasn't one of understanding.

It was anger.

More static filled the line. I heard my dad talking, but I couldn't make out most of it. The words were a jumble, the connection making it impossible to have a good conversation. Until it cleared for one spectacularly awful moment.

"We got married."

I dropped the phone.

30

"Are you okay?"

Not him.

I sat on the steps, my phone on the ground. I brushed furiously at my cheeks. I should have gone to the privacy of my room. But when I tried to get up, my legs were rooted to the spot. Everything in my world had gone still. Everything was different now.

"I'm fine."

I sounded anything but.

Samir sat next to me. "Are you sure? You don't look okay."

"I'm fine," I repeated, this time making my voice sound more forceful. Maybe I could will him away.

"Boy problems?"

I turned my head slightly to face him. Our eyes locked. The concern I saw in his gaze caught my breath. I laughed bitterly, the irony and horror of the situation sinking in. "I guess in a manner of speaking."

Samir's eyebrow rose.

I shook my head. "Not like that. It's my father." More tears escaped. I wiped at my cheeks. Suddenly I couldn't contain it anymore. I had to say it aloud, had to acknowledge it was real.

"He got married." I broke out in sobs, my shoulders shaking with each movement. "I didn't even know he was dating anyone. And now he calls me out of the blue—he never calls me—to tell me he got married. To someone I've never even met. To someone I didn't even know about." More tears spilled down my cheeks.

What I didn't say—what I couldn't say in front of Samir—was how betrayed I felt. It kept playing over and over in my mind, the same thought on loop. My father didn't have room in his life for me—couldn't make the time to be a dad to me. But he could make the time for a wife. He could love a wife.

He couldn't love me. No matter how hard I tried, I couldn't understand why.

"You guys aren't close?" His voice was surprisingly gentle.

I sucked in a deep breath, trying to get control of myself. I was sure that the last thing Samir wanted was to have to deal with me losing my shit. It wasn't his fault he'd decided to come outside for a smoke.

"Our relationship isn't the best." I stared straight ahead at the street in front of me, watching the cars drive by.

"I can relate," he replied.

I turned to face him. "Really?"

Samir nodded, staring ahead. "Yeah. Believe me, I've spent my whole life not measuring up to my parents' expectations."

Surprise filled me. "What are they like? Your parents, I mean."

"Busy. Important. Cold."

I was fascinated by the pain in his voice. I'd learned more about Samir in the past week than I had in the past few months combined.

He shrugged. "I'm just a big disappointment to them."

"Why?"

"My dad's a big deal in Lebanon. He's big in business and politics. He wants me to get serious about stepping up and taking over the family legacy. He's running for political office in two years, and he wants me to be part of his campaign. Sometimes I wish he would just let go a bit. I don't need all the pressure to carry on the family legacy. He never even considered that I might want to do something else with my life. Be something else. Have my own opinions about my country. So yeah, I get what you mean."

"It's just frustrating—"

"Because you wish things were different and they aren't?"

"Exactly."

Samir sighed. He pulled a pack of cigarettes out of his jeans pocket. I watched, fascinated by the motions, as he pulled out a lighter, lighting the cigarette with a little flame. The smell of tobacco filled the air. He took a drag. As he blew out the smoke, he held it in midair, offering it to me.

I shook my head. I'd never liked smoking. But somehow on him it fit.

"Parents suck sometimes," he offered wryly.

"Yep."

He took another drag, blowing a circle of smoke into the air. "You said there was other stuff you were upset about. What else happened?"

"I live with my grandparents in South Carolina and the deal was that he would come visit when he got a chance. He hasn't exactly lived up to his end of the bargain."

"How long has it been since you last saw him?"

"Thirteen months, five days and a few hours. But who's counting?" I laughed bitterly.

"You didn't spend Christmas with him?"

"No." The word was barely a whisper. I wrapped my sweater tightly around my body. "He promised he would be home this time. But something came up and he ended up not making it."

"What about your mom?"

"She left a long time ago." Sometimes I didn't blame her for leaving. I understood how much she must have hated always coming second to the military. I just wished she hadn't left *me*.

"That has to be hard."

I opened my mouth to give my standard answer—*Eh, it's not that bad*—but something else came out instead. "It is."

"How old were you?"

"Five."

"What happened?"

No one had ever asked me that. Everyone seemed to know my mom was off-limits. I treated her as if she were dead rather than alive somewhere, living her life without me. When I was younger, I used to tell people she died; it seemed like an easier answer, and it was the closest thing to the truth.

She was dead to *me*.

I met Samir's gaze, surprised by the emotion I saw flickering in his eyes. I felt stripped bare before him, more exposed than during any of the times we made out. I'd never wanted to talk about it before, and hadn't even told my dad.

I wanted to tell Samir.

I expelled a harsh breath. "It started off like a normal day. I don't remember much about it, but I remember she made me a bowl of my favorite cereal. Lucky Charms."

He grinned. "I love the little marshmallows."

I had, too. I remembered picking them out of the cereal to eat first when I was a kid. I hadn't eaten them since that day. I tried once, but the marshmallows had tasted like sawdust.

"After breakfast she told me to get dressed for dance class. Ballet. I wore a pink leotard." I shook my head, my fist clenching. It all came back in startling clarity. I remembered parts of it so vividly; others were just a haze.

Samir reached out, his free hand grasping mine. I stared down, surprised by the sight of my pale hand entwined in his tan one. He squeezed my hand.

"I got out of the car. I gave her a hug. It was quick—I was

in a hurry to get to class. I was so excited to dance that day. It's such a little thing, but I remember being annoyed by that hug."

"I wish I hadn't pulled away so soon." A tear slipped from my eye. "I wish I could have stayed there, with her. Maybe she would have stopped and thought about what she was doing. Maybe she would have stayed."

"Maggie—"

With my free hand, I wiped furiously at my cheek. "And that was it. I walked away from her. I didn't even turn around. I never saw her again. She never came to pick me up. I waited for an hour, sitting outside the school, waiting with my dance teacher. I had this knot in the pit of my stomach. I think I knew somehow, when she didn't come. I think I knew she was gone."

Samir squeezed my hand, wrapping his fingers around mine, infusing me with his strength.

"My grandmother came. My father was gone for work somewhere. But my grandmother came for me. She took me back to their house, and that was it. My father never spoke of it."

"Never?"

"In the beginning I would ask about her. But he would never answer me. Finally, he told me she was dead. When I was older, I realized that wasn't true. I found their divorce papers one day and I knew what happened." My voice broke. "He got full custody. She didn't want visitation. She didn't want me."

"Maggie."

Samir wrapped his arms around me, pulling me against his chest. One arm hooked around my body, sliding me onto his lap. I sat there, his arms around me, cradling me, tears falling from my eyes.

"I still remember the last thing she said to me. She told me to be good."

And I'd been good ever since.

"When I was younger, I just thought if I was good that maybe she would come back for me."

That maybe she would love me.

"Maggie." Samir's voice was raw with emotion. He reached out, his hand stroking my face. "It's her loss."

My heart thudded. "You don't have to—"

"Listen to me," Samir interrupted. "It's her loss. If she left you, it's on her. It wasn't you." He kissed the top of my head, his lips brushing against my hair. A shiver slid down my spine. "I promise you, it wasn't you."

Emotion—thick and heavy—clogged my throat. "Thank you." Embarrassment flooded me. "I should go." I wriggled off his lap.

Samir held me there. "Maggie—"

I stared back at him, a question in my eyes.

His lips claimed mine.

This time the kiss was nothing like the ones before. It started softly—hesitantly—a tentative meeting of lips. He sucked on my bottom lip gently, his tongue curling into my mouth.

His kiss was easy, almost sweet. My response was anything but. This time I took over the kiss, my mouth moving against his, devouring it. I gripped his arms, pressing his body against mine.

I felt his arousal pressing against me. A moan escaped from my lips.

"I want you."

Three words. Three words that slipped from my mouth without me even realizing it. Three terrifying words.

I jerked back from Samir, my heart racing.

"I don't *want* to want you."

I let Samir pull me back against his body, his arms stroking mine softly.

"I know," he whispered, his lips pressed against my hair.

We sat there on the steps, not speaking, watching the cars drive by.

31

Two days before Valentine's Day, the International School descended into a nervous frenzy. There was far too much romantic drama going around for the holiday to not be a huge deal. Some guys had even gotten an early start—enormous bouquets of flowers were delivered to school daily. It became a competition—each girl striving to receive the most ostentatious display of love.

No one was immune. Sadly, not even the inhabitants of room 301.

"You're going."

"No, I'm not."

Fleur leveled me with what I'd affectionately termed The Look. "I hate to break it to you, but he's not going to call."

"He might."

"He told you he might have to work tonight. It's eight o'clock. He's not going to call."

As much as I hated to admit it, deep down I knew she was right. That didn't make it suck any less. I knew the odds of spending today with Hugh were slim since he had to work, but still. A girl could dream. It was my first Valentine's Day with a sort-of-maybe boyfriend. And besides, I needed a distraction—it was Valentine's Day and the last thing I wanted was to see who Samir was taking out for his date.

"I hate Valentine's Day."

"Join the club." Fleur threw a pillow at me. "That's why you're coming out tonight. It'll make you feel better."

"Doubtful."

"The Valentine's Day party is the highlight of the school's social season."

"You say that about all the events. You might as well be the school's social director."

"Well, this time it's true."

"I don't know…"

"You're going."

"Why?"

Fleur paused, her expression clouded. "Last year Costa and I spent Valentine's Day in Paris. This year he's probably celebrating it the same way with his new girlfriend. I don't feel like being by myself tonight."

Whenever Fleur played the Costa card, I knew she was bringing in the big guns. "I'm not really sure I'm in a social mood tonight."

What I didn't say was that I didn't want to see Samir. Ever since that night on the steps, I'd been avoiding him. I couldn't believe I'd broken down like that in front of him, or that I'd told him about my mom.

I felt vulnerable, exposed. And I didn't want to deal with it.

"That's the point. No one is in a good mood tonight. But instead of sitting in the room feeling sorry for ourselves, we're going to get dressed up, go out, get drunk and judge everyone's fashion choices. We're reclaiming Valentine's Day."

I grinned, her mood infectious. Fleur had a way of rallying the troops when her mind was set on something. "Fine. You've convinced me."

Given my current dateless status on Valentine's Day I figured it couldn't get any worse.

★ ★ ★

By the time we got to the club, the party was already in full swing. I had to give it to the university—they never did things in half measures. The venue they'd chosen for the event was, according to Fleur, one of London's trendier clubs. The interior was sleek and modern. Cool house music poured from the club speakers.

I followed Fleur over to a table where Mya and Michael sat, already knocking back glasses of champagne.

Michael waved us over. "You came!" he shouted over the music.

"Fleur convinced me."

I slid into the booth next to Michael. He passed me a glass of champagne.

"A toast," he shouted. "To my girls."

We clinked glasses.

I caught sight of George across the room. I grinned, waving at him. I'd seen less and less of him as the year progressed.

"Hey, guys, I'll be right back." I left the table and walked over to him. "Hey."

He grinned. "Hi. How's it going?"

"Good. You?"

"Can't complain."

"I'm surprised you came out tonight. It's good to see you, though."

George didn't seem to be big on going out. He ran with the quieter crowd within the International School.

He shrugged. "Residence Life sponsors the party every year. Mrs. Fox wanted everyone to come."

"Well, I'm glad you did."

George gestured to a point over my shoulder. "I see you're hanging out with the Ice Queen now."

My gaze jerked to where Fleur sat with Mya and Michael.

I grinned, turning back to face him. "She's kind of amazing when you get to know her."

George shrugged, taking a swig from his bottle of beer. "I'll just have to take your word on that one."

"She is," I insisted. "She's really loyal and fun. And believe it or not, she can be pretty sweet."

George tossed me a skeptical look.

"Do you want to go for a run sometime soon?" he asked, changing the subject.

I nodded. We'd started running together at the beginning of last semester, but the busier school got, the less time I had for working out.

We talked for a few more minutes before I headed back to my friends.

I slipped into the booth between Fleur and Michael. Fleur sipped her champagne, surveying the room. She had that look in her eyes I'd quickly learned spelled trouble.

"I'm going to play," she announced, wiggling her eyebrows suggestively.

I groaned.

"Maggie likes her men older," Michael teased with an exaggerated drawl.

I elbowed him in the side.

Mya leaned in. "Who are you going to hit on?"

Fleur scanned the crowd, tapping her fingers against her champagne flute. Her eyes narrowed. "Him."

We all followed Fleur's gaze.

Of course.

Alessandro Marin was arguably the hottest guy at the International School. He was Italian and looked every inch the Roman god. He was also, as far as I could tell, pretty much untouchable. Possibly even for Fleur. He didn't even run with the European group; he pretty much did his own thing. There were rumors he modeled on the side and had dated a Swedish pop star.

"Nice choice." Michael let out a low whistle.

I had to agree—the boy was majorly fine.

She grinned. "Excuse me, I'm going to go meet my latest—"

"Victim?" I teased.

"Exactly."

After Fleur left, I sat with Mya and Michael, watching the crowd. Fleur was right; it did look as if most if not all the school was here.

And then I saw him.

32

Samir stood across the room from me.

A flush spread across my cheeks.

He grinned. His gaze ran over me from head to toe, his grin widening.

I froze. I couldn't stop staring at him. A part of me wanted to cross the room and say hi. Hell, I wanted to say more than hi. I was losing my mind.

"Oh, shit," Michael exclaimed.

I tore my attention away from Samir.

"What's up?" I asked, recognizing his tone immediately. It was his something-major-is-about-to-go-down voice.

"Shit is about to get ugly."

I scanned the crowd, but nothing seemed out of place to me. No one was wearing the same outfit; no one seemed to be messing with someone else's guy. My gaze settled back on Samir's group. He'd turned away from me, his attention focused on something else. A low murmur seemed to spread throughout the crowd. Whatever was happening, Samir was clearly about to be part of it.

"What's going on?"

Mya's eyes widened, ignoring me. Her gaze settled on someone in the crowd. "Oh, she didn't." Her voice had the same eager anticipation Michael's did.

"What? What am I missing?"

Mya gestured toward a dark-haired girl standing in the corner, her arms wrapped around a boy's waist.

"That's Amira. She's Omar's ex-girlfriend."

Samir's BFF Omar. Awareness dawned. "And that's not Omar."

"Nope. That's Abdul. He used to be part of Samir's group, but he and Amira hooked up while she was still dating Omar. They've been lying low ever since."

"Apparently not any longer," Michael commented, his gaze jerking back and forth between the couple and Samir's clique.

Sure enough, Omar had broken away from his group and was now heading toward Amira and Abdul. The expression on his face said it all. This was not going to go over well.

"You don't think they're going to fight, do you?"

The words were barely out of my mouth before Omar shoved Abdul. Amira shrieked, moving away from Abdul.

Samir and his friends moved into the fray, backing up Omar with the same support I'd seen them show all year when we were out. Whether it was running an errand for a friend or defending a friend's honor, it was unquestionably clear they had each other's backs.

Mya frowned. "This is about to get real."

Samir came at the group, a mass of guys behind him. I wasn't surprised he was the first one to stand up for a friend considering the loyalty I'd seen him display all year, but my heart thudded. "Oh, no."

"Really, really real," Mya added.

She wasn't kidding. I'd never actually seen a fight in person. My high school hadn't been particularly rowdy, and while there were a few fights, I'd always seemed to miss them. Here I had a front-row seat.

Through the mass of people it was impossible to see who threw the first punch. But inevitably someone did, and the instant fist connected with bone, things got ugly.

Without realizing it, my eyes tracked Samir's movements. He threw punches, his movements sharp and quick. He might not have been a big guy, but he was fast. And by the looks of things, this definitely wasn't his first fight. I winced as one of the other guys landed a blow to his jaw. Samir's head jerked back.

Nausea welled up. "Isn't security going to break it up?"

Michael shrugged. "Would you want to go into that?"

He had a point.

The three of us watched in shock as the fighting continued. I couldn't even tell who was fighting anymore; gone were any clear alliances or sides. This was a brawl—arms shoving, hands punching, legs kicking. I half expected people to start biting each other.

In the melee I lost sight of Samir.

Suddenly club security began moving into the crowd, breaking the fight apart. The bouncers pulled people off each other. A guy grabbed Samir, yanking him off Abdul. Samir's shirt was ripped at the bottom. Blood ran down his face from a cut on his cheek.

"I'm glad you called," I told Hugh, linking my fingers with his.

After the police arrived, we bailed on the party. Fleur left with Alessandro; Mya and Michael headed back to the dorms. The thought of going home to my room had been too depressing. I couldn't stop wondering about Samir. Finally, I ended up sending him a text.

Are you ok?

He hadn't responded. The suspense was driving me nuts.

"I'm glad I called, too. It's good to get to see you, even if

Valentine's Day is almost over." Hugh leaned down, brushing a soft kiss to my temple. "I'm sorry your party didn't go well."

I laughed. "That is the understatement of the year."

I'd been too embarrassed to fill Hugh in on the fight. Somehow, I didn't think nearly thirty-year-old men spent their Valentine's Days engaging in public brawls. Plus, he still thought I was in grad school. I felt a twinge of guilt at the weight of my lies.

We held hands, walking through Chelsea. I'd taken a cab to meet Hugh at Cobalt just as he finished up work and he'd offered to walk me home, not that we had gotten very far.

"Come here," Hugh whispered, pulling me into a dark alley. His arms wrapped around me, his hands slipping under my long coat. It took some maneuvering before his hands found the bare skin beneath my top. I shivered. His lips found mine, his mouth opening, plundering mine with his tongue.

My back hit the stone wall of the mews. Pressed between Hugh and the building, I felt every inch of his hard body against me. We stayed like that, making out in the dark mews, until something wet landed on my nose. I broke apart from Hugh and looked up at the sky. White drops fell from the sky in a lazy pattern, covering my face and coat. I laughed, the sound echoing through the narrow mews.

Hugh grinned, white drops of snow falling around his face and hair. He leaned down, kissing the snowflakes off the tip of my nose. He wrapped his arm around me, pulling me up against the warmth of his body. "Come on. Let's get you out of the cold."

We walked down the streets, our arms wrapped around each other. With the snow falling, the streets of London were remarkably quiet, most people driven inside by the weather. A few other couples walked around us, but for the most part it felt as if we had the town to ourselves. We walked past big glass store windows with elegant dresses and shoes on display. I paused in front of one, catching the image of the girl walking by in the glass.

I wasn't sure I even recognized her anymore.

She still looked like me. It was the same brown hair I'd had my entire life, the same brown eyes. But this girl—her smile was brighter than mine ever was, her clothes just a bit sharper. But what made me stop in my tracks and stare was that for the first time in my life, the girl staring back at me was one of those girls. The polished girls. She was happy and confident and had this glow about her I never had in South Carolina.

Her glow scared me. *She* scared me a little.

Up ahead a man stood outside one of the restaurants selling roses.

Hugh winked at me, pressing a swift kiss to my cheek, breaking me out of my reverie. "Wait here."

He crossed the street in long, smooth strides. Something fluttered in my chest.

Hugh walked over to the guy, his long strides loping over the pavement. It was impossible to not feel admiration at the way he moved. With Hugh's back to me, I couldn't see his face, but I *knew*, and in response my heart pounded in my chest.

He turned around, a red rose dangling from his right hand. The pounding in my chest intensified. He closed the distance between us until there was merely a foot of space separating our bodies. A slow smile spread across his face. "Happy Valentine's Day."

I stared down at the vibrant red rose, something like hope flickering in my chest. No guy had ever given me flowers before.

I reached out, taking the rose from him, our hands brushing against each other. For a moment I didn't speak; emotion clogged my throat. I wanted to tell him how much it meant to me—this simple gesture made me feel special in a way no one ever had before.

"Thank you," I replied, struggling to keep my voice light.

It was just a flower. A flower that made up for all the dateless dances, the missed prom and the Valentine's Days when the only flowers I received were carnations from Jo.

I closed the distance between us, the rose fisted in my hand, careful to avoid getting pricked by the thorns. I stood up on my tiptoes, even then his mouth was just out of reach. Hugh leaned down, meeting me in the middle, his head brushing against mine. His lips found mine, the kiss taking more than it gave. I lost all sense of time, forgot we were standing on the sidewalk of a crowded London street.

Hugh broke apart first, his lips traveling up my face, grazing my ear. Hovering there. Teasing there. "Maggie," he whispered. I shivered in a way that had nothing to do with the weather. "You have to decide. Soon."

I could feel the looming deadline. I wished I could be casual about it—I didn't know why sex was such a big thing for me. But it was. And despite how hot Hugh was, I just didn't feel ready, and I wasn't sure how much longer he would wait.

We finished our walk back to my place, our hands linked. Hugh gathered me close for a good-night kiss. My phone beeped.

I jerked back. "Sorry. I need to take this. I think it's from Fleur," I lied, my heart pounding in my chest.

I pulled out my phone, relief rushing through me as I read the message.

I'm fine. Sorry you had to see that. Happy Valentine's Day. xxxx.

"Everything okay, babe?"

I nodded mechanically, even though I was anything but.

With Hugh's rose clutched in one hand and the text from Samir in another, I'd never felt more confused—

And I couldn't help but think—I didn't even know what I wanted anymore.

33

"Raise your hand if you had the worst Valentine's Day."

Four sets of hands went up. I was the lone dissenter. Four pairs of eyes shot me dirty looks.

"Sorry?" My expression was sheepish. "My Valentine's Day wasn't exactly perfect, either."

I might have spent Valentine's Day with Hugh. But when I came home, I dreamed of Samir.

Samir snorted. "Try spending it locked in a cell."

I shouldn't have felt any sympathy for him. He was a big boy; he never should have gotten into that fight in the first place. But I couldn't help hating the bruise on his face.

"Whose fault was that?" Fleur snapped. "I'm the one who had to get you bailed out. Not exactly how I wanted to spend my Valentine's Day."

"I'd much rather hear Maggie's Valentine's Day story," Michael interjected. "What happened?"

It felt awkward talking about this in front of Samir. But if I started acting weird around him, everyone was going to figure out something was up. Besides, he'd made it clear he wasn't looking for a relationship; he didn't get attached to girls.

It shouldn't matter.

"Things are getting complicated with Hugh, and I don't know what to do," I explained, looking away from Samir.

"Having a hot guy with an accent make out with you is *not* a bad Valentine's Day," Michael countered.

I blushed. "Okay, fine. It wasn't bad. But I am freaking out."

Samir's head jerked up. His cheekbone was bruised; there was a cut over his right eye. He looked like hell. His mood didn't appear to be much better. "Coffee. Now."

I winced, passing him the pot of coffee.

He took it from me, our fingers grazing each other. It took a ridiculous amount of self-restraint to keep from curving my fingers around his. I jerked my hand back, placing it in my lap.

My lips twitched at the expression on his face. He was so surly it was kind of cute. "Okay, fine, maybe Samir wins."

Fleur jumped into the conversation. "Uh-uh, I win."

"Why do you win?" Mya countered. "You were the one who ended up leaving the party with Alessandro Marin."

Fleur stabbed her eggs. "He wasn't interested."

We all stopped what we were doing and gaped at her. Only Samir was immune to the news. Either that or Fleur had already filled him in. He continued eating breakfast as if she hadn't even spoken.

Michael leaned forward. "What do you mean he wasn't interested?" His voice sounded just a touch scandalized.

"He wasn't. We started making out and then he stopped. And walked me to the door."

Silence filled the table.

"Maybe he didn't want to move too quickly?"

Fleur shot me The Look.

Yes, I was grasping at straws. But given how fragile things were with her and Costa, the last thing she was prepared to handle was more rejection.

Samir laughed at my comment, looking up from his coffee

mug, his gaze piercing mine. "You can't possibly still be that naive."

I glared at him. Trust this to be the time he decided to get involved in the conversation. "Don't be pissy with me because you got your ass kicked last night," I snapped, annoyed with him for making a dig at me and Fleur.

His eyes narrowed. "I did not get my ass kicked."

"Your face suggests otherwise."

Fleur groaned. "It's too early and I'm too hungover to have to deal with the two of you bickering right now."

"We're not bickering," Samir argued. A hint of a smile crossed his face for the first time all morning. "This is just how Maggie and I talk." He winked at me. "She likes it."

My face heated before I turned my attention back to my breakfast.

The fucked-up thing was—I sort of did.

"I gotta head out," Michael announced, getting up from the table. "Catch you guys later."

Mya left with him, leaving me and Fleur sitting with Samir.

We ate in silence for a few minutes. Fleur broke it first. "Maggie needs dating help," she announced.

I paused, midbite, choking on a piece of lettuce.

Samir's gaze shifted to me. "Really?" he drawled.

I shot Fleur a look that said *drop it*. She ignored me.

"I don't need dating advice."

She ignored me. "You're a guy. Help her out. Maggie hasn't given up the goods yet."

"Fleur!" The last thing I needed was for her to be talking to Samir about my *sex life*.

Samir didn't speak for a moment. He groaned. "I'm not having this conversation. I haven't slept. I spent last night in jail. I'm tired. I'm tired of listening to you two complain about guys." He paused, taking a bite out of his sandwich. "Why can't you be more like Mya? She never bothers me with inane questions about what men want."

He had a point. Mya was ridiculously calm about this stuff. I wished I could be like her.

He leveled me with a steely glance. "You don't need guy advice, you need to calm the fuck down."

"I'm calm," I argued.

"You're not calm. This—" Samir gestured around me "—this energy you've got going on...the guy can tell."

Fleur grinned at both of us. "Well, on that fun note, I gotta run to class. See you guys later."

"Thanks," I muttered, my teeth clenched. Trust Fleur to open Pandora's box and then leave me to deal with it.

"Why are you scowling?" Samir asked.

I glared at him. "You're totally useless."

"Why? Because I don't tell you what you want to hear?"

Yes.

"Because."

Because I want to know if you care.

"Why?" Samir pressed.

"Because I never know when you're being serious. I never know when you say things to be nice or when you're trying to be an ass."

"Do you trust me?"

I hesitated for a moment. My answer surprised me. Despite his attitude, he showed up when it counted. He could definitely be an asshole. But he was dependable. And he didn't ask for much in return. He was always taking care of all of us in his own way—rescuing us, paying our way, providing a shoulder to cry on in unexpected moments.

I sighed. "Yeah, I do."

"I tell you the truth," Samir continued. "I always tell you the truth. I might not be telling you what you want to hear,

but I'm telling you what you need to hear. You're just ridiculously stubborn and refuse to listen."

"I'm not stubborn."

It was Samir's turn to sigh. "Sure, you aren't." It really wasn't
a good sign when Samir was beginning to sound like the voice
of reason. He cocked his head to the side, studying me carefully. "Why are you so bad at this?" His tone wasn't judgmen-
tal; he genuinely seemed curious.

"I don't know. Why do you suck at giving pep talks?"

He shrugged, a grin forming. "I'm not exactly the pep talk
guy. I have other skills." He winked.

I choked on my drink. "Ew, gross. Trust me, I don't want
to know anything about your skills."

Those skills filled my dreams.

He didn't respond. Instead, he just stared at me, daring me
to keep talking. I broke our stare first, the first one to lose the
game of proverbial chicken.

A pause filled the table.

"I think you know about my skills." His voice was matter-of-
fact, but I could hear the underlying challenge in his words. It
was the same challenge that always seemed to linger between us.

Just the memory of his skills had me warm all over.

Samir chuckled at my reaction. "You're so cute when you
blush. I don't think I'd ever kissed a girl who blushed before
you."

"Shh," I hissed. "Do you want everyone to know we kissed?"

"I'm not embarrassed."

"Maybe I'm embarrassed," I countered.

Samir has bad idea *written all over him.*

"Hardly. I'm a catch."

"You're so full of yourself."

"It's not being full of yourself if you can back it up."

"You can't back it up. Not at all."

"That's not what you were saying when you kissed me."

I glared at him. It was beyond annoying that he'd maneuvered the conversation back to the one topic I didn't want to discuss.

Samir grinned. "You're so easy to play. I'm pretty sure anyone in this cafeteria can figure out what we're talking about just from the expression on your face."

It was a colossal effort not to look around to see if he was right. Samir's lips twitched.

Ass.

"What emotion am I wearing right now?" I asked tartly, flipping him off.

He laughed. "Don't tease me."

I tried to ignore the fluttering in my chest. And the desire coursing through my body.

34

I reclined back in the passenger seat of the Ferrari, my hand linked with Hugh's. It was our first date since Valentine's Day. Hugh had texted with a dinner invite—and an invitation to meet his friends.

"You'll like my friends. They're all nice."

I nodded, pretending I wasn't as nervous as I felt. I hadn't met any of his friends yet. The fact that I was likely a decade younger than most of them hadn't escaped my notice. With Hugh it wasn't a huge deal since we spent most of our time together—well, not talking. But with his friends—

It wasn't as if I could distract them by making out with one of them.

"I'm excited to meet them."

I burrowed deeper in my jacket, trying to ward off the cold. It was late February and London still hadn't warmed up. Hugh was a big fan of driving with the top down, which was totally fine except for the fact that it both ruined my hair and made me freeze. Tonight, I'd opted for putting my hair in a high ponytail in order to avoid looking like a mess when we finally got to the restaurant. I ran a hand over the top of my hair, relieved to feel everything seemed to be in order.

"How many of your friends are coming?"

Hugh shifted gears, changing lanes with ease. "I think six. My best mate Mike is bringing his girlfriend, Violet. You'll like her—she's really sweet. Julia and her sister, Katie, will probably come for a bit. And Dan and his wife, Megan."

"Did you all grow up together or something?" I was aware of how little I knew about Hugh. We had talked a bit about our childhoods, but considering how much of mine was fabricated due to my fake age, I hadn't exactly been eager to delve into childhood experiences in any detail.

"Well, Julia, Katie and I grew up together. Our mums are friends, and we lived a few streets over. I met Mike and Dan at uni."

He had told me before that he only went to school for one year.

"What did you study?"

I was curious to know his interests. I knew he liked movies, and he liked working out. But he never really talked about books he read or subjects that interested him.

"Mostly just general subjects. Basic first-year stuff."

"Was there anything that interested you?" I prodded gently. I didn't want him to think I judged him for not graduating—especially since he was so obviously successful without a degree. But at the same time school was such a huge part of my life; it wasn't easy to not talk about it.

"There wasn't really anything that interested me. Uni was pretty boring. I spent my first year working at a bar to make some extra cash and after that I knew I wanted to own my own place."

"You've done well for yourself, then."

"I'm happy. Cobalt is a good business. We do a good profit and I get along well with my partners. I can't really complain. There are worse jobs I could have."

He pulled up in front of a fancy hotel on the fringe of Mayfair. Hugh maneuvered the Ferrari into a parking spot before getting out and opening the door for me.

He took my hand in his, leading me in through the hotel's separate entrance. Pride filled me. He wore an olive green military-style jacket that fit his broad shoulders perfectly. Dark jeans tapered down to a pair of brown leather boots that had to be Italian. I didn't blame everyone for noticing him. He was the kind of guy you couldn't miss.

Hugh looked down at me, a smile on his lips. "What?"

"Has anyone ever told you you're too perfect?" I teased.

He laughed. "Definitely not. But I'm not going to complain if you want to tell me." He pressed a kiss to the top of my head.

I wrapped my arm through his, the feel of his strong forearm under my hand sending pleasure through my body. He was gorgeous. And I was on his arm tonight.

"Well, you are. Perfect, I mean."

Hugh winked. "You're looking pretty hot yourself."

One of my Christmas shopping finds was a tailored black leather jacket I was obsessed with. I paired it with my best jeans and these amazing black leather boots that were a TJ Maxx find. It felt good to know I had his approval. When he told me I was beautiful, I felt it in every pore of my body.

Hugh waved at a large group of people sitting at a table in the corner. I straightened my shoulders, studying the group as we approached. They all looked older. I said hi to everyone, slipping into the booth next to the girl Hugh introduced as Katie.

The conversation was stilted at first, probably more from my own nerves than anything else. But little by little I relaxed. I didn't talk much; instead I watched Hugh interact with his friends. It was obvious they were close—there was plenty of teasing and joking around. I answered a lot of questions, but it felt comfortable.

When the meal was done, we gathered our stuff, saying

goodbye to everyone. Hugh leaned over and pressed a kiss to my cheek.

"You were great tonight." He flashed me a smile that had my heart tumbling in my chest. "They loved you."

It was sad how much those three words meant to me, the hope I hung on them. We hadn't even had *the talk* yet. There had been no discussion of exclusivity—of boyfriends and girlfriends. It wasn't a talk I even knew how to begin. I wasn't naive, despite what Samir might have thought. I saw Hugh exactly as he was. The odds he was seeing me alone—that I was enough to hold his attention in a city as vast and slick as London—were slim. And yet, meeting his friends left me with enough hope for the possibility of us, that I felt a sense of calm with him I hadn't felt before.

For the first time, I could see a future.

And still, my dreams were full of Samir.

35

"What are you doing for spring break?"

I looked up from my book. Fleur stood in front of me, a huge smile on her face. I shrugged, gesturing toward my book. "Probably studying. I need to get my grades up this semester."

"Wrong answer."

Sometimes I wondered if Fleur and I lived on the same planet. School for me was a desperate attempt to keep my grades up so I could keep my scholarship. School for Fleur seemed to be an endless round of parties. Still, at this point I'd learned better than to argue with her. She was tenacious when she wanted to be.

"Fine. What am I doing for spring break?"

Fleur grinned, sitting down on the edge of my bed. "Picture this. A gorgeous apartment near the George V. Paris in the springtime. A group of your favorite friends. A week of shopping, fabulous lunches in cafés, the best nightclubs."

"Sounds too good to be true."

"It's happening. Mya, Samir and Michael are in. I think Samir was talking about inviting Omar, but they can keep each other company. Besides, Omar's the best person for handling Samir when he gets into one of his moods," she added. "It's

going to be amazing. Samir's offering up his parents' apartment for the trip. It's gorgeous and there's plenty of room for everyone."

There were way too many mentions of Samir. The secret to not hooking up with Samir seemed to be avoiding him completely. The dream thing I couldn't control. But the rest of it? I had Hugh now. Things were good with us. I didn't need to confuse things by hanging out with Samir again.

"I don't think it's a good idea."

Fleur pulled a face. "What's wrong with you? How is Paris not a good idea? Everyone's going. You have to come."

"I don't want to leave now. Things are good with Hugh."

"Hugh will still be here when you get back. If you can't go to Paris without worrying about him, then you have bigger problems."

She was right, of course.

I hesitated. "What about Samir? Does he know I'm coming?"

Fleur shot me a weird look. "Of course Samir knows you're coming."

"And he's cool with it?"

Her eyes narrowed. "Yeah. Why? Has he been a dick to you lately? 'Cause I can totally talk to him."

"No, please don't talk to him. He's been fine." I grimaced. "Is his family going to be there?"

"They're going to be in Lebanon or Switzerland or something. It'll just be the staff and us. The place is huge."

I sighed, shades of the Venice trip coming back to me. "Is it even worth it for me to bother arguing?"

"Nope."

I desperately wanted to go. Paris was on my list of places I wanted to see before I died. And we were only, like, two hours away by train.

"It sounds amazing," I admitted.

"We need this trip. It's the perfect opportunity to let loose for a little bit."

I hesitated for a moment. Fleur did have a point. School had been pretty hectic this semester and my classes were even worse than the fall. But…things were good with Hugh. The idea of leaving London for a week, of not seeing him, wasn't exactly ideal. Neither was the idea of spending a week with Samir.

On the other hand, it was Paris. And I'd never been.

How much trouble could I possibly get into?

We took the Eurostar from London to Paris. Samir went on ahead with Omar. That left me, Mya, Fleur and Michael on the train. The trip was two hours, but thanks to everyone's insistence that we travel first class, the ride was smooth and way more elegant than I ever expected. Dressed in a trench coat and a scarf Fleur assured me was very Parisian, I felt like a character in one of the Agatha Christie novels my grandmother loved.

We posed in front of the Eurostar while Michael snapped our picture.

"You ready?" Mya called out, waving me over to one of the train doors. "It's time to board."

This was a moment I wanted to freeze. So that later, when I was stuck working my summer job at TJ Maxx, I could remember I had this. That for a moment I went to Paris like something out of an Audrey Hepburn movie.

I just needed the big black glasses.

"I'm ready."

I followed Mya up the train steps, filing down the narrow aisle, past businessmen reading copies of the *FT* and elegantly dressed women sipping glasses of champagne. I slid into a seat next to Fleur.

Once the train departed the station, I spent most of the trip with my nose pressed against the glass, watching the scenery pass us by. Mya and Fleur spent most of the time drinking in

the bar car. They were both excited to be spending spring break together, but the feeling wasn't the same for them.

I was the only Paris virgin in the group.

"So how are things with your man?" Michael asked, draping his arm around the back of my headrest. He slid into Fleur's seat as soon as she left.

"He's good. We went out to dinner with some of his friends a week ago."

Michael's eyebrows rose. "Meeting the friends? That sounds important."

"I guess. It was pretty low-key. They didn't grill me or anything. They were really nice."

"Does that mean he's a boyfriend yet?"

"We haven't talked about it. I'm not even sure if we're exclusive."

"How is the whole sex thing going?"

"So far, it's not. I mean we make out a lot and that's great—"

"But you haven't actually gotten naked in front of him?"

I laughed at Michael's bluntness. "Basically, no."

Truthfully, things had gone further with Samir than they had with Hugh.

"What are you waiting for?"

"I don't know. Don't get me wrong, I want to." I didn't add that I'd already gone to the student health center and gotten birth control. *That* had been an experience.

"Nervous?"

"Ridiculously so."

"I was nervous before my first time."

"How old were you?" I couldn't help but be curious. Both Mya and Fleur seemed pretty used to having sex, so they didn't really understand my reservations.

"Eighteen. It was last year."

I hesitated, not sure how much I should pry. Michael was pretty open about being gay, but for as much as we all complained about our love lives (or lack thereof), he mostly played things close to the vest.

"Did you always know you liked guys?"

"Pretty much, yeah. I mean, I never really had to come out to my parents or anything. I think they always knew. They were really supportive about it."

"That's gotta be nice, to be close to your parents."

"They're great. Honestly, I don't know what I would have done if I hadn't known I could talk to them about it. It made everything so much easier." Michael hesitated for a moment. "Speaking of parents—I don't mean to pry or anything, but I heard about your dad getting married. Are you okay?"

"How did you hear about my dad?"

I hadn't talked to anyone about his marriage, not even Fleur or Mya. The whole thing still felt too new and raw. A couple days after my conversation with my father, my grandmother called me to talk about it. I had pretty much brushed her off, telling her I was fine with everything. The lie had been so much easier than the truth. My grandmother seemed happy he'd found someone. I didn't want to bring her down by sharing my feelings.

Michael hesitated. "I was there when Samir told Fleur."

Of course, Samir.

"He shouldn't have said anything."

"He wasn't talking about you or anything," Michael interjected. "And he wasn't trying to be a dick. He just told Fleur that you seemed upset, and he was worried about you."

Surprise filled me. Michael got along okay with Samir, but he wasn't exactly president of his fan club. I didn't expect for him to be defending Samir's actions.

"I'm sorry if you don't want to talk about it," Michael added. "I didn't mean to upset you. We all just wanted you to know we're here for you if you need it."

I shook my head, regret filling me. "Thanks. Sorry I jumped

down your throat." I paused, searching for the right words. "I'm doing okay."

"Have you talked to your dad since he told you he got married?"

"No. He hasn't called."

"Seriously?"

"Trust me. That's just how he is. He doesn't like dealing with emotions or scenes. He knows I'm upset. He's just not going to talk about it."

"I'm sorry, Mags."

"Yeah, me, too."

I turned away from Michael, staring out the window, pressing my forehead against the cool glass.

I didn't ever want to go home.

Like London, Paris was bustling. Traffic was heavy, the early morning punctuated by the sound of drivers honking at each other. Fleur gave the driver directions to Samir's apartment in rapid-fire French and we all piled in.

The scenery changed from the neighborhood outside the station to fancy streets with elegant apartments and plenty of trees. Women dressed in gorgeous outfits walked down the sidewalk with fluffy white dogs on leashes. Men dressed in business suits and trench coats carried briefcases. Parisians were every bit as glamorous as I'd imagined.

I smiled at Fleur. "This is incredible."

She beamed back at me. "It feels good to be home."

The driver pulled up in front of a gorgeous row of white flats and wrought-iron balconies.

"Nice place, huh?"

I blinked. "It's amazing."

"Glad to hear you approve." Samir opened the car door. "Welcome to Paris."

I got out of the car, Fleur on my heels. She exchanged air

kisses with Samir. I stood there awkwardly, not sure how to greet him. I couldn't do an air kiss with the same aplomb as Fleur and a hug felt way too personal. I settled for what I hoped was a friendly smile and an awkward wave while he greeted Michael and Mya.

"Did you guys have a good trip?"

I nodded, my nerves too jumbled for a proper response.

"Come on, then. Let's get you settled."

We all followed him through the building's front door, past the elegantly dressed doorman, who greeted us with a nod. Everywhere I looked antiques and gold surrounded me. We piled into the small elevator, squeezing in to make room. I ended up squished between Samir and Michael.

Samir got out first. He stopped in front of a pair of large black double doors. He pulled out a gold key, opening the door. I stifled a gasp, following him over the threshold. The floors were marble, the walls covered by enormous oil paintings in heavy gold frames. A huge crystal chandelier dominated the entryway. It looked like a small palace.

"There are five bedrooms. Omar's staying at a friend's place, so everyone can have their own room. The porter will bring up the bags."

An older woman with gray hair walked toward us.

Samir grinned. "This is Lenore. She's our housekeeper." He put an arm around her. "She's amazing. If you have any questions or need anything at all, she's the person you should go to."

Lenore smiled. "I'm happy to help in any way I can. It's always nice to meet Samir's friends."

Samir and Lenore led us through the apartment—pointing out all the various rooms.

I followed Lenore into my room.

"Samir thought you would enjoy this room. It has a beautiful view." She walked over to the window, pulling back the heavy blue drapes.

The Eiffel Tower stared back at me.
It was perfect, absolutely perfect.
It took my breath away.

36

It was our first night in Paris. We ate dinner in a little café in the Latin Quarter. The tables were small and round, votive candles covering the surface. With a guy on the street playing the violin, the night was like something out of a movie.

I liked Venice. I *loved* Paris.

Fleur and Samir ordered for the group, advising us on our choices and translating the menu.

After dinner we went for a walk. Samir and Omar walked ahead of us, laughing and joking around. I walked with Michael, Mya and Fleur trailing behind us. I wrapped my coat around me, the air surprisingly chilly for March. My hair whipped around my face as the wind picked up around us. My gaze shifted and I stopped dead in my tracks.

It rose from the ground, dominating the Paris skyline. Amid all the old buildings, the history of the city, it was this brilliant spot of magic. During the day it was an impressive sight; at night it was nothing short of breathtaking. Twinkling lights lit up the Eiffel Tower like a towering Christmas tree. It sparkled and shone throughout the night sky, each twinkle a spark of magic.

I couldn't look away.

"It's pretty, isn't it?"

My head jerked up in surprise at Samir's voice. He stood beside me, his head tilted up toward the night sky. Omar walked up ahead, alone. The rest of the group trailed behind him, deep in conversation.

I smiled softly. "Yeah, it is."

Samir shoved his hands in his coat pockets, matching my stride. "Some people think it's tacky." He shrugged. "But there's something about it. It's fun."

I grinned, tossing him a sidelong glance. "Yeah, it is."

"You seem to like Paris a lot."

"It's amazing. I love London. But Paris is incredible, too. I don't know. It feels special here." I waited for him to say something about how naive I sounded. Instead, he remained quiet. We continued walking alongside the Seine, the others ahead of us.

Our shoulders nearly touched. I knew I should move away, put some distance between us. But I stayed there, my shoulder occasionally brushing against Samir's. With each touch, my nerves ratcheted up a notch.

Samir turned his head, tossing me a small, sidelong smile.

I couldn't help myself—I grinned back.

We ended up at a club off the Champs-élysées. Just like in London, Samir whisked us through the door, bypassing an enormous line. The club was a lot bigger than most of the London clubs—two floors, with a large balcony surrounding the lower-level dance floor, the decor modeled after an old theater. Foam fell from the ceiling onto the dance floor and techno music blared out of the club speakers.

Fleur's eyes narrowed, linking her arm with mine. "None of that foam better get in my hair. I can't deal with frizz."

"Do they always do foam parties here?"

"One night a week." Fleur's eyes scanned the room. "It's packed tonight."

Mya joined us. "Well, we lost Michael. He met some guy and took off."

"Where are Omar and Samir?" Fleur asked.

Mya shrugged. "No idea. Samir showed me where the table is and then he and Omar headed downstairs."

"I guess it's just us girls, then." I hated the disappointment that coursed through me.

Despite losing our guys, though, the night turned out to be a blast. We spent the night dancing. We met some nice French guys—well, Fleur said they were nice; they didn't speak English and I had no clue what they were saying. We danced with them, each of us pairing off, until Fleur and I were too tired and sat down.

"I think Mya's going to get some action," Fleur joked.

We both sat at the table, watching as Mya made out with her French guy.

"Where do you think the guys are?"

Fleur shrugged. "No idea."

I jerked my head toward the two guys at the bar, struggling to push Samir out of my mind. "What do you think of them?" I had high hopes for Fleur meeting a guy on this Paris trip. She hadn't talked about Costa lately, but she still seemed upset by the whole thing.

"Mine's not that great of a kisser. Yours?"

I laughed. "I haven't kissed him. I'm sort-of dating Hugh, remember? I'm not interested in kissing other guys."

I tried to tell myself Samir didn't count.

"Have you talked to him since you've been here?"

"No."

Fleur pulled a face. "I want you to be happy, Mags. You deserve a good guy. Someone who will treat you right. Trust me—you don't want to be with a guy who isn't that into you."

"I know."

"Have you guys had the talk yet? The exclusivity talk?"

"No."

"You should."

I sighed. "I know."

I couldn't see myself relaxing enough to take our relationship to the next level if we didn't have an understanding between us. I needed to know he wouldn't leave—I needed some sort of a commitment from him. And deep down I knew that if Hugh and I became exclusive, everything would change. Whatever *thing* existed between me and Samir would have to be killed off.

I just wasn't sure I was ready for that.

I couldn't sleep.

I tried to tell myself it was just being in a strange country, sleeping in a strange bed.

It wasn't the boy who should have been asleep a few doors down.

After we left the club, Fleur texted Samir to see where they were, only for him to tell her he'd met up with some of his French friends and not to wait up.

That was three hours ago. Not that I was keeping track.

I stared at the clock next to my bed: *4 a.m.*

I turned over in my bed, punching the pillow with my fist. It was no use; I wasn't even a little bit tired. I sat up, running a hand through my hair. Maybe a glass of water would help. I grabbed my robe from the foot of the bed, wrapping it around me. I padded down the hall, struggling to find the door Lenore had pointed out as the kitchen.

My body connected with an object.

"Ouch." I struggled to catch my balance.

Two arms wrapped around me, steadying me. I stilled, a sense of awareness running through me. I knew the body pressed against mine...intimately. My head jerked up.

Samir stared down at me.

37

"Waiting up for me?"

Samir's husky tone sent a shiver down my spine.

"No."

Maybe.

I backed out of his grasp.

There was enough moonlight shining through one of the apartment windows to just make out Samir's body. He was still dressed in the same outfit he'd been wearing earlier. I scanned his appearance, looking for an untucked shirt, mussed hair, the smell of perfume.

But there were no signs that screamed he'd been hooking up with a French girl. Or anyone else for that matter. His gaze was just as searching as mine.

We both seemed to realize I was wearing little more than a robe at the same time. I grabbed the edges, pulling the robe tighter around my chest, covering myself. Samir's gaze trailed down my body, openly admiring and probing.

"I'm wearing clothes underneath."

Samir laughed, the sound low. "Now you've got me thinking about peeling those clothes off you. You're only tempting me more."

I died a bit inside.

"What were you doing sneaking out this late at night?" he teased.

"I wasn't sneaking out. I was going to the kitchen to get some water."

"A light might have helped."

"Yeah, I figured that out. I couldn't find it."

Samir leaned against the hallway wall, studying me carefully. "Are you tired?"

"Not really."

"Me, either."

Samir leaned in closer to me. The smell of his cologne filled my nostrils. My nerves jumped. If I just reached out… I curled my fingers into fists to keep them in place. Without intending to, my body leaned forward.

A new tension filled the hallway.

"Do you want to—"

Yes.

I knew I shouldn't want to. A part of me even felt guilty about Hugh. Sure, we weren't exclusive, but I'd still never imagined I would be one of those girls who hooked up with two guys at once. But Samir knew about Hugh and never said anything to me—I doubted he cared. And Hugh didn't seem like the type of guy who got jealous. Still…

"Play cards?"

I blinked.

"What?"

Samir grinned at me. "Do you want to play cards?"

Surely, I'd misheard him. "Cards?"

"Yes, cards." He let out a low laugh. "Take your mind out of the gutter."

I flushed.

"Come on, it'll be fun. I'm a great card player."

"Cards?" I repeated again.

Samir laughed, throwing an arm around my shoulder. "Come on. We'll play in the library."

I blinked. "You have a library?"

Samir grinned. "I should have known that would get you excited." He held his hand out to me. "Are you in?"

I hesitated for a beat. I knew better than this. I was only asking for trouble hanging out with Samir on my own. At night. In a robe.

"I'm in."

I let him lead me down the hallway, reveling in the feel of his body pressed against mine, his arm still wrapped around me. He stopped in front of a door down the hall, releasing me to open it and flip on a light switch.

I gaped at my surroundings.

Samir's family library was incredible. The room was filled with wall-to-wall bookshelves nearly bursting with books—thin spines, fat spines, a rainbow of colors and the smell of old leather.

"You should see your face right now."

"What?"

Samir shook his head ruefully, amusement in his tone. "You just look happy. I've never seen anyone who loves books as much as you do."

"I've always liked books."

Samir sat down in one of the leather wingback chairs. "Why?"

This time there was no challenge in his tone; he genuinely sounded curious.

I walked away from the bookshelves, sinking down into the chair opposite his. "I don't know."

"Yeah, you do. Why?"

I should have known he wouldn't let me get off that easily. I shrugged. "I didn't get to travel much when I was younger." *Or at all.* "So, I liked to read. Books let me go places I wouldn't have a chance to go to. They gave me a different life, an adventure."

"Is that why you wanted to go to Harvard?"

My eyes narrowed. "How did you know about that?"

"I talk to Fleur."

"You talk to Fleur about me?"

His lips twitched. "I talk to lots of people about you."

What did that mean?

"So—Harvard?"

I sighed. "Yes. Harvard was a chance to change my life. Or so I thought."

Samir was silent for a moment. I waited for the joke.

"And now you're in London. And Paris."

I smiled softly. "Yeah, I am."

He grinned. "You've done well, Maggie."

I flushed with pleasure. "Thanks."

Samir gestured to the table between us. "Want to play?"

Yes.

I sat down at the chair across from him. Samir opened a drawer, pulling out a stack of cards.

"This is what's called a gaming table."

I grinned. "Fancy."

He laughed. "Something like that." He began shuffling the cards. "So, what do you want to play?"

"I'm not much of a card player. I don't know a lot of games."

"Lucky for you I know plenty of games." A dimple winked back at me. "So, what do you want to play?"

"Go fish? Rummy? Those are the extent of my card games."

He laughed. "I was thinking poker but sure…rummy sounds good." He got up from the table, walking over to an elegant wood cabinet. He opened the doors, pulling out a bottle of alcohol and two glasses. Samir poured the drinks, walking over and handing one to me. "Brandy. Perfect for a night of gaming."

I grinned. Our fingers brushed as I took the glass from his hands.

"To games." Samir raised his glass in the air.

"To games," I echoed, bringing the glass to my lips. "Mmm." The liquid filled my mouth, the taste rich and seductive. "It's really good."

"It's my dad's finest." Samir sat back in his chair and dealt the cards, face down.

I sipped from my glass, waiting for the cards to fall. When he finished dealing, I lifted my cards, staring at the hand. Not too bad.

Samir took a sip from his glass. His gaze met mine. "Want to make things interesting?"

"What do you mean?"

"Let's up the stakes a bit." His tone was huskier than normal. Suspicion filled me. "Up the stakes how?"

Samir flashed me an irresistible grin. "Strip rummy."

38

"I'm not playing strip rummy." I couldn't even say the words without laughing.

"You might like it."

"Doubtful."

Samir grinned. His hands moved, his fingers hovering over the buttons of his collared shirt. "Come on. I'll even give you a head start."

Slowly he popped open the first button, revealing tanned skin and a sprinkling of chest hair.

My gaze was riveted to that spot. *Holy hell.*

"Should I stop?" Samir asked, toying with the next button. *Yes. No.*

Curiosity filled me. I had only seen Samir shirtless in my dreams—despite all the kissing, we'd always remained clothed— it was a chance to make my fantasies a reality. Maybe strip rummy wasn't such a bad idea, after all. I stared at that little patch of skin, temptation taunting me.

"No," I whispered. "Don't stop."

Heat flared in Samir's eyes. Slowly his hand traveled down his shirt, unbuttoning the rest of the buttons. His hands shook

slightly with each motion until finally he reached the last button. His gaze met mine as he pulled the shirt off his shoulders.

Whoa.

His body was covered in lean muscle—his pecs and abs
clearly defined without looking beefy. His skin was gorgeously
tan, just the lightest sprinkling of dark hair across his chest. I
couldn't tear my gaze away even if I wanted to.

Samir flashed me a knowing grin. I took another sip of
brandy.

"Now you have a head start." He gestured toward the cards.
"Ready?"

Not even kind of.

My response came out with a jerky nod.

I struggled to concentrate on the cards in my hands. They
were decent, not great, but hopefully good enough. As long
as I didn't concentrate on the sight of Samir's bare chest. We
played in silence, tension making the air thick and heavy. It was
ridiculously difficult to play cards across from a half-naked guy.
Especially one I struggled to keep my hands off fully clothed.

I sipped my brandy.

"Getting nervous?"

My head jerked up as I struggled to keep my eyes above
shoulder level.

"I only have three cards."

My gaze moved to Samir's hand. *Shit.* I hadn't even been
paying attention to his cards. If I wasn't careful, he was going
to go out soon. And I would lose a piece of clothing.

I took my turn quickly, my heart beating wildly in my chest.
Fear and something else—anticipation, maybe, spurred me on.

Samir reached for the deck—drawing the top card—staring
at it, a slow smile spreading across his lips. You could have heard
a pin drop. He fanned three cards down—the three of clubs,
the three of hearts and the three of spades. He placed a card on

the discard pile, leaning back in his chair, his arms folded over his head, a satisfied smile spreading across his lips.

"I'm out."

Horror filled me. I stared at the cards for a moment, struggling to get my courage up. I could back out now—go to bed and avoid all of this. I knew Samir; he talked a good game but if I bowed out, he would understand.

The gleam in his eyes gave me all the courage I needed.

My hands moved down, shaking slightly, tugging on the knot of my soft pink robe. I untied the silk, hesitating before pushing the robe off my shoulders.

Samir's eyes widened.

It dropped to the floor.

Underneath I work a thin cotton camisole—the fabric so sheer I knew Samir could see my nipples through the material. Thankfully a pair of lace boy shorts gave me at least a bit of coverage. I tucked my legs in front of me in the chair, struggling to cover myself as much as possible.

Neither one of us spoke.

It was a minute before I shuffled the deck, dealing the cards. The entire time I felt the hot weight of Samir's stare trained on my body. Every part of me felt sensitive, electrified. Despite my lack of clothing, I was ridiculously warm.

This hand went faster than the last. I played recklessly now, spurred by the desire to not have to take off any of my remaining clothes. Samir had removed his shoes and socks before we started playing, so now he was down to just his jeans and presumably a pair of boxers.

I couldn't contain my glee when I went out first. "Strip."

Samir laughed. "Gloating now, are we?"

I shook my head. "Uh-huh. Stop stalling. Strip."

Samir's eyes gleamed. "Eager to get me naked?"

I laughed, not denying it. "Better you than me."

Samir stood, reaching for the button of his jeans. All traces of laughter fled. My eyes were mesmerized to the spot where his fingers hovered. He knew it, too. Slowly—too slowly—he unbuttoned his pants, dragging the zipper down. The sound filled the room.

I didn't bother looking away. It was as if all the air had been sucked from the room. I couldn't breathe, couldn't think. All I could do was look.

I wanted to touch.

Samir pulled his jeans off his lean, tapered hips, exposing a lot of skin and a pair of dark gray boxers. His jeans fell to the floor. He kicked them away. He reclined back in his chair, his posture relaxed, his gaze anything but.

My gaze traveled lower. His boxers left little to the imagination. He was definitely as turned on by this as I was.

Fire heated my cheeks.

Samir dealt the next hand in between sips of his brandy. He winked at me, seemingly comfortable playing in his underwear. "Things are about to get interesting."

I wasn't sure I could handle things getting more interesting than this.

I fumbled with the cards, my hands shaking with my movements. Part of me wanted to stop playing, part of me desperately wanted to continue.

The play slowed a bit, making the awkwardness of sitting across from each other in essentially our underwear even more pronounced. I watched in horror on the next hand as Samir went out first.

This time he didn't speak. We both just stared at each other, the silence between us palpable. It was the boy shorts or the camisole. Either way, Samir was about to see a whole lot more of me than anyone had ever seen before.

Never taking my eyes off his, I reached down with both arms, curling my fingers around the soft cotton fabric of my camisole. I hesitated for a beat.

His eyes flared.

I began dragging the soft pink fabric up over my stomach, over my belly button, my hands hovering just below the swells of my breasts. Samir's gaze dipped down, below my eyes, running over my naked skin. A flush spread across my body.

I liked him looking at me.

I pulled the rest of the fabric over my head, the cool air hitting me as I tossed the shirt aside. I could feel the weight of Samir's stare on my breasts, could sense the desire growing within him. For a moment I just sat there, arching my back slightly, letting him look his fill. The desire in his eyes chased away any embarrassment I might have felt. He made me feel beautiful, wanted, brave.

"Samir—"

The door to the library swung open. I instinctively moved to cover myself.

"Samir, man, I'm going to crash here tonight…" Omar's voice trailed off at the sight of me, half-naked in the library. He blinked as if I were a mirage.

Samir jumped up from his chair, blocking me from Omar's sight, rapid Arabic coming out of him. I didn't need a translator to know he was pissed.

Humiliation flooded me. I fumbled with my clothes, grabbing the camisole from the floor, and tugging it over my head, picking up my robe and belting it tightly around my waist.

From the other side of Samir I heard Omar call out, "Sorry about that, Maggie," before he walked out of the library, closing the door behind him with a click.

A flush spread throughout my body. I wanted to die.

Samir turned around to face me. "Are you okay?" he asked quietly.

My chest rose and fell with rapid breaths. "Omar saw me naked. Omar saw my boobs. No, I'm not okay."

"I'm sorry. I had no idea he was even here. He was supposed

to be staying at his friend's. I'm so sorry. I thought I locked the door."

"Apparently not."

"He won't say anything," Samir swore. "I made him promise not to."

For a minute neither one of us spoke.

Samir gestured to the table between us. "Do you want to call it a night? We don't have to finish if you don't want to." He left the last part hanging like a question I didn't know how to answer.

Wanting wasn't the problem. It was everything else.

"We probably should."

Samir nodded.

"Good night," I offered weakly.

A soft smile spread across his lips. "Sweet dreams, Maggie."

39

"Did you sleep okay?"

My head jerked up at the sound of Samir's voice. A flush spread over my body. Considering the dreams I had after our card game, *restful* was the last word I would use to describe my sleep.

I nodded, needing a moment to gather my composure before I trusted my voice. I paused for a moment before gesturing toward the silver coffeepot on the table. "Want some?"

Samir slid into the seat across from me. He grabbed the coffeepot, pouring the steaming liquid into the ivory-and-gold cup in front of him. He reached forward and grabbed a croissant off a platter on the table.

"Those are really good." I was already on my second one.

"Yeah, the chef makes them all the time."

We ate, silence filling the table.

"So, what are your plans for today? Fleur mentioned something about going shopping. Hitting up some of the vintage shops?"

I nodded. Fleur and Mya had been talking about going shopping since we planned this trip. Apparently, there was a district of shops in Paris where you could buy vintage Chanel for good prices. Although I was pretty sure we had very different definitions of what a good price was.

"I'm surprised you wouldn't want to do more of the city. See touristy stuff. That sort of thing. The Louvre is nice. And Montmartre has a great view of the city."

I wanted to see all those things. But Michael seemed just as excited about going vintage shopping as Fleur and Mya were. And I wasn't sure I felt comfortable going off on my own. I knew like three words in French and from what I could tell Parisians weren't eager to help Americans with the language barrier.

"Everyone is really excited about shopping. And I'm not sure I can navigate the city with my mediocre French."

"I can take you."

Surprise filled me. "That's nice of you to offer, but it's fine. I can do Paris another time."

"Why not now?"

"I don't want to screw with everyone's plans."

"Then don't. I'll take you. It's not a big deal." Samir's lips curved. "I think I can live with the disappointment of not getting to go vintage shopping."

I laughed. "I don't think—"

"Are you afraid to be alone with me?" Samir interrupted, a challenge in his voice and a knowing look in his eyes.

"Don't be ridiculous."

Yes.

"Then take me up on my offer. I'm only nice like once or twice a week. Take advantage of a rare opportunity."

I had to laugh at that. It seemed dangerous to go with him. But I didn't know how to come up with a valid excuse other than *I'm afraid I won't be able to keep my hands off you.*

But it was Paris…

"You're sure you don't mind?"

"Trust me. I wouldn't have offered if I didn't want to. It'll be fun. Promise."

★ ★ ★

Twenty minutes later, I stood in Samir's parents' apartment, waiting for him to come down. I tapped my foot impatiently against the marble floor. I wanted to leave before everyone woke up and learned we were going on this little sightseeing adventure. It was too weird to explain.

I stared down at the round wood table beneath a large crystal chandelier that looked as though it belonged at the Palace of Versailles. Various framed photos sat on top of the table. I couldn't resist staring. Pictures of Samir at various ages sat in the frames. I smiled softly at the sight of a chubby baby with dark curls.

"Please don't look at my baby pictures."

My head jerked up at the sound of wry amusement in Samir's voice. I set the picture back down on the table. "Why? You were a cute baby."

He snorted. "I've never been cute."

I laughed at the expression on his face. "You ready?"

I followed Samir out of the apartment, trailing behind him. We rode down the elevator in silence.

"So where do you want to go first?" he asked when we reached the sidewalk outside his apartment.

"You're the tour guide. Lead the way."

He paused for a moment, considering. "We'll go to the Eiffel Tower first. Then maybe the Louvre. It's still early enough that hopefully we can miss most of the tourists."

I cast a sidelong glance at him. "I didn't peg you for the museum type."

"Why?" Samir asked. "I like art."

"I don't know. I just never really thought about it before."

"Well. I do. Like art. And other things." He hesitated. "You know, you really don't know much about me at all."

He had a point. In a way, I was scared to learn more about him. It was easy to tell myself that this thing between us was nothing more than a physical reaction to a hot guy. Anything else was dangerously close to something more. And yet I wanted to know him better. I wanted him to know me. "So, what else do you like?"

"I like to read. Sometimes I like to cook."

"You cook?" I couldn't keep the surprise out of my voice. I never would have guessed that one.

"Of course I cook." He almost looked affronted by my question. "Our chef taught me how."

"What kind of food?"

"Mostly French. A little bit of Lebanese, but not a ton."

I shook my head, a wry smile on my face. "You don't seem to ever stop surprising me."

Samir grinned. "Go on, ask me something else."

"Favorite book?"

"Hmm." Samir paused for a moment. "That's a tough one. *The Count of Monte Cristo*. In French, of course. Or *The Great Gatsby*."

Surprise filled me. "I love *Gatsby*. I never would have pegged you as a *Gatsby* fan."

"Why?"

I shrugged. "I don't know. It's sentimental…romantic, even."

"Hey, I can be sentimental and romantic." I pulled a face. "I can," Samir insisted. He put his arm around me, guiding me out of the path of oncoming Parisians.

"How about you?"

"What about me?"

"What's your favorite book?"

That was a hard one. "*Pride and Prejudice. Gatsby. Great Expectations.*" I grinned. "Honestly, the list could go on and on."

Samir smiled. "You should check out the library in the daytime, then. My dad has some great first editions."

I blushed, the memory of last night assailing me. I tripped on the sidewalk just as Samir reached out a hand to catch me.

The streets and sidewalks were relatively crowded this morning, although less so than London—and the people walked a little slower. But despite all its history and beauty, Paris was still a busy, modern city.

We walked down the street, the Eiffel Tower suddenly coming into view.

"Do you want to go up?" Samir asked, removing his arm from my shoulders. "You can go up on the different levels and look out at the city."

"Have you ever done it?"

He grinned. "Actually, no. It's usually crowded with tourists and I'm not one for waiting in line."

I thought of all the club lines he always bypassed.

"We don't have to. It looks busy already."

Samir shrugged. "I don't mind." He scanned the landscape before settling on a small trailer off in the distance. "Well, if we're going to wait in line, we might as well have something to eat."

I followed his gaze. "What's that?"

"Crêpe stand. Had one?"

I shook my head.

He flashed me a grin, grabbing my hand. "Come on, then."

I followed Samir to the crêpe stand, allowing him to pull me along. Our fingers linked together.

I scanned the options, trying to translate what some of the words meant. Some things I could recognize. Strawberry crêpe. Chocolate crêpe. Others were harder to decipher.

"What are you getting?"

"Nutella. Definitely Nutella." I recognized the name of the chocolate spread; we had it in our school cafeteria.

"I'll try that, too."

Samir ordered for us in French. I took the opportunity to move my hand out of his. The French was hot enough as it was; I didn't need to add touching to the mix.

When he pulled out his wallet to pay, I shook my head. "My treat."

He hesitated. "I'm not letting a girl pay for me."

My lips twitched. "Please? Think of it as a thank-you for showing me around Paris today. Despite what you might say, I'm pretty sure hanging around a bunch of tourists is not your idea of a good time."

He snorted.

"This is just my way of saying thanks. Besides, you always pay for everyone. I beyond owe you."

"It's no big deal. It's how I was raised." He sighed, the expression on his face vaguely uncomfortable. "Fine. But just this once. Thank you," he added.

I grinned. "You're welcome."

40

We spent the day hitting up the major Paris sights. We only made it halfway up the Eiffel Tower, but the view was incredible. From there we walked to the Louvre, following the signs to the *Venus de Milo* and finally, the *Mona Lisa*.

"This is the Louvre express tour," Samir joked. "Next time you come to Paris you should come back and fully experience the museum. It's so big, it can take days to appreciate the artwork."

I wasn't a huge art lover or anything, but something about standing there, staring up at one of the greatest masterpieces ever created, resonated with me. It wasn't about the painting as much as it was what the painting represented. Here I was, this girl from South Carolina, in Paris, no less. Even after months of living in London I still felt as if, somehow, this was all a dream.

"Ready for the next stop?" Samir asked.

I nodded, surprised by how good a tour guide he actually was. Even though he'd offered to show me the city, I'd been fully prepared for him to moan about the number of tourists or get impatient with my desire to take way too many pictures. Instead, he was quiet most of the time, answering my questions and taking the obligatory photos of me in front of various landmarks.

For the most part we took our tour of the city on foot. Occasionally Samir would hail a cab if the distance was too far, but other than that, we walked everywhere. I loved it. My ballet flats were perfect for navigating Paris's cobblestone streets. And Parisians were big walkers.

Throughout the day Samir would put his arm around me, guiding me out of the path of oncoming traffic. A few times he took my hands in his, pulling me along with an infectious enthusiasm.

I'd never felt more aware of his body. Or his hands.

We went to Notre-Dame, Montmartre and an artistic district called The Marais. Samir took a picture of me in front of the Arc de Triomphe and we walked through the Tuileries Garden. It was one of the best days of my life.

"Is there anything else you wanted to see?"

I glanced down at my watch. It was getting late, and the sun was starting to go down. For dinner Fleur planned for us all to go to this Lebanese restaurant she loved.

"I think that's everything." I looked up at him. "Thanks for today. I had a really good time."

He smiled. "Me, too."

We walked along the river, Samir pointing out the sights. Artists set out canvases of Parisian street scenes for sale all along the riverbank. I hesitated. It would be the perfect souvenir to remind me of this day.

"Do you mind?"

His lips twitched. "No. Everyone should have their obligatory Parisian street scene."

I walked over to the paintings, studying them before settling on the one I wanted—a picture of the Eiffel Tower. Samir haggled with the guy in French until they reached a price both seemed happy with. I pulled out the requisite number of euros, flashing Samir a grateful smile. "Thanks for that. It's a little intimidating when you don't know the language. And I noticed not many Parisians speak English."

Samir laughed. "I promise they speak a lot more English than you think."

"Then why don't they try to help out more?"

He shrugged. "Because the French won't deign to speak English. They think their language is superior, so why bother? Besides, you *are* in France. If you were a French tourist in the United States, would you be angry if people refused to speak French to you?"

I guess he had a point. "It's still a little frustrating."

He winked at me. "We can be frustrating. It comes with being French."

I considered this for a moment. "Which are you?"

"What do you mean?"

"Well, at school—in London—when you speak Arabic, it seems so natural. But here in Paris…you fit here, too."

I was still trying to make out who Samir was. Normally I was decent at reading people. But with him it felt as if he was a riddle I was constantly trying to solve.

"I'm both," he answered, his gaze meeting mine. A new kind of tension filled the air. "Always both."

I shook my head, breaking the gaze between us. There was something about his stare—suddenly I felt both warm and cold all over. "I can't figure you out," I murmured softly.

He was silent. For a moment I didn't think Samir heard me. He started walking, heading back toward his apartment. I followed behind him, silence between us. He stopped abruptly, standing still until we were right in front of each other. When he finally did speak, his words were a surprise, his tone a mix of challenge and frustration.

"I can't figure you out, either."

"I don't know what you mean." I looked down at the ground in front of me, unable to meet his gaze. He was so close—if I reached out, I could feel his body beneath my hand, his heart pounding beneath my palm. I could stroke up to the bare skin at the collar of his shirt, my fingertips roaming up his neck, stroking his lips—

"Don't look at me like that."

My head jerked up in surprise, my gaze meeting his. The heat of Samir's stare had me stepping back. He reached out, his arm grabbing me at the waist, pulling my body up against his. His arousal pressed against me.

"Don't look at me like that and think I'm not going to kiss you."

I barely had a chance to register his words before his mouth descended on mine. With each kiss, bite, lick, he devoured me. There was nothing patient in this kiss, nothing sweet. It was nothing like our kiss on the steps. This kiss was a mass of desire and frustration. It wasn't a question. He wanted. He took.

My knees felt weak as Samir plundered my mouth. The only thing I could do was hold on. My hands traveled up his body, running over his chest, moving up to lace around his neck. Without realizing it, I pulled him closer to me. I wanted him all over me, inside me. I wanted everything.

Samir broke away first, his chest rising and falling in heavy pants. He looked deliciously rumpled. "Why are you with that guy?" Anger blazed in his eyes—anger and something else, something that might have been hurt.

I stared at him, my mind struggling to keep up. "What?"

"The British guy," Samir ground out.

Oh.

"Why, Maggie?"

"Why do you care?" The words just slipped out, driven by frustration and the need to know, once and for all, where I stood with him.

"You know why."

My eyes narrowed. "Do I? Why do you care that I'm with Hugh? Why?"

He raked a hand through his hair. Frustration filled his tone. "I don't know, okay? I don't know. I just do."

I waited for him to say something, waited for him to tell me he had feelings for me. But instead, he just stared at me, confusion flickering across his face.

"I see you."

I couldn't tear my gaze away.

"I see you," Samir repeated. "I see you, exactly as you are. Can you say the same about him? Can you say that about yourself?" His voice was raw, hypnotizing me with each word. "Do you know what it's like watching you make a mistake by hanging out with some guy you clearly don't fit with? Do you know what it was like watching you walk away with him that night? Imagining you fucking him? Imagining him touching you? Do you know what these past few months have been like?"

I did know. It was the same feeling I suffered every time I saw him out with another girl.

"I had to talk to Fleur. I've been pumping her for information for months. Trying to find out if you were having sex with him or not."

I stared at him incredulously. Who was he to push me like this? What did he know about anything? About how I felt inside?

He was a magnet I couldn't escape from. And he was a chance I couldn't take.

I turned away from him. My heart pounded in my chest. All this time, all he did was jump from one girl to the next. He was so casual about things; he always treated me as though we were just having fun. How dare he push me on this? How dare he make me doubt things with Hugh?

"Do you love him?"

I whirled around. "Why? Does it matter? Give me one reason why I should walk away from Hugh. He's nice and he's good to me. He makes me feel good about myself. I can breathe around him." My voice broke. "I don't want to be a random hookup. I see you, too. I see you with a different girl every night. I hear the stories. So yes, I want Hugh. I'm happy with Hugh. The only mistake I've made is hooking up with you. This ends now. No more kissing. No more strip rummy, no more hooking up. We're done."

Samir's eyes closed for a moment, and he staggered backward as if absorbing a blow. Then he turned his back to me and walked away.

41

After our trip to Paris, the pace at school picked up considerably. I barely saw my friends. We didn't have any classes together and we were all so busy with school. Fleur and I were like two ships passing in the night. We talked a bit at night in our room, but otherwise I spent most of my time in the library or hanging out with Noora. I avoided Samir. Somehow—eventually—we managed to be cordial around each other, but we never spoke of that night in Paris. And whatever friendship we'd had seemed to be gone.

Exams were coming, and with them, the stress of final grades. And soon—far too soon, if you asked me—I'd be leaving London. Not just for a few weeks, either. For four months.

Four *very long months.*

I walked up High Street Ken, heading toward the Tube station. Hugh had invited me over to his place and for the first time since I'd known him, I hadn't invented an excuse not to go. I wanted things to work between us. Needed them to. And if I didn't change quickly, I was worried I'd lose him for good.

I lengthened my stride, weaving through the crowds of people. The weather had warmed a bit, and with the changing season came a whole new host of visitors to London. Tourists descended on the city, blocking the sidewalks. When I complained about it to Hugh, he laughed and told me I was officially a true Londoner.

I liked the sound of that.

I turned into the station entrance, elbowing my way past a group of American tourists. I walked toward the turnstiles—

Fleur was walking in the opposite direction. I opened my mouth to call out her name—

She wasn't alone.

Costa stood beside her, his arm draped casually around her shoulder. He said something that made Fleur laugh and then he leaned in, pressing his lips against hers.

"Excuse me, miss?"

My gaze jerked away from Fleur and Costa, turning to face the man who spoke to me. He was dressed in a business suit, annoyance on his face.

"You're blocking the entrance."

My cheeks flamed as I mumbled my apologies. I moved out of the way, my thoughts full of what I had just seen. When I looked back at the stairway, Fleur and Costa were gone.

How could she have kept something like that from me? Were they back together? I had seen him recently at school with his girlfriend, so I didn't think he was single. I just couldn't believe Fleur would get involved with him again.

By the time I got to Hugh's flat, I'd pushed all thoughts of Fleur from my mind. I leaned against the glass window, staring out onto the city. Hugh lived in a modern building with a doorman and a killer view of the river. This was the part of London I always thought of as "modern London." Here the buildings were taller, the architecture more contemporary. I liked it, but for me, London would always be a celebration of a time long since passed. I loved the history that flooded the streets, loved the feeling that I was in another era when I walked down my street in Kensington.

"Enjoying the view?"

I turned around, anticipation filling me as Hugh walked toward me. I turned back to face the window. My eyes closed as his arms wrapped around me; his muscular body pressed against me. I was short enough that Hugh could fit my head under his chin, giving me the sensation that my entire body was encased in his.

It was so different from being in Samir's arms.

Hugh bent his head, his lips finding the sensitive spot behind my ear. He kissed me softly there, his lips leaving goose bumps in their wake. I turned in his arms, leaning up on my tiptoes and pressing a soft kiss to Hugh's cheek. His hands stroked down my back. Our bodies were locked against each other, his fingers probing, hands stroking. He reached up and tugged at the edge of my shirt, lifting it up over my bra, pulling it over my head. A rush of cold air hit my bare skin.

Hugh's eyes flared. "You're so beautiful." He leaned down, pressing a swift kiss to my neck. My head tilted back, giving him more access to my bare skin. His tongue swept down my neck, his teeth giving little bites along the way. He pulled me closer against his hard body. "Bed," he murmured, taking my hand and leading me through the flat.

I followed him on shaky legs, a mass of confusion running through my head. Part of it was the enormity of what I was doing—the fact that if this continued, I wouldn't be a virgin anymore. And part of it, damn him, was the memory of that night in Paris and what hung between Samir and me, lingering, unresolved.

Hugh flicked on a light switch. I blinked. His room was big by London standards, but most of the space was dominated by a large bed covered with black silk sheets.

Hugh guided me over, pressing more kisses on my neck. He

pushed me down on the bed, his body following mine, covering me. I could feel every inch of him pressed against me.

I pulled off his shirt, tugging it over his broad shoulders. When he shrugged it off, I gaped at the sight before me. *Holy shit.* I reached out, my fingers stroking the powerful muscles on his stomach. He was beautiful. Hot, sexy and absolutely beautiful. But I couldn't help but think something was missing, something was off—

"That feels so good," Hugh murmured,

I pushed the traitorous thought from my head. "Good."

Hugh shifted slightly, reaching behind me to unhook my bra. The move was effortless, one-handed. Apparently, all that practice came in handy.

I stiffened slightly as he peeled away my bra, exposing my breasts. He hadn't bothered to turn off the light; my body was completely on display.

His lips claimed mine in an erotic kiss, his tongue plundering my mouth. His hands raked over my body, stroking my breasts, teasing my nipples.

And suddenly, I was back on a street in Paris, standing by the river, Samir's arms wrapped around me, Samir's lips on mine. It was like a bucket of cold water had been thrown over my body.

"Wait."

I broke away from Hugh.

"I can't do this."

Surprise flickered across his handsome face. "Are you serious?"

I reached down, grabbing my bra and shirt. I bunched the fabric in front of my chest. "I'm sorry. I'm so sorry."

"I don't get it. What happened? I thought you were into it."

"I was. I mean, I am."

"Then what is it?"

For some horrible reason, I can't get Samir out of my mind.

"It's nothing. I'm just tired." My voice was pleading. "I just thought maybe our first time could be special. I thought I would buy sexy lingerie—"

Hugh groaned.

"I just think having rushed sex on a Tuesday might be a bad idea." I struggled to sound convincing. "When we do have sex, I want it to be amazing."

Hugh was silent for a moment. He sighed, moving closer to press a swift kiss on my lips.

"I should go," I murmured against his mouth.

"Stay."

I shook my head, pulling away from him. "I can't. I have class tomorrow morning. I can't afford to miss it."

"Are you sure that's all there is?"

I could hear the frustration in his voice, could see it in his brown eyes. I hated lying to him. But honesty didn't seem like the best idea, either. I settled for evasion. "What do you mean? I told you. It's just the timing."

"Every time I try to get you alone, you seem to have some kind of excuse. I just don't get it. I thought we talked about this. I thought we were on the same page about where we wanted things to go."

"It's not you," I answered honestly. "I do want to stay. Really. But my grades have been down this year, and I can't afford to lose my focus this close to finals."

Hugh pulled away from me. "I forget sometimes what it's like being with a girl who's still in school," he responded.

"I'm sorry."

He waved me off. Gone were the good-natured smiles, the playful tone. "It's fine, don't worry about it. I'll drive you home."

I glanced down at my watch. It was after midnight; the Tube had stopped running. "You don't have to do that. I can get a cab or something," I protested. The last thing I wanted to be was a pain in the ass. Unfortunately, the frustration in his voice seemed to suggest that was exactly how he felt about me.

I'd worked so hard to get him. The real question was—how hard was I willing to work to keep him?

42

"How are things going with Hugh?"

I flipped through racks of clothes. We'd decided to take a much-needed study break and do some shopping. We settled on a store that was cheap enough for me to maybe get lucky on the sale rack and nice enough for Fleur not to be embarrassed wearing their clothes.

"I'm not sure. We sort of had a fight the other night." I hesitated. "Okay, maybe not a fight. But I annoyed him."

"What happened?"

I turned toward where Fleur was looking at skirts. I hated not being able to tell her the full story. And I desperately needed advice. But there was no way I could bring Samir into this.

"I don't know really. We were at his flat and he wanted me to stay over." Her eyes widened. "I wanted to. Honestly. But I've just been so tired and stressed lately with exams coming up. It didn't feel right."

"That seems to be your problem a lot."

"What do you mean?"

She shrugged, pulling a skirt off the rack, and holding it up in the air. "It just seems like there have been plenty of opportunities for you guys to have sex and it never happens. Maybe you don't really want it to."

Her words hit a bit too close to home.

"What are you saying? You think I'm sabotaging myself or something?"

Fleur frowned at me. "Don't shoot the messenger. I'm just saying that it seems weird, that's all. I can kind of see his frustration. He shouldn't pressure you, but at the same time, you need to be honest with him. You like him, he likes you. It really isn't that big of a deal. Just have sex with him and get it over with."

"That's romantic."

"Who's talking about romance?" Surprise filled her voice. "Maggie, he's old. There's no way this is going anywhere."

"What are you talking about?"

"What did you expect would happen? At the end of all of this he's going to fall in love with you and you guys are going to get married?" Her voice was incredulous. Her tone wasn't cruel, but it did little to ease the sting in her words. "There's like a decade between you. You have nothing in common. Not really. At most this is a fling. He's a hot guy, but come on? Do you really think this is going to be long-term? You read *War and Peace* for fun. He owns a bar. You guys have nothing in common. He's a player, you're a hopeless romantic."

I stared at her, feeling the weight of each word. "I thought you were my friend. I thought I could count on you to at least support me."

"I *am* your friend. I care about you, and I don't want to see you get hurt. None of us do. But I never thought you meant for things to be serious between the two of you. I thought this was just something fun."

"Well, it wasn't just fun for me. I like him. I don't do flings."

"I know you don't." Her tone gentled somewhat. "I know you like him. But he isn't right for you. Can't you see that?"

Anger bubbled up, replacing my earlier hurt with a need to

lash out, to wound her as she was wounding me. "You aren't exactly one to give relationship advice," I challenged.

She stiffened. "You're right, I'm not. I've been through hell this year and the last thing I want is to see someone I care about suffering the same way."

She was such a hypocrite. I couldn't hold it in any longer. "I saw you with him." Fleur blinked. "The other day—I saw you and Costa making out in the Tube station at High Street Ken." Something that might have been embarrassment flickered across her face. "What was that? You just having fun? Don't talk to me like I'm an idiot for having feelings when it's so obvious you and Costa are hooking up again."

Fury flashed across her face. "You know nothing about me and Costa. You've never had a boyfriend. Look at you, you never get involved, you always play it safe and then you sit and judge the rest of us for making mistakes. It must be nice to always feel so perfect and superior, but guess what? You don't know anything about me and Costa, so back off."

"You're right. I don't know anything about you and Costa. I'm just the friend that's been putting up with your bullshit all year. I'm the one who's been there when he's been making it clear to everyone around that he wants nothing to do with you." Fleur's cheeks colored. "You want to talk about being naive? I'm not the one putting out for a guy who doesn't want me."

With that parting blow I left her shopping alone.

"I fucked up."

Samir lowered the volume on the TV in the common room. It was late enough that he was the only one in there watching movies. The fight with Fleur was enough to have me breaking my attempt to stay away from him. I needed him.

"What happened?"

I closed my eyes, an overwhelming sense of relief crashing

over me. After the fight with Fleur, I couldn't bear the thought that things were awkward with Samir, too.

"Honestly? I don't know. Fleur and I had a fight. I said some horrible things to her." Guilt flooded me. "What do I do?" If anyone would know how to handle Fleur, it was Samir.

"How bad was it?"

"Bad. I said something about the whole Costa situation." My words came to mind again. "It was really bad."

"Well, yeah. You did pick Fleur's one big sensitive spot. Can you just apologize?"

"I hope so." I walked over to the couch, sitting down next to him. "I don't know what got into me. I've never fought with anyone like that before. I was just so angry…"

Samir shrugged. "Fleur knows a thing or two about pushing buttons."

"Apparently so do I," I added wryly. "Except I didn't exactly fire a warning shot. I went straight into full-on nuclear attack."

A smile tugged at Samir's lips. "I'm not surprised."

My heart pounded in my chest. This was good. Things felt normal. Almost as if we were friends again.

"No?"

He shook his head. "You've had this sort of tenuous grasp on yourself for a while now. You forget—I've seen you lose your inhibitions more than the others have."

I blushed. That was a polite way to put it.

"You have a temper on you." His gaze connected with mine. "And you're not as self-contained as you like people to think."

I raised a brow. "You make me sound difficult."

His lips quirked. "I prefer *challenging*."

"Okay, so I'm *challenging*." The word slipped from my lips with a whiff of distaste. "So, what do I do about Fleur?"

"Apologize. Trust me. Fleur's challenging, too. She'll understand."

"And if she doesn't?"

"She will."

I hesitated for a second, silence stretching between us. "Thanks for the advice. I knew I could count on you to know the right thing to do."

A ghost of a smile touched Samir's face. "No problem. I'm just surprised you came here to talk to me. I would have thought Mya was the more obvious choice."

"Mya has a lot on her plate right now." I didn't elaborate. I figured she didn't want me sharing her dad's infidelity with everyone. From what I could tell she hadn't even mentioned it to Fleur. "Besides, you know Fleur better than anyone. I figured you would give me the best advice on how to handle her..." My voice trailed off uncertainly.

"And?"

I flushed slightly. "And what?"

"You were about to say something about what a great friend I was? How wise and helpful?"

That teased a smile from my lips. "Something like that."

He hesitated for a beat. "It's good to see you smile. It's been a while."

I flushed. "I've been stressed with exams and everything."

"I've missed you." His voice was so low I had to strain to hear him. My heart pounded madly in my chest.

"I've missed you, too."

Samir's expression turned serious, his gaze piercing mine. I held my breath, waiting to hear his next words. "Maggie, that night in Paris—"

The door swung open, and a group of drunk kids filed into the common room. I jerked away from Samir, the noise breaking the moment between us. They filled the room with their chatter, sitting down on the couch opposite ours.

A tense line formed around Samir's mouth.

"I should go back. I've been hiding from Fleur for long enough."

His phone rang. Samir made no move to answer it.

I hesitated for a moment. I thought about asking him what he had been about to say. But I let it go.

With Samir I wasn't sure I wanted to know.

43

"I'm sorry."

I blinked in surprise. I hadn't expected Fleur to apologize as soon as I walked into our room. I wasn't entirely sure I deserved it.

"I'm sorry, too," I blurted out, setting my bag down on my bed. "I got upset with what you said about Hugh, and I lashed out."

"No. I shouldn't have said anything about Hugh. It isn't my business and you're right, I am definitely the last person who should be judging anyone on dysfunctional relationships."

"You were being a good friend."

Fleur shook her head. "Good friends support each other. I shouldn't have discounted your feelings about Hugh. Things might work out with you guys. You never know."

I knew her well enough to know she didn't entirely believe what she said. But she cared enough to try and that was enough for me.

"I'm sorry about everything I said to you about Costa. It's not my business. I was just so surprised when I saw the two of you together. And I'm worried about you. I don't want to see you get hurt." I paused. "And I guess, honestly, it hurt me a bit that you didn't tell me you guys were together again. You're one of my closest friends here and it just felt weird not being in the loop."

"We're not together again," Fleur interjected, guilt flashing across her features. "We're just talking about things."

"Why?"

"There's some stuff we haven't resolved yet. And I miss him." She shrugged. "I'm not like you. I don't want to be single. I like having a guy. Things were good between us once. They can be good between us again."

There were so many things I wanted to say to her. But looking at the determined glint in her eyes, I knew there was nothing I could say to change her mind. She was going to have to see this thing with Costa through, even though it was a near certainty that it would end badly.

All I could do was be there for her when it did.

I sat with Samir at dinner, picking at the food on my plate. Silence loomed between us. A week had passed since he'd helped me with Fleur. We'd barely seen each other since then. I hadn't meant to be alone with him, but I got to dinner late and everyone else was nearly finished before I started. Only Samir remained.

Finally, the tension at the table got to a point that I couldn't take anymore. I had to break the silence. "I made up with Fleur."

"Good. I'm glad. I figured you guys would. Is everything okay now?"

"Yeah, it is. Thanks."

He continued eating, not speaking.

"So how was your weekend trip?" I asked, searching for something to smooth over the weirdness that had sprung up between us. Travel plans seemed like a safe topic. Fleur had mentioned Samir went home for the weekend. This was the first time I had seen him since he'd been back.

The fact that I'd missed him wasn't something I was proud of.

Samir's head jerked up. Something that might have been surprise flickered in his eyes. "It was good."

"What did you do?" Whatever weirdness we felt, I was determined to chase it away. Somewhere along the way, Samir's friendship—albeit completely different from that of my other friends—had become just as important to me.

As long as we kept our hands and lips away from each other, everything would be okay.

"I didn't do much. Just spent most of the time hanging out with my girlfriend."

For a moment, my world came to a crashing halt. I could do no more than stare at him as I struggled to process the words coming from his mouth. Whatever I had expected Samir's answer to be, I hadn't been expecting that. *I went to a few clubs* or *I hooked up with some random girl* were the sort of responses I expected to hear from Samir. But this? A million thoughts ran through my mind. Was he back with his ex? Did he meet someone new? How did Samir have a girlfriend? How was that even possible?

"You have a girlfriend?" I couldn't do more than stupidly repeat the question that had been running through my head. The words came out scratchy and hoarse.

"Yes, I have a girlfriend. As of this weekend, at least." Samir frowned at me, his gaze piercing. "You don't have to say it like it's so surprising. Some girls do find me attractive, you know."

I heard the underlying hurt in his voice. It wasn't obvious, but it was there, lurking underneath the surface. Like so many things with Samir, I'd learned you had to listen, really pay attention to pick up on what he really thought. He didn't always say what he meant and often the subtle nuances were the most important cues.

I studied him from across the cafeteria table, this time think-ing before I spoke again lest I blurt out something else that of-fended him. I didn't want to hurt his feelings. I just didn't know how to process this latest development.

Did he like her when he was kissing me?

I pushed the thought aside, horrified it had even sprung up. I struggled to change the subject. My voice was strained. "So, is she Lebanese?"

He studied me for a minute before turning his attention back to his food. His answer came a moment later. "Yeah."

"How did you guys meet?" My mind couldn't quite grasp what was happening. I knew I was interrogating him, but I couldn't help it. Part of me didn't want to know any of this; part of me had to know everything.

"We grew up together. Our parents are friends."

My heart thudded. I felt like an idiot. This whole time, there had been someone else.

"Congrats." The moment the words left my mouth I real-ized how insincere they sounded.

"You don't sound like you really mean it."

I didn't. And of course, Samir picked up on it. All along he had been doing the same thing to me that I had been doing to him—noticing me, my quirks. And in that moment, I knew that he knew I wasn't entirely happy for him.

Shame filled me. He was my friend. I should have been happy for him. I should have been happy he found someone to be with. But no matter how hard I tried I couldn't wrap my head around the fact that this was Samir—our Samir—my Samir, with another girl.

"How are things going with the British guy?"

"What?"

The question jarred me from my mental freak-out.

Samir repeated the question, his head cocked to the side. It hadn't escaped my notice that he never referred to Hugh by name despite the number of times we'd talked about him.

"They're fine," I hedged, realizing I wasn't quite telling the truth about that, either.

"Good. I'm glad to hear it." His tone sounded just as sincere as mine had.

Suddenly I didn't want to be there. I felt like my sweater was too tight, like the room was too warm; everything just felt off. For an irrational moment I hated this anonymous Lebanese girl who had taken Samir away. There would be no late-night movie nights in the common room, no joking around at dinner. It shouldn't have felt as though everything was changing—she was, after all, a long-distance girlfriend; it wasn't like she would be here in his pocket. But somehow it felt as if everything was different now. There was a wall between us that hadn't been there before.

There would be no more kisses.

"Did you hear Samir has a new girlfriend?" I asked Fleur, struggling to sound casual. I kept my voice low. There was no such thing as privacy in the halls. Besides, I had pretty much accosted her outside of her English class, hoping someone else would be as freaked out by this latest development as I was.

At least then it might not feel so weird.

Fleur frowned. "Is that what he's calling her these days?"

My heart thudded. "Do you think Samir is serious about her?" Once again, I struggled to sound like her answer didn't really matter, like I was just making casual conversation.

"I don't think Samir is serious about anyone. It's not his style. She's probably someone his parents pushed on him. Now that Samir's going to be a senior next year, they're likely making plans for when he graduates and goes back to Beirut." I wasn't sure that made me feel any better. In fact, I was pretty sure it definitely didn't. This whole time I'd forgotten that Samir only had a year left of school.

"He's a player. Always has been. Always will be," Fleur continued. "I mean, sure, he's my cousin and I love him, but he's hell on girls. And anyone who gets involved with him has to realize what they're getting themselves into. He wears his rep like a badge of honor."

That seemed a bit unfair. "He's not that bad. He has his moments."

Like when he flew to Venice to bail out Fleur. Or held me the night on the steps when my world was rocked. Or took me on a tour of Paris.

Fleur flipped her hair over her shoulder, moving through the crowd of students waiting between classes. I lengthened my stride to keep up with her.

"He told me he had a girlfriend. Vanessa? It seemed like he was good to her."

Fleur stopped in her tracks, glancing at me in surprise. "He told you about Vanessa?"

I nodded.

"Fine—yes—there was one girlfriend he was loyal to. I liked Vanessa. But in the end, he broke things off with her, too."

I remembered what Samir said about Vanessa that time in the cafeteria, about how she cheated on him. Did he really tell me the truth about that, but not Fleur?

"You're right, he can be nice," Fleur added. "When he wants to be. He's nice to me, to Omar. He's even okay with you and Mya. But there's a point where that ends. He'll never let anyone get close to him. He'll never let anyone love him. He's smart, really, really smart." Frustration seeped through her tone. "But he doesn't go after smart girls. He only goes after girls who just want another night out at a club, girls who won't make him feel. Girls who are with him for what he can do for them, for what his name is. He doesn't really want a girlfriend, because if he had a girlfriend he would have to let his guard down. And I promise you that will never happen."

It was a fascinating insight into Samir, probably from the person who knew him best.

"You worry about him."

She sighed. "Yeah, I guess I do. I don't know. I just want him to be happy. And I don't think some girl his parents pushed on him is going to make him happy."

"Fair enough."

We said goodbye, making plans to meet up later to do some shopping on High Street Ken. I walked away, telling myself the talk with Fleur helped. We could all still be friends. Nothing would have to change.

Except the kissing.

I was pretty sure the whole purpose of Fleur's speech hadn't been to make me feel sorry for Samir. But the more Fleur described Samir, the more she talked about his relationships and the way he treated people, the more I realized how much she might as well have been describing me. On the surface we couldn't have been more different. He was so confident and arrogant. I tended to blend in the background more than stand out and my confidence was something I was still growing into. And yet that wall Fleur described? How many times had I used that in my own life to push people away? Wasn't that what I always did to Hugh?

That was why I could always talk to Samir when I was freaking out. Why he made me feel better the night I found out my dad got married. We were more similar than I cared to admit.

And that scared the shit out of me.

Considering how close-knit the International School was, there was only one person who I could think to confide in.

I called home. My best friend answered immediately.

"It's Maggie. Do you have a minute to talk?"

"Of course I have a minute. I haven't heard from you in forever." Jo paused on the other line. "Are you okay? You sound kind of funny."

I didn't blame her for being surprised by my phone call. It was almost midnight in South Carolina. And I hadn't been the best about keeping in touch lately.

"I'm sorry to call so late." I sucked in a deep breath. "Yeah, I'm fine. It's just been a bit of a weird day."

I heard rustling on the other end of the line. "What's up?"

I gripped the phone, struggling to keep my voice low. I'd been going around and around about the Samir situation in my mind, coming up with just one solution to explain my bizarre reaction. I hoped I was wrong. It came out of my mouth in a panicked rush, the words smashed and jumbled together.

"How do you know when you like a guy? As more than just a friend?"

I felt like throwing up.

There was a pause on the other end of the line and then Jo laughed. The sound was so familiar; it filled me with waves of homesickness.

"I don't know, Maggie. That's not normally something I have to think about a lot. I know if I like someone or not. It isn't exactly rocket science."

"Yeah, but how?"

Jo sighed. "I don't know. I just get that feeling."

"The slightly feverish, nervous, am-I-going-to-throw-up feeling?"

Jo laughed. "Yes, exactly. That feeling. Why? Is this about the British guy? Hugh, right? Did he call?"

I felt a rush of guilt. It had been ages since Jo and I had last talked. I hadn't filled her in on the fact that Hugh and I were dating now.

"Yeah, he called. We're actually dating now."

"Your first boyfriend. That's amazing." She paused as the rest of our conversation clearly set in. "Wait. I don't get it, though. If you're dating, how do you not know that you like him? You seemed so sure when you came home over Christmas break. What changed?"

A trip to Paris. My dad telling me he got married. A series of ill-advised kisses. All these little moments that, pieced together, most likely accounted for the feeling of acute nausea in my stomach.

I sucked in a deep breath, ready to let the other shoe drop.

"I'm not talking about Hugh."

44

"Who are you talking about?" The surprise in Jo's voice came through over the other end of the line. I didn't blame her. I wasn't exactly the type of girl you'd expect to be torn between two guys.

"This guy at school." I wanted to keep things as vague as possible. Fleur and Noora were out for the night, but still. This wasn't exactly the kind of thing I wanted to shout from the rooftops.

"A British guy?"

As much as I tried to explain it, my friends back home didn't seem to understand just how international the International School actually was.

"No, he's actually Lebanese. And French."

"But I thought you were dating that British guy?" I could hear the confusion in Jo's voice. I was pretty sure it matched the confusion in my own life.

"Yeah, I am," I answered glumly.

"But you like them both." There was no judgment in her voice, just uncertainty. I sounded nothing like the Maggie she had known most of her life.

"I wouldn't go so far as to say that I like Samir."

"Then what is it?"

I had been asking myself that same question for hours now. "I don't know. It's just this feeling I get when he's around. It's weird."

"What kind of feeling?"

"I don't know." I couldn't keep the frustration out of my voice.

The not knowing was the worst part. I couldn't put a name to the feelings going through me. They were just this jumbled mess of guilt and confusion. I racked my brain to think of a better way to describe it. I tried to remember all the times we'd spent together. "It's like I always seem to know where he is. Or what he's doing. And he makes me uncomfortable," I added, thinking that was somehow important.

"Uncomfortable how?"

"Just uncomfortable. Itchy. Warm. Incredibly turned on."

"Well, does he like you?"

"I don't know." I was starting to sound like a broken record.

"Why not?"

"Let's just say that's not really his style." I didn't even bother explaining the girlfriend development.

"But this guy Hugh likes you."

"Yeah, I guess."

"So maybe you should forget about this other guy and just focus on Hugh."

She had a point. If only it were that easy.

Operation Avoid Samir worked out better than planned. Partially because I suspected he had his own Operation Avoid Maggie going on. Which was fine with me. I had much bigger things to worry about than Samir's love life. My going-back-to-the-US deadline was looming near, not to mention the fact that exams were breathing down the back of my neck.

On Friday, Hugh took me to dinner for our last date before I started my final exams.

"You're quiet tonight," he commented, stroking my wrist.

"I have a lot on my mind."

"I can't believe you're going to spend the whole summer in the US." His voice was teasing. "What are you going to do there, anyway?"

"Work, I guess."

"Where will you work?"

"A retail shop. I sell clothes." I couldn't quite keep the embarrassment out of my voice. "It's not the most glamorous job."

"Maybe I'll come visit you in the US."

I coughed, choking on my wine. "That would be nice," I managed.

"We could go to New York or maybe Miami for the weekend. I haven't been before, but I've heard there's a great club scene there. I have a friend who runs a bar in South Beach. We could check it out."

I nodded, guilt filling me. Here he was making plans for us, and I couldn't even be honest with him. I couldn't go out to clubs or bars in the US. Hell, I couldn't even drink in the US. And I doubted that my grandparents would let me go off with a guy for the weekend. I couldn't keep lying anymore. Even if it meant he was going to hate me, even if he was going to break up with me—I had to be honest. I was sick of him not knowing me. And maybe a part of me had to know if Samir was right. Was I making a mistake with Hugh?

"I have to tell you something."

"What's wrong?"

I took a sip of my wine, trying to calm the pounding in my heart. I could do this. "I wasn't exactly honest with you when we first met. I didn't mean to lie, but when we met in Babel that night and you seemed interested in me, I wanted to impress you. And so, I told you I was doing a master's rather than telling you the truth."

I had his full attention now.

"I'm not doing a master's degree." I focused my gaze on the stem of my wineglass to avoid watching his reaction. My fingers clutched the stem, my knuckles turning white. "I'm at uni here in London. I'm an undergraduate. I'm not twenty-three."

"How old are you?"

I sucked in a deep breath. "Nineteen."

For a moment he didn't speak. I lifted my gaze, the suspense no longer bearable. I studied his reaction carefully, waiting to hear his response.

"I'm sorry."

He shook his head.

"It just got out of control. I never imagined when I told you that it would matter because I never thought someone like you would be interested in me. And then when you were, I was so happy that you were interested that I didn't want to do anything to spoil it—"

"Maggie—"

I closed my mouth.

"I knew you were probably younger than you said." He ran a hand through his hair. "I admit, I didn't think you were nineteen—"

"I'm sorry," I repeated.

He shook his head again. "It's not even the age that bothers me that much. We're both adults. I just don't understand why you couldn't be honest with me. If you didn't want to tell me that night in Babel, then fine. But why didn't you tell me any of the other nights? Why didn't you trust me?"

"I wanted you to like me." I knew how hollow the words sounded. I didn't even fully understand my actions myself. I never even gave him a chance to like me, never let him see the real me.

"I do like you."

The waiter came over and dropped off our check. Hugh stared down at it, frowning for a moment, before reaching into his coat and pulling out his wallet. His jaw clenched.

"Are you mad?"

He hesitated. "I'm not mad. I'm just not sure what we're doing here. Things are getting complicated, and I don't know. I'm just wondering if this is really working."

"I know things have been tough lately. I've been distracted with school. And I know I could make more of an effort." I reached forward and grabbed his hand, running my finger down his palm. He didn't move away. "I want to be with you. Just give me two more weeks to finish with exams. And then I'm all yours."

He was silent for a moment before he squeezed my hand. "My friend Tony is getting married two weeks from Saturday. I need a date. Are you interested?"

I grinned, the first waves of tension falling away. "I would love to."

We left the restaurant together, our hands entwined. I felt as if a weight had been lifted off me. I'd been honest with him. And he didn't seem angry. Fleur was right—if I was going to have a relationship with Hugh, it had to be real. It was time to take things to the next level. As he drove me home, I told myself everything was going to be okay.

He didn't invite me back to his place.

45

"Which one will he like?"

Mya's eyes narrowed, her gaze shifting from me to Fleur. "I don't know. What do you think, Fleur?"

"The black. Definitely the black."

I hesitated, turning back around to look at my reflection. "I kind of like this one."

"It's too virginal," Fleur interjected.

"I *am* a virgin."

"You won't be much longer in that outfit," Mya teased.

I stared at myself in the mirror. The black lace bra and thong set that I had tried on earlier might have been Fleur's favorite, but I wasn't sure it was mine. It was sexy and glamorous, perfect for Fleur. I just wasn't sure it was right for me.

The outfit that stared back at me wasn't exactly sexy. Not in an obvious way at least. The corset was boned, the ivory satin fabric cupping my curves. The cut of the corset made my boobs look amazing; the matching lace thong was delicate and feminine. It made me feel beautiful.

"I think I like this one," I protested stubbornly. "It's more me."

Fleur shook her head. "I like the black."

"Why don't you get them both?" Mya suggested. "At least then you have options."

"I think I will."

I changed back into my regular clothes and followed them out of the dressing room, the two outfits in hand. I handed the shopgirl my credit card. She wrapped the lingerie in tissue paper, placing it gently in a large shopping bag.

It felt like such a momentous purchase.

"Are you sure this is what you want?" Mya asked, coming to stand next to me as I paid.

I thought back to my last conversation with Hugh, to the feeling I had when I told him I was only nineteen—and the fear that he wouldn't be interested in me anymore. I thought about that awful moment when Samir announced he had a girlfriend.

"I'm sure."

For two weeks I lived like a hermit, mostly to atone for my earlier slacking. Finals began at the International School and suddenly a student body that had spent the last four months partying buckled down and focused on the exams that would decide their final grades. It was an interesting transformation to see—one that even my least academically motivated friends succumbed to. Rather than spending our nights in the clubs, we fled to the library, cramming a semester's worth of knowledge into a few marathon study sessions. It was two weeks of hell, filled with late-night food runs and copious amounts of caffeine. *This* was the other side of college. The not-so-glamorous side.

At the end of two weeks, after my fifth and last final, I finally stopped and looked at myself in the mirror. The girl staring back at me would have scared small children.

Fleur looked up from her magazine. She had been lucky enough to finish her exams a few days ago. Now she was in full-on relaxation mode.

"I figured you made the decision to let hygiene go after your second final," she teased.

I threw my brush at her.

Fleur moved out of the way, a grin deepening on her face. "You know, I'll never understand why you Americans think sweatpants are clothes to actually be worn out in public."

I rolled my eyes. "Please. I remember seeing you rocking some Uggs last week."

"They're comfortable," she replied, nonplussed, turning her attention back to her magazine. "So what time is this wedding?"

I glanced at my watch. I still had a few hours left to transform myself into Hugh's elegant date. "Seven p.m."

Her eyes widened, taking in my appearance. "I mean this with as much love as possible, but you definitely have some work to do." She grinned. "*We* have some work to do," she corrected.

I groaned, rubbing my face in my hands. "I know." I turned to face her. "I beg of you. Take pity on me. I need makeup and hair help. Do you have any plans for tonight?"

Fleur hesitated for a fraction of a second before turning her attention back to her magazine. "No. No plans. I can help you."

My eyes narrowed. "What's up?"

She looked up at me, her expression innocent. "What?"

"I don't know. Something is obviously going on with you. You're being weird."

"I'm not being weird."

I tapped my foot against the cheap linoleum floor, suddenly impatient. I knew what was coming. "You're hiding something. What's going on? And why do I think this has everything to do with Costa?"

Fleur set down her magazine, guilt flashing across her face. "Promise me you won't judge me."

"I can't promise that."

"Well, at least know this—I know what I'm doing. I'm not going to get hurt."

"This doesn't sound good."

Fleur waved her hand dismissively. "It's nothing."

"It doesn't sound like nothing."

"Costa—"

I shook my head, worry filling me. I had already seen her go off the rails once with this guy. I didn't want to see it again. "He's not worth it, Fleur."

"We're just going to talk—"

"No. I'm sorry, but no, I don't believe that you guys are just going to talk. I saw you together. That didn't look like talking. Besides, after everything he has put you through, why on earth would you agree to meet with him to talk about anything? The guy is an asshole. Everyone knows it. Why can't you believe it and move on? You deserve someone better. Hell, at this point I feel like anyone would be a better choice." I softened my tone. "I don't want to fight again. I just hate seeing you hurt and in pain."

"I know. I just need to get some closure on things."

"I don't understand what closure he can possibly give you. I think he's going to hurt you again."

Fleur lifted her chin, a stubborn look flashing in her eyes. "You don't get it. You've never been in love before."

Maybe she was right. I hadn't ever been in love before. But if this was what love looked like, I wanted no part of it.

The wedding was beautiful. The hotel was decorated in white roses and candles. The setting was hopelessly romantic. The couple was so obviously in love—the entire ceremony they kept exchanging smiles and whispering to each other.

"It was a gorgeous wedding," I mused, smiling up at Hugh.

We danced together on the dance floor to the sound of a jazz band.

"It was." He paused, a smile tugging at his lips. "Have I told you how beautiful you look tonight?"

"Thank you," I responded, feeling a bit shy. "You look nice, too."

Hugh twirled me, the sudden motion catching me off guard. He caught me as I ended the twirl, his arm grasping my waist, pulling me closer to him. I could smell the scent of scotch and mints on his breath.

I shivered. Under my gown I now sported the ivory boned corset I'd bought two weeks ago with the girls. Tonight was the night.

The song stopped playing and the band announced they would be taking a short break.

"Do you want to go outside and get some fresh air?" He didn't answer me. "Hugh?"

He ignored me, staring at the entrance to the ballroom. Curious, I followed his gaze, scanning the crowd for what had taken his attention.

And then I saw her.

There were those girls who always looked flawless. Their hair was always silky, with none of the visible signs of frizz I seemed doomed to combat on a daily basis. Their makeup was always impeccable—no stray smears of eye shadow or days when they put on just a little too much blush. Their outfits were never wrinkled; they seemed impervious to coffee stains and loose buttons. Those were the intimidating girls—the girls who carried themselves as though the world was their oyster, as if they could never take a wrong step.

I was not one of those girls. She was.

My head jerked back to Hugh. He stood in the middle of the dance floor, his gaze riveted to the entrance, his jaw clenched.

"Hugh?" I repeated, my arm grazing his sleeve. We were both rooted to this invisible point on the dance floor, our focus on this one girl—

This girl who was very clearly someone to Hugh.

He shook his head, as if to break himself from his stupor. He turned his attention down to me. "Sorry. What did you say?"

For a moment I couldn't answer him. Questions pounded through me. "I asked if you wanted to get some fresh air."

He frowned for a moment, his dark eyes hooded. "Sure."

I led the way out to the balcony, navigating through the crowded ballroom. Hugh followed behind me, his hand loosely pressed against the small of my back. Despite his physical presence, the whole time I could feel his distraction. He might have been with me physically, but it was obvious mentally he was somewhere else entirely.

I wasn't sure I wanted to know where.

When we reached the balcony, I walked out to the edge, planting my hands out on the railing. I took in the London scenery—the dark streets, the skyline I had come to love. I sucked in a deep breath, the cool air filling my lungs. I struggled to calm the nerves raging inside of me.

Neither one of us spoke, silence filling the space between us. With the silence came a new tension, an awareness that something had just happened. Something we both had no desire to speak of. The worst part, the thing that lodged in my throat, wasn't the truth of what had just happened. It was the question of what would happen next. I knew in that moment that no matter how hard I tried, it would be nearly impossible for me to forget the look on his face when he saw that girl—woman, really. And I knew, without a doubt, that there would be no need for my lingerie adventure.

"I'm sorry." The words came from behind me. I heard the regret in them. I recognized that he wasn't just apologizing for his reaction to the girl. It was an indication of things to come.

"Who is she?"

"My ex-girlfriend."

I absorbed the impact of this with little more than a tight

nod. Hadn't a part of me known who she was from the first moment I saw her? Given his reaction to her, it all made perfect sense. She looked like a match for Hugh. In a way that I doubted I ever would.

Somehow, I found my voice. "You still love her." I didn't even bother asking the question. His eyes said it all.

"Yes." Hugh sighed. "I'm sorry, Maggie. This isn't working."

"I know." My voice was barely above a whisper.

"It's not the sex thing."

We stared at each other across the balcony. On some level we both knew he lied.

"It's not totally the sex thing," Hugh amended.

I couldn't bear the answer to the question I desperately wanted to ask. *Why not me?* But maybe the most telling question of all wasn't the one I wanted to ask him—it was the one I wanted to ask myself. The same question Fleur had posed: Why hadn't I ever let my guard down with Hugh? Why hadn't I let myself fall for him? Because as much as this hurt, as much as the pain overwhelmed, I didn't doubt that there was a part of myself that I kept locked away. A part I wouldn't let him touch.

Hugh moved in closer, his tall frame blocking my view. "I'm sorry." He leaned in, running a finger across my cheek. His voice filled with regret. "I'm too old for you. I tried to tell myself that the age difference wasn't that much, but it is, Maggie. We're in different places in our lives. You know that."

"I'm mature for my age."

He nodded. "You are mature for your age. But you're still so young. And there's nothing wrong with that. You should be young. You should experience all the things that you haven't had a chance to explore yet. We're in different phases of our lives. I always knew it—I just thought if we kept things casual between us it wouldn't matter. But it does. There's just too much of a difference."

"I know."

Something that might have been regret passed across his face. "I really liked you."

I sucked in a deep breath. Somehow that only seemed to make it worse. I really liked him, too. But I understood now what I hadn't understood in the beginning. Really liking each other wasn't enough. There was too much standing in the way—ourselves included—that kept us from having anything real.

Hugh sighed. "It's hard seeing my ex again. I haven't seen her since we broke up." His gaze was hooded, his tone pleading. "I tried to tell you from the beginning—I wasn't looking for a girlfriend or anything serious. But you're not that girl. And I don't want to hurt you. I don't think you can do casual. And I can't give you anything else." Hugh shifted, shoving his hands in his pants pocket. "I'm sorry. I think we should just be friends."

There it was. The end that I had been dreading all along. And there was nothing I could do to fight it.

"I should go."

Hugh moved closer to me, his arms slipping around me. "I'm so sorry." He sounded nearly as upset as I was. It struck me then that he didn't like being the bad guy. And he wasn't. He had been good to me, honest from the beginning. It just wasn't the right fit.

46

It wasn't until Hugh had gone back inside that I realized I didn't
have any cash in my bag to get a cab. And my debit card was
useless considering how little cash I had left in my account. I
stared up at the sky. It was getting dark out, night beginning to
fall. The walk would be half an hour tops. Not ideal in a long
dress and heels, but I couldn't imagine the alternative—having
to go back in and face Hugh.

I gathered the hem of my skirt in my hand, making my
way through the exit, turning toward Knightsbridge. I walked
through the city, my head ducked low, all too aware of the stares
coming my way. The evening dress stood out, even in London.

My phone started ringing. I hesitated before pulling it out.
The last thing I felt like doing was talking to anyone, but curiosity won out. I pulled out my phone, feeling a flash of relief
at Fleur's name on my caller ID.

She was the only person who would really understand how
I felt right now.

"Hello?"

"Maggie?" Fleur's voice sounded on the other end of the line.
Except that it didn't sound like Fleur at all. The Fleur I knew
was confident, her voice cool and crisp. This Fleur sounded

anything but confident. She sounded as though she had been crying—my name coming out in a muffled whisper.

"What's wrong?"

"It's Costa—"

My heart sank. "What happened?"

"It's over. This whole time, he was lying to me. He told me he loved me, but it was all just a game with him. He just wanted sex." Her voice broke off. "I thought he cared. After what happened between us, I thought it meant as much to him as it did to me. It never meant anything."

Anger filled me. I wasn't exactly surprised, but I wanted to kill him for hurting her. "Are you okay?"

She didn't say anything.

"Fleur?"

"I don't know. I don't know what I am." I could hear the tears in her voice. "I loved him. I loved him so much. And I thought he loved me. I thought that if we just worked through our shit, we might be able to work things out between us. I thought we could fix what happened. I feel so stupid."

I sighed. "I know. But you'll be okay, Fleur. There are other guys out there. Better guys. Guys who will love you the way you deserve to be loved. I promise."

Fleur laughed harshly. "Maybe what I had with Costa was what I deserved."

"It isn't," I insisted. "I promise you, you deserve better."

"I'm just so sick of feeling this way. I wish it wouldn't hurt anymore."

"I know." A lump formed in my throat. "I know how you feel."

"Are you okay, Maggie?" Worry filled Fleur's voice. "You don't sound great. Are you still at the wedding with Hugh? I'm sorry I bothered you. I just needed to talk."

"No. I'm not okay. And I'm not at the wedding. Or with Hugh." The words came out with a strangled sob.

"What happened?"

"He broke up with me."

There was a pause. "What an asshole," Fleur spat out.

I shook my head, wiping furiously at the tears spilling down my cheeks. As much as a part of me welcomed Fleur's anger, I knew it wasn't fair.

"He wasn't an asshole about it. He was nice. He was right, there was just too much of an age difference—too much of a difference between us for it to ever work. He wasn't looking for a girlfriend. And that was all I wanted to be." I didn't even bother adding the part about the ex-girlfriend. I could share that part later. Preferably with alcohol and chocolate involved.

I moved to the side of the sidewalk, hovering under the green awning at Harrods. I turned toward the windows, struggling to hide my tears from the crowd. Samir had been right all along, I was an idiot.

"Where are you?"

"Knightsbridge. I'm in front of Harrods."

"What are you doing?"

"Walking home."

"In your dress?"

"I didn't have money for a cab, so I've been walking."

"He didn't drive you home?"

"It was his friend's wedding. I couldn't exactly ask him to leave. Besides, I'd already told him I was fine before I realized I didn't have any cash."

"It's raining."

I looked up in the sky. It was the quintessential London night—the weather not bad enough to be a full-on storm and yet gloomy enough to suit my mood. "It's not bad. Barely drizzling. I'm almost back, anyway."

"When you get back can we just get miserably drunk tonight and eat lots of chocolate?"

I couldn't help but laugh. "Yeah, that sounds like exactly what I need."

★ ★ ★

I punched in the code to the room. I had tried knocking, but Fleur hadn't answered.

I pushed the door open, the room dark and quiet. I closed the door behind me, fumbling for the light switch, my elbow hitting the wall.

"Ow." I cursed, flipping the switch.

Fleur lay face down on the ground in front of her bed, a pile of vomit next to her.

"Fleur?" I rushed toward her, my heart pounding madly. "Fleur!" I reached out and shook her, turning her body over. She was pale. Too pale. Her eyes rolled back in her head. "Fleur!"

I reached down, fumbling for a pulse, trying to remember any first aid I knew. Her pulse was faint, but it was there. I scrambled over to my bag, pulling my cell out. Fingers shaking, I dialed the emergency number as I fumbled over the keys. "Please, please, please."

A woman picked up on the third or fourth ring. Her clipped British accent filled the line. "What's your emergency?"

"My roommate. She's lying on the floor, unconscious."

"Is she breathing?" The woman's voice was remarkably calm as she fired off questions at me.

"I think so. Her breaths seem shallow." My voice reached a high pitch, the words tumbling from my mouth in a mad rush.

"Did she take anything?"

I scanned the floor near Fleur's body. My gaze settled on a small baggie. There were two pills in the bag. My heart sank. "Yes. There are pills on the floor."

"Where are you?"

I gave her all the necessary information for the school, panic filling me with each second that passed. She asked me a few more questions, which I struggled to answer.

"Help is on the way. They should be there in a few minutes."

Tears ran down my cheek, my heart pounding madly in my chest. I turned my attention back to Fleur. "Stay with me, Fleur, stay with me." She moaned. "Fleur!" She moaned again, her eyelids fluttering.

I cradled her head in my lap, waiting for the paramedics to arrive. I thought about running to get help, but I quite simply couldn't bear the thought of leaving her. So I sat with her, praying she would be all right.

She was breathing, shallowly, but she was breathing.

After what felt like an eternity, the paramedics pounded on our door. I released her, gently setting her head back down on the ground, jumping to my feet and rushing to let them in. "She seems unconscious," I babbled by way of a greeting. "She's not responding or anything."

They spoke to me briefly, asking questions about when I found her, how long she had been unconscious, if she had any allergies or drug habits. I answered them as best I could, all the while staring at the paramedics working on her. They moved me out of the way, crowding around Fleur's body, yelling things out to each other—in words that might as well have been a foreign language for all I understood them.

"Maggie!"

I whirled around.

George came through the door. "I'm on duty for Residence Life tonight. What happened?" His gaze flew to the ground where Fleur lay, the paramedics loading her on a stretcher.

"I came back to the room, and she was like this." My voice broke. "I called for help."

"What's wrong with her?"

I hesitated. "I think she took something." George's expression darkened. "She was upset..."

The paramedics lifted Fleur up on the stretcher, motioning for us to move out of the doorway.

I grabbed my purse off the dresser. "I'm going with her."

George nodded. "I'll come, too."

We left in an ambulance.

The wait in the hospital was agonizing. Mya had already left on vacation with her parents. Michael was flying back to the US tonight. I sat with George, waiting for any news from Fleur's doctors.

Mrs. Fox came down to the hospital to handle things until Fleur's parents were able to fly in from France. But there was only one person I wanted with me right now. I dialed the number, panic bubbling in my chest as the phone rang and rang. Finally, voice mail picked up.

"This is Samir. Leave a message."

I waited for the beep. "It's Maggie. Fleur's in the hospital in Chelsea. She's alive but she's not doing well." My voice broke off with a strangled sob. "Please come."

I disconnected the call, leaning back in the waiting room chair, fear and panic coursing through my body.

And I waited.

An hour later he came bursting through the hospital doors.

Samir rushed toward me. "What happened?" he demanded, his voice hoarse. "Are you all right? What happened to Fleur?"

I nodded, tears flowing down my face. "I found her in our room. They think she took something. They don't know." I brushed furiously at my face, batting away the tears. "She called me earlier. She was upset about Costa. I was on my way back. We were going to have a girls' night. Drink wine, that sort of thing. I don't know where she got the drugs."

"Is she going to be okay?"

"I don't know." I couldn't make the tears stop. "They won't tell me anything. Mrs. Fox is talking to the doctors now."

Samir wrapped his arm around my waist, gathering me against his body. He tucked my head against his chest. "Shh," he whispered, his lips grazing my ear.

"She can't die." The words slipped out amid a rising panic building in my chest.

"She won't."

I couldn't get the image of Fleur lying on the floor, her body pale, her eyes lifeless, out of my mind. I shivered.

"Are you cold?"

I nodded. I realized then that in my haste to make it to the hospital I hadn't even grabbed my coat. I still wore the same evening gown I wore to the wedding. My hair had long since escaped its updo, tumbling down my shoulders.

Samir pulled away from me. Shrugging out of his jacket, he draped it over my shoulders. "Better?"

I nodded, barely trusting my own voice. "Thank you." I filled him in on what Fleur had told me about her last conversation with Costa.

"I'm going to kill Costa."

"That makes two of us." I was a mix of emotions that bubbled up, threatening to spill over the surface. There was anger—a burning, deep anger. I wanted revenge, wanted to punish this boy who hurt my best friend. Fear gnawed at me, settling deep in my belly. It was the same fear that had my heart pounding madly in my chest from the first moment that I discovered Fleur's body lying on the floor of our room.

Samir released me abruptly, turning toward the long hallway opposite the waiting room. Mrs. Fox walked toward us.

"She's going to be fine," Mrs. Fox announced.

Relief flooded me. I sagged against Samir.

"She's tired now, and she's resting." Her gaze flickered between me and Samir, her voice gentle. "For right now the doctors are only letting family visit with her. But tomorrow I'm sure you can visit, Maggie. I know she'll want to see you. Her parents should be here soon."

"She's going to be okay, then?" Samir asked, his expression still tense.

"She's going to be fine, Samir. I'm sure she'll be happy to see you." She turned to me. "Would you like to go back to school together?"

I hesitated, reluctant to leave Fleur.

"I'll take care of her. I promise," Samir interjected, his gaze on mine. "You should get some rest anyway." He gestured toward my outfit. "And you should probably change."

"Are you sure you're all right by yourself?" I hated leaving him.

"You heard Mrs. Fox. Fleur's parents will be here soon. It's probably easier for them if it's just family. Go, Maggie. Rest."

I waited while Mrs. Fox finished speaking with the doctors. I gathered up my stuff to leave with her and George, saying goodbye to Samir.

I had only taken a few steps down the hall when I heard his voice behind me.

"Hey, Maggie…"

I turned.

Samir stood in the middle of the hospital hallway, his hands shoved into his coat pockets. I could still smell the scent of his cologne on my skin. It clung to me, invading my pores. Samir hesitated for a moment, looking uncharacteristically unsure of himself.

"You look beautiful tonight."

I froze for a moment, standing there blinking like an idiot. I had no idea how to respond. Saying thanks seemed insignificant somehow.

Before I could answer him, he was gone.

47

I didn't sleep all night. Every time I closed my eyes, I saw Fleur's body lying on the floor. Unfortunately, not sleeping also meant I had plenty of time to think of my breakup with Hugh—and Samir.

I packed instead.

I threw stuff into my suitcase, rising feelings of panic bubbling up inside. It had been a shit couple of days, and I wasn't sure how the hell I was going to move forward. For the first time I actually was looking forward to going home. I needed to get the hell out of here.

Fast.

"Is she going to be all right?"

I looked up at the sound of Noora's voice. She had spent last night at her aunt's flat, but clearly the International School gossip had made its way to her.

I smiled weakly. "Yeah, I think so. Her family is with her now." Samir had texted me earlier to tell me that Fleur's parents had arrived from France.

"I can't believe you found her. You must have been terrified."

"I was."

Noora reached out, wrapping her arms around me. "Do you need anything?"

"I'm fine. Thanks, though."

She released me, walking over to her side of the room and sinking down on the bed. "Are you going home soon?" She gestured toward my suitcases.

"Yeah, I leave tomorrow."

"I'll just miss you, then. My flight leaves tonight."

She stood up, grabbing a few books off her shelf. Her side of the room looked so barren, her things all packed. "I have to run and meet some friends from class." She enveloped me in another hug. "I'll see you next year."

"See you next year."

After she left, I returned to my packing. I grabbed a stack of papers from my desk, pausing when I came to a photo of me, Mya and Fleur standing on a bridge over the Grand Canal in Venice. We were all smiling, our hair blowing in the wind, arms linked. Back then everything had seemed shiny and new, the world full of possibilities. Now it just felt as though everything was falling apart.

"Knock, knock."

My head jerked up, my face lighting up at the sight of Michael standing in my doorway, his arm propped against the door.

"Michael!" I ran to him, throwing my arms around him. He caught me easily in his arms. "I thought you had left already. What happened?"

"I missed my flight and the next one they could put me on was tonight."

I pulled back. "Did you hear?" My voice broke. "Have you seen her?"

Michael nodded, running a hand through his hair. "Yeah, Samir called me. I visited her today. Samir asked me to check on you, too."

"How is she?"

"She's doing okay. Her parents were with her." He smiled wryly. "I think she likes all of the attention."

I shook my head. "I don't know how you can joke about it. You didn't see her. You didn't see what she looked like, lying on the floor…"

"She's going to be fine," Michael promised, his tone serious. "I expect from now on Fleur won't party as hard. It's probably better that she learned the lesson on her own this way rather than something worse. She was lucky you were there for her. It could have been a lot worse."

Anger filled me. "I don't get you guys. You act like a drug overdose is no big deal. She could have died."

I knew I wasn't mad at Michael, but I couldn't help but direct some of my anger at him. He was here; Fleur wasn't.

"You guys?" He quirked a brow at me. "You aren't one of us?"

"I don't think I was ever one of you." I tucked my hair behind my ear. "I wanted to be. It was so glamorous, the parties, the clothes, the cars, the guys…" I shook my head. "But this? Finding my roommate on the floor?" I grabbed a stack of sweaters and set them down in my suitcase with an angry motion.

"I know you're upset, but you're freaking out. Fleur's going to be fine. You're going to be fine. We're all going to be fine," he repeated as if saying it was enough to make it true.

I met his gaze evenly, suddenly feeling so tired. "Why does everything feel so fucked up?"

"Because it is. For a moment. But things will get better."

"I don't think so anymore."

"What else is wrong?"

I bit my lip. Given what just happened with Fleur, my problems seemed so trivial. "Nothing."

Michael frowned. "It's not nothing. You're upset. What happened?"

"Hugh ended things with me. Last night."

Michael rolled his eyes, an impatient sigh escaping from his lips. "Hugh dumped you, so what? Do you want to be another Fleur and spend a year pining over some guy who didn't have his shit together? Or do you want to be someone fabulous? Don't let a few setbacks make you change who you are. You were born for this. Own it."

I scowled at him. "I wasn't exactly looking for a pep talk."

"Well, tough shit. You're getting one. Stop feeling sorry for yourself. You can do better than this. Who are you, Maggie?"

"I don't know. I don't know who I am anymore. I don't know what to do anymore."

"Bullshit. Who are you? Who do you want to be? Someone mopey and sad or someone fabulous?"

I couldn't help but laugh. "I want to be someone fabulous."

"Good girl." Michael reached into his pocket and pulled out a handkerchief.

I took it from him, gingerly blowing my nose. I stared down at his monogram etched into the fine linen fabric. "I don't know any guy our age who carries a handkerchief."

Michael grinned, tossing me a wink. "That's because you don't know anyone else like me."

"True."

"Listen. Go put some makeup on. Clean yourself up and go be fabulous. Go see Fleur. You have one day—and one night— left in London. Make it count."

48

Make it count.

The hospital was far quieter in the day than it had been last night. Still, the memory of rushing in with Fleur, desperately hoping she would be all right, sent chills down my spine. The feeling stayed with me all the way to her room. It filled my throat as I stared at her, lying in her hospital bed, amazed by how small she seemed.

"You can't do that again."

Fleur blushed. "I know. I didn't think I'd have that reaction— I thought—"

"I thought you were dead."

"I know. I'm sorry," she replied. It was the first time I had ever seen true remorse on Fleur's face. "Thank you for saving me. If you hadn't been there…"

I shook my head. "Of course. I'm just glad you're okay." I gave her a firm stare. "He's not worth it."

"Yeah, I know that, too. Now," she added bitterly.

"I wish you'd learned that lesson months ago."

Her voice was quiet. "It wasn't just about Costa."

"What do you mean?"

She looked down at the sheets, playing with the cotton fabric. "No one knows this. Not even Samir. Just my parents and Costa. Did you hear about how I missed a month of school last year?"

"Yeah, Mya told me."

"I was pregnant."

My jaw dropped.

Tears filled her eyes. "We were always careful, but one time we weren't and that was all it took. I was terrified when I found out. I told Costa. He was nervous—we talked about all our options." Naked pain filled her eyes. "But even from the beginning, I couldn't get the idea of this baby out of my mind. Would it have my eyes or his? I wanted a little girl."

I couldn't believe it. Couldn't believe she'd carried all of this with her for over a year now.

"I decided to have the baby. I was so excited. I didn't tell anyone, wanted to keep it a secret for as long as I could—until we could figure things out."

This was a different side of Fleur, one I'd never seen before.

"About a month in, I woke up one morning. There was blood everywhere. I miscarried."

I moved forward, sitting next to her on the bed, wrapping my arms around her.

"I'm so sorry."

A tear fell down her cheek. "I didn't just lose him. I lost our baby."

"I had no idea. I'm so sorry for everything I ever said—"

She waved me off. "There's no way you could have known. I haven't been myself lately."

"That's understandable."

I released her and walked to the edge of Fleur's hospital room, stopping in front of the large window. Below us the streets of Chelsea were crowded, filled with people on their way home from work. It was still light out, if you could call the gray mist covering the city light.

It fit my mood perfectly. I turned away from the window.

"Are you angry with me? I'm sorry you had to deal with everything."

"No. I was just scared. Really, really scared. You're my closest friend here. You and Mya. I just couldn't imagine—"

"I know." Fleur swallowed tightly. "I didn't do it on purpose, you know. I wasn't trying to do anything. I just wanted to forget for a while. I just wanted a break."

"I know." I leaned over, sitting back on the edge of her bed. I reached out, squeezing her hand in mine. I echoed the words Michael had told me. "You're going to be okay, Fleur. I promise you, you'll be okay."

"I'm starting to think so." She ran her free hand through her hair. "My parents are sending me to a spa retreat in Saint-Tropez for the summer. They think that will help out a bit."

"There are worse places you can end up."

"True. I'm hoping for hot masseurs." Her voice cracked. "Are we still friends? Is everything okay with us? I know how you feel about drugs…"

I squeezed her hand. "You don't even have to ask that. Of course we're still friends."

"Then will you be my roommate next year? I was thinking maybe you, me and Mya could get a triple."

We had discussed it all semester, but it wasn't something we had decided on. "Yeah. Sounds good to me."

Fleur smiled weakly. "Next year is going to be our year. I can feel it."

"I sure hope so." I leaned over the bed and gave her a hug. "Take care, Fleur. Have a good summer. If you need to talk about things, let me know."

"You, too."

"Hey, Maggie."

I stood in the hall, waiting for the elevator. I had left Fleur in her room when the nurses came in to give her the next round of meds. George walked toward me, a bouquet of yellow roses in hand.

"What are you doing here?" I asked him.

A faint flush crossed his cheeks. He pointed toward the flowers. "These are from Residence Life. For Fleur. I'm just the messenger."

I studied him, my gaze shifting from the flowers to the embarrassed expression on George's face.

"Do you think she can see people?" He shifted his weight uncomfortably. "I don't want to bother her or anything. I can come back another time. Or just give these to you to give to Fleur." He thrust the flowers out at me.

I stared at the yellow roses. They were elegant and lovely. They were so Fleur. I cocked my head to the side, my curiosity piqued. "Who picked out the roses?"

George hesitated for just a beat too long. "Well, I did. I just guessed what I thought she might like best."

"I think they're perfect. Very Fleur."

And then it all clicked into place. George was totally into Fleur.

George looked toward the empty doorway. "I guess I should go in, then."

He looked terrified. I offered up a silent prayer to the heavens. *Be gentle with him, Fleur.* I leaned over and pressed a swift kiss to his cheek. "You're a good guy."

"I didn't do anything," he protested. "They're just flowers."

"It's more than the flowers."

George's gaze focused to a point off to my right. My gaze shifted.

Samir walked down the hall toward us. I heard George say goodbye and wish me a good summer before he headed in to see Fleur. His words barely registered with me. I couldn't stop looking at Samir. He wore the same jacket he had put over my shoulders the night before. He stopped a few feet away from me, his gaze on mine.

"Should I be jealous?"

"What?"

Samir nodded toward the doorway. "You and George." His tone was teasing. But his eyes seemed to contradict his voice.

I rolled my eyes, struggling to keep things light, easy. "He's a friend."

"Maybe I like being the only friend you kiss," Samir teased.

My face flushed in response. I didn't bother responding to *that*.

Samir gestured toward Fleur's room. "How is the patient doing?"

"She seems better." I hesitated. "Maybe wait for a bit before going in there."

Samir paused, his eyebrow raised as it clicked for him. "George? Residence Life George? Really?"

I grinned at the surprise in his voice. "You never know. Stranger things have happened."

"True." He shook his head. "Still. Sorry but I just can't see my cousin going for George."

"George is nice."

"George is boring," Samir countered playfully.

"Maybe Fleur needs boring right now. Maybe we all need boring right now." Part of me wanted to tell him about the baby. He loved Fleur and she needed all the friends she could get right now. But it wasn't my secret to tell.

Samir studied me quietly before speaking. "You holding up okay? Did Michael stop by?"

I nodded, running a hand through my hair. "Yeah. Thanks for that, by the way. He helped. I'm fine, just tired. I've been packing all day. I didn't sleep much last night."

"When is your flight?"

"Tomorrow morning at ten."

"I leave tomorrow, too."

"Going back to Beirut or Paris?"

"Beirut. I'm going to see my girlfriend."

My heart sank. I tried to pretend his answer didn't affect me.

"What about you? You still going out with that British guy? Are you spending your last night in London with him?"

My heart pounded. "No."

"No, you're not going out with him, or no, you're not spending your last night with him?"

A pause filled the hallway. "Both." I couldn't look up to gauge his reaction. I stared down at my feet instead.

"Want to talk about it?"

My heart thudded. "Nope."

I dragged my gaze away from my feet to look at him. At the same time, Samir turned away. He jerked his head toward Fleur's room again.

"Did you get to see her for long?" he asked, changing the subject.

"Yeah, for a bit. She says she's fine. Physically the doctor seems to think she's doing well enough to go home soon. Her parents are flying her back to France tomorrow."

"Emotionally?"

"Not so good." I hesitated. "It wasn't intentional—"

"I know."

My eyes narrowed, my tone sharpening. "I want to kill him. She needed him and, apparently, he never gave a shit about any of it."

"Oh, I wouldn't worry about that. I don't think Costa is going to be bothering Fleur anymore."

"What did you do?"

"Let's just say I taught him a lesson."

"Did you fight him?"

Samir's lips pulled back into a fierce grin.

"Are you hurt?" I couldn't keep the concern out of my voice.

My hand reached out of its own volition, searching his face for any sign of bruising. I touched his chest, my fingers brushing against the fabric of his jacket.

Samir's eyes widened slightly. He didn't speak. I jerked my hand back.

"Sorry."

I doubted his girlfriend liked other girls touching him. I shoved my hands in my jeans' pockets, staring down at the cheap hospital floor.

"Are you around later?" Samir asked.

I jerked my head up. I nodded wordlessly.

Something flickered in his eyes. "Good. Maybe I'll see you around." The words were casual enough. But his eyes—

There was a world of promise in those brown eyes.

49

I retreated to the common room, take-out sushi and a bottle of wine in hand.

My bags were packed and ready to go. Our room was stripped of any sign that we had all been there. It was depressing to see it so empty and the memories in room 301 were too much to bear. The common room had seemed like the best place to spend my last night alone in London.

I *definitely* wasn't sitting here waiting for Samir.

"Want some company?"

My heart pounded. I took a swig from the bottle of wine, turning to face the doorway. Samir stood in the entrance, wearing a black shirt and jeans. His hands were shoved deep into his pockets.

He hesitated for a moment, standing in the doorway.

"Sure."

I didn't know what I was doing, but I didn't want to be alone tonight. No, that wasn't entirely true—I wanted to be with Samir.

I gestured toward the screen in front of me. "Want to watch TV?"

Samir hesitated in the doorway for another moment before coming into the room. "Why not?"

Hands shaky, I tossed him the remote. It completely missed the mark, bouncing off one of the sofa cushions on the couch opposite mine.

Samir grinned. "Smooth move."

"Are you going to play nice today?" I hadn't intended for my tone to be flirtatious, but somehow it came out that way. The air fairly sparkled with some unspoken tension.

He cocked his head to the side, as if considering my question. "Sure, why not." He turned his attention to the TV screen. "What're we watching?"

I shrugged. I hadn't been paying attention to the movie in front of me. "You pick something. I'm cool with whatever."

Samir leaned over and grabbed the remote off the other sofa, flipping around between the channels. He closed the space between us, coming to sit next to me. "Is this okay?"

I gazed at the screen. An action movie flickered in the background. Mindless entertainment was exactly what I needed. "Works for me." I held out the nearly empty wine bottle. "Want some?"

Samir took the bottle from me, taking a long swig. His face scrunched up. "Ugh. What is this crap?"

"It's chardonnay." I frowned at him.

"This stuff is shit."

"Some of us don't go around drinking thousand-dollar bottles of champagne."

Samir rolled his eyes. "Whatever." His Rolex glinted under the harsh fluorescent light as he pulled out a cigarette, holding it out to me.

"Want one?"

I wrinkled my nose in disgust. "No, thanks. No lung cancer for me."

"Suit yourself." He pulled out a fancy-looking silver lighter.

"You aren't seriously going to smoke in here?"

Samir paused, the cigarette in midair. "Why not? School's

out. No one is around. I doubt the administration is going to freak if I light up."

"There are fire alarms." I raised my gaze up to the ceiling to illustrate my point.

Samir laughed. "You really are a good girl, aren't you? The fire alarms don't work. I've done it plenty of times."

He held the lighter to the edge of the cigarette until the paper lit up. He took a long, slow drag, smoke filling the room. The fire alarms remained silent.

I bristled, his words hitting way too close to home. "I'm not a good girl."

"Sure."

"What are you—reformed now? Because of the girlfriend?"

Another shrug. Followed by a long pause. I waited for his answer, all my concentration focused on Samir.

"Not really. Layla and I haven't been serious for that long. A couple weeks at most."

"Let me get this straight. You have a girlfriend. Who is apparently enough of a girlfriend that you're going to visit her in Beirut. But apparently not enough of a girlfriend to factor into your decision-making on whether you should hook up with some other girl."

Samir's lips twisted into a grin. "Pretty much, yeah."

"You're disgusting."

His gaze lingered on me for a moment. "You're one to talk—what about the British guy?"

I grabbed the bottle of wine, taking another swig. Okay, he was right. It wasn't the best wine. But it was cheap. And given the sad state of my bank account right now, cheap was good.

Samir turned up the volume of the TV, effectively terminating the conversation. His shoulder brushed against mine. We sat there like that for an hour. I barely paid attention to the movie, my thoughts drifting between my conversation with Samir and my breakup with Hugh. I didn't get guys. I'd never really thought I did, but now, after this year, I realized just how utterly clueless I was.

Samir lowered the volume on the TV, turning to face me. I could feel the full weight of his attention on me. "What happened with the British guy?"

"I don't want to talk about it."

"Why? I thought you really liked him. I thought he was the one. I thought you'd want to spend your last night in London with him."

I blushed. "He broke up with me because I wouldn't have sex with him. Partly." I sucked in a deep breath, not quite believing I was going to share *this* much with him. "He said it was the age difference. And I'm sure that was part of it. But the sex thing was part of it, too. Even if he couldn't admit it. And he had this ex-girlfriend who had perfect hair." My eyes narrowed. "Does your girlfriend have perfect hair? I bet she does."

Samir chuckled softly. "How drunk are you?"

"I'm not drunk," I protested, glaring at him.

"Good."

It was a moment before Samir spoke, but when he did—

Samir's voice was low, his tone strained. "Why wouldn't you have sex with him?"

The TV was muted now. I stared at the flickering images on the screen, unwilling to meet his gaze. I couldn't believe we were having this conversation.

"I don't know. He was hot. Like seriously, seriously hot. Tall, and built, and hot. Really, really hot."

"So you mentioned." His voice was terse.

I ran a hand through my hair, fidgeting with the ends. "I liked him—a lot. And I tried." Embarrassment crept into my voice. Everything came tumbling out now. "I even bought lingerie. But every night I thought to myself, *Okay, this is the night*, nothing happened. We kissed and stuff. But I could never move past that." I shook my head. "I knew he was getting frustrated with me. I knew it was only a matter of time before I lost his attention. And I just couldn't make myself do it. And then we saw his ex…" My voice trailed off bitterly. "It all just fell apart."

For a moment Samir didn't say anything. When he finally did speak, all I could see was his profile.

"You shouldn't feel pressured into having sex with someone. It's a good thing you didn't have sex with him. It sounds like it wasn't what you really wanted."

Why did everyone keep saying that?

"I did want it," I protested.

Samir shook his head. "Sorry, but I don't buy it. I don't think you did. I've known you for, what—almost a year now? Maybe you came here shy and feeling out of place. But that's not who you are anymore. If you'd really wanted to have sex with this guy, you would have."

I blinked.

"Trust me. You dodged a bullet on this one. You don't want to have sex with some guy you aren't that into."

I laughed—a harsh, jaded sound that filled the common room. "That's a little rich coming from you."

"Believe what you want." Tension sparked between us; the air now visibly shimmered with it. "You should expect more from some guy than having to fight for his attention. Don't sell yourself short. You deserve more. You deserve everything."

I had nothing. I just sat there staring at him. "Why?" I whispered, knowing it was the one question I shouldn't be asking. I was starting something, something I had no business starting. Something I doubted I could see all the way through.

The question hung between us.

Samir's eyes flared with heat. I watched the slow simmer before his lips curved and his face relaxed. "I only get involved with girls who can handle it. Someone like you will end up getting attached. I'm just looking for fun. Some girls are okay with that. They're just looking for fun, too. Everyone has fun and it's all good. Is that what you want?"

"I don't know. No."

"See that's the thing. If that's all he's offering you and you want more, then you deserve better than a guy like him…hell, you deserve better than a guy like me. You need a good guy. A guy who will treat you right. A guy who can give you what you want, what you need."

His words were so close to Hugh's that they hit uncomfortably close to home.

My eyes narrowed. "I think I might hate you."

We both knew how much I lied. He'd been right all along. This was how we handled each other. And in a strange way, we both liked it.

Samir laughed. "You don't hate me. You just hate that I'm right. Look, there's nothing wrong with the way you are. But know your limits. Find some nice, boring guy somewhere and date him."

"I don't like nice, boring guys," I muttered between clenched teeth.

"Then you just might have a problem."

No shit.

My mouth parted, frustration filling me. I wanted— something. I just didn't know what. *It had been so long since we kissed.* And then I knew. At that exact moment—

I liked Samir. Couldn't get him out of my mind, didn't want to keep my hands off him, wanted him and only him, liked him.

Make it count.

"What if I want something else? What if I'm tired of playing it safe?"

For a moment he didn't answer me. And then words in French escaped Samir's mouth. I may not have understood the words, but I knew the emotion behind them. He leaned in closer to me, a gleam in his eye.

He wanted me. I knew it in my bones.

"Samir?"

"Yes?"

It was now or never. Our bodies were inches apart. I itched to wrap my legs around him. To feel him pressing up against me—hot and hard.

Samir stiffened. For a moment he just sat there, his gaze devouring me. And then he moved closer...

"What are you doing?" I asked, my voice tense and breathless.

"Breaking the rules."

50

Samir moved forward another inch, our lips so close they were nearly touching.

I leaned in, closing the gap between us. Rational thought fled, replaced by a need that would no longer be ignored. I wouldn't see him for months. Now was all that mattered. My lips brushed against his, hesitant at first. Then, bolder. My tongue darted out, sliding into his mouth. It was all the invitation he needed. Samir's hand traveled up, his fingertips brushing along the side of my face. His mouth opened, his tongue licking into my mouth.

Just like that, he took over the kiss.

It felt good. Really, really good. Mind-numbingly good.

I wanted more. I wanted *him*.

I moved from my spot on the couch, letting Samir pull me forward onto his lap. My legs wrapped around his waist. I felt him—lean and hard against me. His hands moved along my body, cupping my curves, fisting in my hair. He was everywhere, his hands molding and shaping my body against his. He was sculpting me, learning every inch of me. Remembering it. His lips moved from my mouth, running alongside my neck. His tongue darted out, licking at the delicate flesh.

I shivered. Desire rammed into me. I needed more. *Now.*

"Take off your shirt," he whispered.

I fumbled with my sweater, distracted by his lips and hands.

Impatient, Samir reached down, his hands gripping the edge of my sweater. He lifted the fabric up, the cold air hitting my skin. He tossed the sweater onto the common room floor.

For a moment, Samir stopped moving. He leaned back, his gaze roaming over my naked torso, his eyes lingering on my bra. "You are so fucking gorgeous." He trailed a finger along the bra's scalloped edge.

A grin escaped.

"I wanted to touch you here—" his fingers dipped lower, grazing my nipple "—the night we played rummy. I wanted to play with you, to kiss you, to lick every inch of your gorgeous breasts."

"Now's your chance." My voice was breathless as I reached down, grabbed his shirt and pulled it over his head.

For a moment I simply stared. My gaze devoured Samir's body. My fingers itched to reach out and touch his skin, to press my flesh against his. I wanted to kiss him, to run my tongue along his skin.

I ran my fingers along his chest, tracing the skin there, running my hand down over his flat stomach. My fingers hovered just above the waistband of his jeans.

Samir groaned.

I bent down, pressing a swift kiss to his collarbone. I licked the skin there, nibbling at his chest, my mouth working its way down his body.

"I've been wanting to do this since the night we played rummy. And before."

Samir groaned.

I was going on pure instinct now, indulging every rush of desire. We'd been dancing around this for so many months. Now I wanted what I had only dreamed about.

I stroked downward with my hand, over his flat stomach, molding the shape of his arousal underneath his jeans. Samir pulled back at my touch. My hand hovered in midair, caught between us. Samir's chest rose and fell with deep breaths. His eyes blazed with intensity.

"God help me, Maggie, if you're going to stop, tell me now. Is this what you want? Are you absolutely sure?"

I paused for a moment, staring at my outstretched hand. My fingers curved into my palm. I waited for the usual array of questions to run through my head. Waited for the doubt.

There was only silence.

Whatever doubts or questions I had were gone. It wasn't the wine talking this time. It was me.

I'd never felt more in control.

I'd never felt more powerful.

My gaze met his, my heart thudding at the lust I saw blazing there. I was pretty sure it mirrored the look in mine. I reached down, lacing my fingers with his. He brought our joined hands to his lips, pressing a swift kiss there.

"I'm sure."

Samir's eyes closed for a moment. He shifted me off his lap. His voice filled with desire. "Come upstairs. I want you in my bed."

That was all the invitation I needed.

We pulled our shirts back on, dressing quickly, struggling to look presentable even though our hair was mussed, our lips swollen. I took Samir's hand, the feeling of our fingers laced together inexplicably right. We'd held hands enough now throughout the past year that this felt familiar—comfortable, even. And yet exciting at the same time.

I felt alive. And I felt safe.

I followed Samir up the first flight of stairs, grateful for the late hour and the fact that most students had already left for the summer. Whatever this was, I didn't want anyone else to know about it. I wasn't ready to deal with the questions or judgment. Tonight, was just about us.

It was a slow process to get up to his room. Every few steps Samir would snag an arm around my waist, pulling my body flush against his. He would nibble on my lips, my ear, cupping my breasts with his free hand, teasing my nipples, pressing his body against me.

I'd never wanted anything as much as I wanted him.

We reached the top of the stairs, turning down the hall until we stopped in front of the door to his room. It was strange that in a year I had never been up here.

Curiosity filled me.

Samir broke apart to punch in the code to the room. Our bodies brushed against each other as he held the door open for me. Anticipation filled me.

The room was dark, slivers of moonlight escaping from the blinds. He didn't move to turn on the light. Instead, Samir sat down on the bed, kicking off his shoes and lying back against his pillows. He crossed his ankles, stretching out his legs. His eyes watched me.

The air crackled with anticipation.

I stood in the middle of the room, studying my surroundings. His room was a lot like ours, only smaller and a single. There were no pictures of family or friends. Just a flat-screen TV propped against the wall. As much as I couldn't wait to jump him, I couldn't help indulging my curiosity about how he lived. I wanted to know everything about him.

The soft sound of house music punctuated the night. I turned. Samir pressed a few buttons on a small stereo next to his bed. The beat of the song matched the pounding in my blood, the music perfect for the night. My heartbeat sped up. The music wound its way into me as I stared at Samir across the room. His stare tracked my every move.

"Come here." His voice was barely above a whisper, but I heard the intensity behind it. His voice was soaked with lust.

He looked so comfortable there on the bed. It seemed like the most natural thing for me to join him, for my body to curve against his.

The first stirring of nerves filled me. My legs carried me forward as I joined him on the bed. I sat on the edge, staring down at his face, marveling at how long his eyelashes were, at the deep brown color of his eyes.

I eased myself down onto the bed, my body lying next to his. Our faces were mere inches apart. His hand reached out, his fingers tracing the curve and shape of my face. With each touch he seemed to memorize me. The sounds of our breathing mixed with the low, heavy beat of the music.

Samir shifted in the bed. He leaned over me, his lips joining mine. His weight settled against my body. I gave myself over to his lips, to the touch of his hands roaming all over my flesh.

We stayed like that for what felt like hours, exploring each other's bodies. He undressed me layer by layer, stripping away whatever inhibitions remained. When he pulled off my top and released my breasts from my bra, I felt only delicious anticipation.

He leaned down, his mouth covering one nipple, his hands working the other breast, teasing and stroking.

"Finally," he murmured against my skin.

I moaned.

My body was wet, wild for him. There was an ache building inside me, an ache only he could ease.

His head lifted from my breast, his gaze meeting mine.

The intensity of Samir's stare nearly undid me. I felt beautiful, as though he saw me differently than I saw myself. I felt like I could be me, not some girl pretending to be older or cooler, but me.

He saw *me*.

Samir reached down, his hands fumbling between us, unbuttoning my jeans, pulling the zipper down. It struck me then, as his hands shook with the movements, that he was nervous.

A soft smile spread across my lips.

I lifted my hips, allowing him to pull the denim from my body until a thin scrap of black lace was the only thing I wore. I reached over, unbuttoning Samir's jeans, cursing at the long row of buttons. My fingers shook as I struggled to undo each one. With each movement, my hand brushed against the weight of his arousal.

My mouth was dry with anticipation.

When I reached the last button, Samir tugged the jeans off, exposing a pair of black boxer briefs.

"Straddle me."

Desire filled me.

I shifted my body, swinging my legs around Samir. Only the thin layers of our underwear separated our bodies. I rocked against him—once, twice—reveling in the feel of his body beneath mine. I leaned down, capturing his mouth in a long, slow kiss.

His hands stroked my bare skin, lighting a fire with their path. Slowly his hands journeyed downward, moving to cup my ass, squeezing.

Samir tossed me a grin. "You have a gorgeous ass."

I grinned back at him.

I stilled when he reached the edge of my thong. All traces of laughter fled. My skin tingled as his thumbs hooked under the lace.

For a moment his fingers hovered there, a question in his eyes. "We can stop if you want."

Stopping was the furthest thing from my mind. "Don't you dare." I wrapped my arms around his neck, pressing our bodies together, kissing him with all the passion and intensity I felt. Samir tugged on the edge of my thong, drawing it down over my hips. I raised my hips, helping him until the black lace slid off my legs.

Samir moved, turning on his side, bringing my body with him so we faced each other.

He kissed me, his hand drifting down my stomach, dipping into my belly button before moving farther. His fingers stroked me, sliding inside me, sinking into wetness and warmth. I moaned, the feeling unfamiliar and yet everything I wanted. I could feel the intensity building there, felt the need for a release. I was hot all over, desperate for him.

I pulled at his boxers, sliding them off over his hips. I wanted to feel his skin against me. I wanted to feel all of him. I wanted him inside me, filling me, pushing me over the edge.

There were plenty of moments when I could have stopped things. And the more time we spent in bed together, the more sober I became. I didn't feel pressure to put out, to keep him interested. He had no expectations of me, or I of him. But I trusted him. I was with him because I wanted it.

Samir broke away from me, reaching over to the drawer and pulling out a condom. Thanks to all my near misses with Hugh, I was on the pill.

I watched as he rolled the condom on, his expression fierce.

"Are you sure?" Samir asked again, his hand reaching out and squeezing mine. He pressed a swift kiss to my lips.

"Yes."

His lips found mine in a fierce kiss. He slid his body between my legs, wrapping my ankles around his back. There was a moment of adjustment, of delicious anticipation. And then little by little, he slid inside me, fitting our bodies together, filling me up completely.

And then I wasn't a virgin anymore.

I had always thought the moment I finally had sex would be momentous. That in that instant, I would feel transformed, like a new person. Now an adult. I thought it would make me feel different. Like so many things, the reality was much different.

It wasn't anything like I expected. It didn't hurt as much as I thought it would. Just a twinge. A tightness. And then it was gone, replaced by something so foreign and yet completely natural. It felt right to be joined with Samir, our bodies locked together, a thin film of sweat covering our skin.

"You okay?"

I nodded, words failing me. I was so much better than okay. I felt alive. I was filled with a sense of awareness that everything would change from here on out. Not because I had sex. Because I had taken a chance, thrown caution to the wind.

I was okay with that.

Samir began moving inside me, the movement exquisite. With each thrust, the pressure inside me built, each stroke sending a thrill down my body. He slid in and out of me, his gaze locked with mine, setting a rhythm my body naturally followed. The pressure rose inside of me, the tempo building, until everything came crashing down and I rode the wave of my first orgasm, tremors slamming through my body. Samir's gaze darkened, his movements increasing, quicker now, until words in Arabic spilled from his mouth. His body clenched inside mine. For a moment he was still, his weight pushing me into the mattress, his body covering mine until it was difficult to tell when his flesh ended and mine began. He stayed like that for a moment before he rolled off me, our bodies still joined, bringing me to lie on my side, facing him.

He leaned forward, pressing a soft kiss to my temple. His hand stroked my hair.

I wrapped my arms around his neck, my breasts rubbing against the hair on his chest. I grinned. "That was kind of amazing."

"Amazing" was the understatement of the year.

Samir kissed me, slowly, his tongue curling inside my mouth. "Good thing we have all night."

Desire flooded me.

It wasn't supposed to mean anything. It was just sex. Just one night. That was all I needed.

Hours later I fell asleep in Samir's arms, his fingers laced with mine, our hands pressed against my heart.

51

"Flight 2810 to Charlotte, North Carolina, will begin boarding shortly."

My head jerked up at the flight announcement. I stared down at my watch, my eyelids drooping slightly. Twenty more minutes. In twenty minutes I would be back on a plane, headed home.

Not that South Carolina even felt like home anymore. I wasn't sure what did.

I stared down at my phone for what felt like the hundredth time. No new messages. I wasn't sure what I even expected. One night. That was all I wanted. All I still wanted.

It was stupid of me to wonder if Samir would text.

When I'd finally left his room, it was 6 a.m. He'd kissed me softly before I slipped out of bed, mumbling something about staying. He'd been half-awake. We hadn't let loose of each other all night.

In the clear light of day, last night felt more pronounced. What seemed unimportant under the cover of darkness now made me feel as if I was wearing a bright neon sign, blinking to announce I was no longer a virgin. I was pretty sure everyone in the airport could see it, that everyone knew what I had done. Not only lost my virginity in a one-night stand but even worse, lost my virginity in a one-night stand to a *guy who had a girlfriend*. I had broken every rule in the girl code. Three times.

I couldn't even say I'd forgotten about the girlfriend. She'd been there, somewhere in the periphery of my mind. I'd pushed her out. She'd been in the way of something I wanted. And for the first time in my life I hadn't hesitated; I'd taken.

I was equal parts ashamed and proud.

"Now boarding zone A for flight 2810 to Charlotte."

I stared down at my ticket. That was me.

I shuffled through the boarding queue, ready to settle into my seat on the plane and fall right asleep. I made it to my seat with little fanfare, squeezing in between two older guys.

I was asleep before we even taxied down the runway.

When I woke the flight attendants were handing out landing cards. I blinked, staring at the little map screen on the seat in front of me. I'd slept the whole way to Charlotte.

"Were you in London for vacation?"

I turned to face the guy next to me. He had a slight Southern accent, his hair peppered with gray.

"No. I go to school there. University," I added.

He smiled. "What year are you?"

"I just finished my first year."

He nodded. "You must be excited to get home. The first year is the worst. College gets better afterward."

Did it? I wasn't so sure. What could I say about my freshman year? Parts of it hadn't been great—Fleur's overdose, my breakup with Hugh, my dad's impromptu marriage. But then I thought about the rest of it. My trip to Paris. My friends. Samir. Last night. Everything felt jumbled somehow, all my carefully ordered plans, the things I thought I knew about myself a scattered mess. But in its wake, I saw possibilities.

That was enough for now.

We landed smoothly. When we touched down, a beeping

noise started from the direction of my purse. *Shit*. Of course, I had forgotten to turn my cell off. I stared down at my phone. The screen blinked back at me. Two new messages.

My heart raced even as I told myself to calm down. I shouldn't get my hopes up. This was Samir we were talking about. He was probably too cool to call a girl after he hooked up with her. I knew better than to have expectations. But that was the thing about hope—it was sneaky and unexpected, winding its way through you, tying you up in knots before you even realized it.

The first text was from Fleur: My flight sucked but I'm here. They wouldn't give me alcohol and I forgot to take a Valium. If you get bored in the U.S., come visit me in France. Miss you!

I grinned. Classic Fleur.

The next message left my mouth dry as the name flickered across the screen.

Last night was amazing. We should do it again. Often. See you next year. xxxx.

A grin spread across my face. I couldn't wait for summer to be over.

★ ★ ★ ★ ★

Maggie and Samir's story has only just begun.

Look for London Falling,

*from Chanel Cleeton
and Canary Street Press*

1

Maggie

I wasn't looking for Samir. At least that's what I told myself.

I shouldn't be looking for Samir.

"We spent most of the summer in Saint-Tropez. You should have seen the guys. There was this one guy…" Fleur took a sip of her soda, brown eyes sparkling. She wiggled her eyebrows suggestively. "He was so fine. You would have died."

I flashed her an easy smile, my gaze glued to the door behind her. Classes started tomorrow. Where the hell was he?

"How was the US?"

I tore my gaze away from the cafeteria door, like a kid caught with their hand in the cookie jar. Which I pretty much was, come to think of it.

"It was fine." *Boring. Frustrating. Agonizing.*

I turned my head to the side, the cafeteria door just barely visible out of the corner of my eye. *Come on.* Three more students walked in, laughing and talking about their summer break. My heart sank.

"Are you listening?" Fleur's voice was impatient, two shades away from pissed off, as she nudged my plate. "You seem like you're somewhere else."

"I'm paying attention," I lied with ease, turning my body toward the open doorway. I glanced at the clock against the wall. The dining hall closed in fifteen minutes. If he was going to make our first family dinner back at school, time was running out.

I shouldn't have cared. I should be better than this. I shouldn't be sitting here, waiting, my stomach in knots, my nerves frayed. I'd already made it through four months with only two, one-line texts from him. What was another day?

Everything.

I tore my attention from the empty doorway, the gaping hole taunting me. "Is anyone else going to join us?" I asked Fleur, my voice deceptively casual. I couldn't say his name, but I was desperate to hear it. He was a secret I both wanted to keep and needed to spill.

I'd spent the whole summer talking about him to my friends back home, until even Jo was sick of hearing about my boy woes.

"No idea where Mya is. You know how she is. She's been MIA practically all summer. I think her parents' divorce is hitting her hard. Michael said something about going out to dinner with other friends."

Mya's dad's infidelity had apparently led him to ask for a divorce. Mya was spending most of her time with her mom and not speaking to her dad. She seemed to be handling it pretty well, all things considered. But still—Mya's priority right now was her family.

I waited for Fleur to continue, to say the one name that had been flooding my head all summer long. But in classic Fleur fashion, it appeared she was going to make me work for it.

"And Samir?" I kept my gaze trained on my plate, hoping she hadn't heard the hitch in my voice.

"No idea. You know how Samir is, you can't exactly predict what he's going to do next."

No kidding. Not being able to predict what Samir would do was exactly what had gotten me in this mess. Not that I regretted our one night together. I just wished to hell that he'd given me more to go on than a text the morning after, followed by one in July consisting of three little words. Even worse?

There hadn't even been any chances for me to casually interact with him online. Trust me to hook up with the one guy who seemed allergic to social media.

I tucked a loose strand of hair behind my ear, not bothering to resist the urge to smooth down any stray flyaways. My hair was just the tip of the iceberg; brand-new black sandals adorned my feet, their heel height more aptly suited to a nightclub rather than a university cafeteria. Relentless hours at the gym, combined with endless hours working overtime, had squeezed my curvy five-four frame into a pair of designer jeans so expensive, I'd been too afraid to eat for fear of spilling. A new black halter top completed the look in what an hour ago I thought screamed I-look-good-without-trying-to but now felt more like I'm-desperate-over-here.

"Maggie!"

I jerked my head up. Fleur stared back at me, an annoyed expression on her face.

"Sorry," I mumbled, my cheeks heating.

"What is up with you?" Her tone was a mix of concern and petulance. Classic Fleur.

For the millionth time I wanted to tell her. *Last semester on my last night in London I lost my virginity to your cousin, and I can't stop thinking about it. Or him.* I wanted to confide in Fleur. But if I did, I wasn't just admitting to a one-night stand. It was so much worse. *Yeah, he was still with his girlfriend when it happened. No, I don't know if they're still together. No, I don't know if he likes me. Or if he regrets it. Or if he thinks about that night at all. No, we haven't talked in 124 days save for one text but who's counting?*

"I'm sorry, I think I'm just jet-lagged." That, at least, wasn't completely a lie. My flight from Charlotte to London had been particularly brutal. I stared back at the clock. Five minutes left.

Unfuckingbelievable.

I'd been camped out here for, like, four hours. No way I'd missed him. Was he avoiding me?

I sighed, pushing back my chair slightly. I knew when to admit defeat. "I'm going to head up to the room and lie in bed."

"Can I join you?"

I froze, my entire body prickling with awareness. I knew that voice. It had been haunting me for months.

"Samir!" Fleur shrieked, jumping up from the table and launching herself at her cousin.

I turned, time moving in slow motion. Fragmented images and thoughts flew at me. Flashes back to that night—his body pressing into me, his hands molding my curves, his lips devouring mine—mixed with the reality of Samir in the flesh. My gaze ran over his body, greedily drinking in the sight of him.

He'd cut his hair. The black curls I'd once run my fingers through were shorter now. The skin I'd kissed, tasted on my tongue, was a deeper color. Whatever he'd done this summer, clearly, he'd spent time in the sun. Impossibly, he looked better than I remembered. His shoulders looked broader, his body toned and hard. The memory of his naked flesh, his muscled chest, his abs...

I flushed.

Would I always look at Samir and see him naked?

It was an excellent trick and exquisite torture all rolled into one. Just being here, a foot away from him, was enough to tempt me. I ached to reach out, brush my fingers against his skin and curl into that warmth.

And then I heard that voice again—sexy and sultry, the husky tone winding its way through my body, sending a shiver in its wake. I could drown in that voice.

"Hi, Maggie."

Samir

It was like being punched in the chest. Fuck me.

She sat there, inches away. All I could do was stare, like a man lost in the desert, faced with a mirage. I could smell her perfume; the memory of that subtle scent had been haunting me for months. I remembered exactly what it smelled like on her bare skin. Remembered kissing every inch of that gorgeous skin, nibbling on her, my tongue tracing patterns across her flesh. Kissing, licking down her body...

The rush of arousal hit me like another punch.

"Samir? Are you paying attention?"

I jerked my gaze away from Maggie, taking one last look, before turning to face my cousin. I slid a smile on my face, struggling to get my body under control. I knew it would be weird seeing Maggie after...well, after seeing *all* of her. But this?

Somehow, I missed the memo that seeing her under the harsh cafeteria lights, surrounded by the aroma of crappy food and the presence of other students, would make me want to take her back to my room and strip her bare. Hell, at this point a cafeteria table would do.

I wanted to bury myself in her body.

"Samir!"

I rolled my eyes. "Give me a minute, Fleur. Can you chill?"

I needed a moment. A moment of quiet before I had to look back at her. I needed a moment to get my shit under control.

"There's no need to be pissy," Fleur snapped, dark eyes flashing.

"I'm tired, Fleur. I just flew in from Beirut. Give me a second."

Fleur rolled her eyes. "There seems to be a lot of jet lag going around."

My gaze jerked to Maggie. Her head was turned, her gaze focused on the plate in front of her, her face partially hidden by the curtain of her hair. I remembered all too well having that hair wrapped around my fist, pulling her head back, exposing that delicate, pale neck—

"Samir! Are you going to sit or are you just going to stand there staring?"

"Chill," I muttered through gritted teeth, sliding into the chair next to Fleur so that I could have a perfect, uninterrupted view of Maggie. If only she'd look at me.

"So how was Lebanon?"

"Fine." I needed to get Fleur on another subject fast. Lebanon was the last thing I wanted to talk about right now.

"How's your girlfriend?"

The word *girlfriend* passed so easily from Fleur's lips, sending a wave of dread through me.

My head filled with curse words—in English, French and Arabic. I couldn't look at her now. This wasn't how I imagined this going down. I needed a chance to talk to her—to explain everything in private, without Fleur and the rest of the damn school listening in.

But Fleur said the word I'd been dreading, the word I never wanted Maggie to hear from anyone but me. Hell, let's be real, I would have rather eaten glass than told her what Fleur casually told her now.

I didn't want to look at Maggie. I couldn't look at Maggie. I owed her an explanation—an apology—so much more than what I could give her. But I just felt frozen, unable to move, unable to think of anything I could do that would save this moment.

Her head jerked up from the plate and the anger flashing across her face was a knife slashing me open. But it was nothing compared to the hurt that followed, clouding her beautiful brown eyes. Shame filled me. Not for the first time, I wished

I could go back and undo everything that happened this summer. I wished things were different. I wished I was different. I'd never been one for regrets. Until now.

This girl brought me to my fucking knees.